COLD SNAP

Bulgaria stories

COLD SNAP

CYNTHIA
MORRISON
PHOEL

Southern Methodist University Press / Dallas

Requests for permission to reproduce material
from this work should be sent to:
Rights and Permissions
Southern Methodist University Press
PO Box 750415
Dallas, Texas 75275-0415

Some of the stories in this collection appeared previously
in slightly different form in the following publications: "A Good Boy"
and "Never Trust a Man Who—" in *The Missouri Review*; "Satisfactory Proof"
in *Harvard Review*; and "Galia" in *The Gettysburg Review* and *Cerise Press*.

Cover photo: © David Turnley/CORBIS
Jacket and text design: Kellye Sanford

Library of Congress Cataloging-in-Publication Data
    Phoel, Cynthia, 1971-
    Cold snap : Bulgaria stories / Cynthia Morrison Phoel. — 1st ed.
        p. cm.
    ISBN 978-0-87074-561-4 (alk. paper)
    1. Bulgaria—Social life and customs—Fiction. 2. Short stories. I. Title.
    PS3616.H59C65 2010
    813'.6—dc22

                                                                    2009052306

Printed in the United States of America on acid-free paper
10   9   8   7   6   5   4   3   2   1

For Wayne

ACKNOWLEDGMENTS

This book would have no beginning, middle, or end without my husband, Wayne, who sent letters and packages to Bulgaria and who now takes our little people to the playground so Mom can write. In every respect, we shared this endeavor.

My parents, Terry and John Morrison, have encouraged me in countless ways. I am enormously grateful to them for the sense of adventure they fostered in our family—and to my sister, Linda Davies, and my brothers, Mark and Jason Morrison, who made sure adventures were approached with tenacity and humor.

I have enjoyed incredible support from a brilliant and bighearted community of writers. Many thanks to Fred Shafer, who first helped me find a path, and to the members of the Warren Wilson community, who furthered me along the trail. Special thanks to Tom Paine, Kit McIlvoy, Robert Cohen, Robert Boswell, Margot Livesey, and Pete Turchi for their wisdom, generosity, and patience. Thanks also to my trusted readers, especially Vyvyane Loh, Rebecca Winterer, Tracy Winn, Julia Hanna, Jasmine Beach-Ferrara, Lara Wilson, and the Thursday night group. And many thanks to my editor,

Kathryn Lang, for laying down the finish line and wrangling me across it.

I gratefully acknowledge the Massachusetts Cultural Council for financial assistance in the creation of *Cold Snap*.

Finally, I owe a world of gratitude to my friends and students in Bulgaria who welcomed me into their lives and homes during my Peace Corps years. Above all, I am indebted to my dear friends, Miroslava Mateev and Tanya Dimova, who read these stories backward and forward. (I accept full responsibility for any errors in the Bulgarian language—some made with intent, where I simplified the language to make it less confusing to a broader readership.) I'd also like to thank Anton Dimov for his elegant artistry and Anissa Paulsen for her joyful companionship. And my enduring love and thanks go to Stefka Atonasova for so many trips to the garden up the mountain.

CONTENTS

A GOOD BOY

For hours now Dobrin has been begging Stassi to stop it, shut up, are you *trying* to make her mad? "Put those down," Dobrin hisses, whispering, though his *maika* lags too far behind to hear.

Stassi has plucked two tomatoes from his bag and is holding them to his chest, the stems pointing out. "Dobrin," he says, cupping the undersides of the tomatoes with mock tenderness. "You want a squeeze?"

"*Molya ti se,*" Dobrin pleads. He has had enough of his friend. They have spent the entire afternoon together, helping Dobrin's mother in the garden she keeps a half-hour's walk up the mountain. Until today Dobrin had almost liked the garden, mostly for the gratification it brought his mother, who hardly had time for it. Now Stassi has tainted the place, not to mention the tomatoes, which no amount of washing will ever make clean. "Your mother's tomatoes are so *firm,*" Stassi said the first time she turned her back. "So *ripe.*" By the time they were finished in the garden, Stassi was saying things right in front of her, as if his comments were so clever she would never catch on.

He finally shut up when they began the walk home, but at the crest of the hill overlooking their town, Dobrin's mother stopped to talk to an old woman. It irritated Dobrin that there could be so many old women and his *maika* could not pass a single one of them without stopping to say hello. He continued down the road with Stassi, which turned out to be a mistake. Away from Dobrin's mother, Stassi started up again.

"Some nipples really are green, you know," he says now, admiring his handheld protrusions.

Dobrin can see his mother inching away from the woman, trying to extricate herself from the conversation she started. It is still early, and already they are on the brink of evening, the sun low over the mountain. Dobrin is ready for the summer to be over. Stassi will be in his class again, but others will be there to dilute his energy and Ms. Kuneva there to squelch it. Many of his classmates think it unfair they should be stuck with crabby old Kuneva for a second year in a row, but Dobrin doesn't mind so much—certainly not so much as he minds Stassi fondling the tomatoes.

"If you don't stop it—," he begins but is distracted by a tomato bouncing down the mountain. He squats to trap it, and another hurtles by, another and another. A throng of tomatoes has escaped from one of the bags. Above him, his mother stands in the middle of the street shading her eyes. Her bag of tomatoes, what's left of it, is tipped at her feet.

A quickening in Dobrin's stomach and he follows her gaze, panning church steeple and bakery stack, flagpole displaying limp Bulgarian flag, rusted metallic beams of the new post office, started but never finished, the skyline of flat asphalt roofs. Finally, with Stassi beside him pointing, Dobrin sees it. In the hours they have been at the garden, the large white disk of a satellite dish has appeared on top of an apartment building. Block 103. Theirs.

"*Bozhe,*" Stassi says, "Do you think your father—"

"I think you should go home," Maika says. She is walking fast now, about to overtake them.

Stassi nods politely to Dobrin's mother, and then, looking at Dobrin, his face splits with a grin too wide to be merely a smile. He makes a great show of running down the mountain unencumbered, flailing his arms out from his sides, going out of his way to stomp on tomatoes lolling in the road.

Dobrin's mother continues down the mountain. By the time Dobrin is balanced with Stassi's bag in one hand, his own in the other, she is several paces ahead. Something advises him to keep his distance.

After a block or so of trailing Maika, of silence, the bags bumping, leaking smeary tomato juice down his legs, the satellite dish disappearing from his vision but growing larger in his mind, he wishes Stassi were still there.

Dobrin's *tatko* greets them at the apartment door with jumpy hellos. In the next room a cheery, televised voice offers a more articulate welcome. "Your ticket to the best in sports," it promises. "World Cup soccer. Watch it here."

"You," Maika says and rushes past him.

Dobrin's father flinches, though only for a moment. He has been expecting this. This is not the first time Tatko's accepted *electronica* instead of wages, though this piece, this infraction, is the biggest by far.

In the following days, Dobrin can hardly last an hour without going outside to admire the dish. Up close it's dizzyingly large, and Dobrin is at once thrilled and sickened by its size. His queasiness doesn't go away if he heads up the mountain and views the dish at eye level: even from a distance it is otherworldly and menacing. Such dishes may be commonplace in Sofia, but sixty kilometers east of the capital city, the small town of Old Mountain has never seen one like this. At night, the dish looks larger than the moon.

Stassi says with a dish like this Dobrin can have any girl he wants. He says girls can't resist a really big dish. This dish is going to change Dobrin's life.

Dobrin wonders if it already has, though not in the way Stassi thinks. Of course there have been fights before, too often having to do with the cost of Dobrin's notebooks or the condition of his shoes or the new jeans, too tight too soon. Though small for his age, Dobrin would be willing to stop growing if it would make things between Maika and Tatko a little easier.

But Dobrin cannot think of one fight where the crime was committed with intent. He does not like trouble, least of all with his mother, who has skinny shoulders and is not at all pretty when she's angry. Tatko, on the other hand, does not seem to mind trouble—a thing Dobrin can't quite grasp. Sometimes he wishes his father would be nicer to Maika or at least not make her so mad. Other times, he thinks it takes a lot of guts. It takes a lot of guts to get a dish this big. He wonders if guts grow along with belly, muscle, and bone.

Sitting on his mountain perch, Dobrin stares absently at the dish, which looms over their home like a big white cloud. Beneath its shiny orb the rest of the building looks shabby and old. Better when he makes his eyes into slits and looks only at the dish. Then, what he sees is glory.

How long can Dobrin's parents go without speaking to each other? A week has passed, and so far nothing more than the

occasional spray of words spat out like watermelon seeds—
necessary, unwanted. Dobrin is on the lookout for a sign—a
Bless you or *Excuse me*, a stifled giggle—any indication they
will be okay.

Stassi assures him the silence is normal. Parents can go for
long periods of time without talking. He asks if Dobrin can
hear sex noises coming from their bedroom, because if they're
having sex, then they're going to be okay. "Sex can cure anything," Stassi says. "Even cancer."

What does Stassi know? His parents have been divorced
since he was four. He has never known anyone with cancer *or*
a satellite TV.

Dobrin thinks if Maika would just sit down and watch one
of the TV's programs, she might learn to appreciate it. But
she refuses to enjoy it. It's foolish to own a satellite TV, she
says, when you can barely afford heat. This year she is teaching
Bulgarian literature at both high schools in town. At night and
on weekends she tutors private students at the dining room table. During these hours the TV should not be on, though Tatko
has watched more than a few crucial matches—Barcelona,
mostly, and sometimes Hamburg—with the volume muted.

Dobrin has to agree with Tatko the satellite TV is a blessed
thing. Even with his parents not talking he loves it. After years
of watching the same three stations through a thick haze of
electric fuzz, it seems like a miracle there can be so many programs playing at once and no matter where the program is
coming from, the picture is clear—clearer than the hand in
front of your face. Clearer even than the mural pasted to their
living room wall of a sun setting on a crystalline lake, an image that always looked remarkably sharp until now. Soccer and

basketball all day long, and if there isn't a new game on, they replay an old one. At night, after Maika goes to bed, girls appear on the screen—girls like Dobrin has never imagined, like the centerfolds on the front of the bus only better, touching themselves, undulating with passion. It is better than his cousin's Madonna video, better than anything he has ever seen.

During the matches Dobrin cheers and Tatko jumps up and down, calling fouls and assigning penalty shots like a true referee. But the girls they watch in silence. Tatko—and Stassi, when he's there—on the sofa, Dobrin in an overstuffed chair. Dobrin's favorite is a girl called Lana, schoolteacher by day, hooker by night. At school Lana wears heavy glasses, long skirts, and blouses buttoned up to the neck. Dobrin thinks if he were her student, he would only consider her a little bit beautiful. Then, the camera does this great thing where it peers between the buttons of her blouse and transports you to the other Lana, the unconscionably gorgeous Lana with parts Dobrin can hardly believe are real.

They watch the girls with the volume turned low, because Maika is sleeping in the other room. Tatko insists there are parts of a man's education a mother shouldn't know about, and for the wondrous hours with Lana and others, Dobrin is willing to agree. Besides, he suspects the girls might make Maika's migraines worse than they already are. As it is, on most nights she goes to bed without even having dinner. Sometimes, through the closed door, Dobrin can hear his mother's gasps as the pain grips and squeezes her brain. If he goes in to check on her, he finds tears soaking her pillow. Tatko says the headaches are an act to make him feel bad. Dobrin is not so sure; nevertheless, he can feel his father's sadness, the way he slumps over the arm of the couch and peers at the TV from beneath the low visor of his hand. Even when they are watching girls, he can feel it.

It's almost impossible to believe the girls on TV and Ms. Kuneva are of the same species. Stassi says people shrivel up if they don't have sex. Dobrin points out neither he nor Stassi is having sex, and neither is as withered and sorry as Kuneva.

"Who says I'm not having sex?"

"*Stiga be.* Who would have sex with you?"

"Your mother," Stassi screams and slaps his leg. "You thought you had her all to yourself, didn't you?"

Dobrin punches Stassi in the arm—*stop with my mother!*—and Stassi laughs harder. This is the Stassi Dobrin hates. In seventh grade he was responsible for the extra homework their class got almost every night, homework Stassi himself never did. He was always rocking his chair, tipping his desk, dropping bits of chalk into Ms. Kuneva's cups of espresso, spoiling what little stamina she had to get through class. As they embark on eighth grade, Dobrin expects more of the same. To Dobrin, sameness is more ominous than change.

On the first day of school, Ms. Kuneva addresses them as *ladies and gentlemen.* "Ladies and gentlemen, take out your English workbooks," she says with such propriety for a moment Dobrin thinks she may have forgotten where she is. He looks at his classmates—Stassi with his head bent over the desk, using a protractor to engrave his name in the already-mutilated surface—and wonders if it's possible they have become *ladies and gentlemen.* Indeed, they have grown. Taller, wider, moister. They have more hair. But *ladies and gentlemen?*

From Stassi's corner of the classroom comes a fit of coughing and inaudible words.

In their second year with Kuneva, Dobrin's classmates know to be skeptical of their teacher's broad optimism. Last year she was always making them out to be more than what they were. "You are very well prepared for this exam," she would say as they began a test half of them would fail. "You know all the words in this dictation," she'd promise before she read an impossible passage. "You are the most considerate group of students I have ever had," she told them a week before Women's Day, and still they gave her only a paltry bouquet, picked from a garden near the school and wrapped in napkins. Time and again they witnessed the rise and fall of her hopes. And still, Dobrin believed maybe he would do well on this exam, this dictation.

This first day of school, Ms. Kuneva seems to be hoping for an awful lot. She is all dressed up like a lady out of one of those films from the British Council she is always making them watch. She wears a pink dress, cinched at the waist. Dobrin thinks it might look nice if her breasts weren't so saggy and thin. Her hair is curled, pinned just above the ears. She looks like an antique—girlish and nicotine yellow—and you can tell she fancies herself a beauty, the way she walks around kicking her pink shoes out in front of her. Dobrin wishes she looked prettier than she does. It's a shame because he can tell how hard she's tried.

Later Dobrin catches Kuneva grimacing at her saggy self in the smudged classroom window. Already she has confiscated the protractor and a soccer ball from Stassi and worked herself into a healthy rage over their poor memories. She has dictated a passage she pledged would be "so simple they would enjoy it." Sharpening his pencil, Dobrin momentarily believed in his proficiency in the English language—he would start this school year off with a high mark—only to stumble first on *Somerset,* then on *Maugham.* By the second sentence, he knew he would be lucky to get a passing mark.

Ladies and gentlemen, Kuneva says as she bids them goodbye. When he tells his mother about this, she catches her breath—*Gospodin? Kak mozhe?*—then starts to cry. She says she is not ready for him to be a man just yet.

After school, Stassi invites himself over to watch the satellite TV. Soon this becomes a habit. "Only if you leave before my mom gets home," Dobrin says, feigning irritation. The truth is, he is glad for an ally when he returns to the apartment at the end of the day.

In just a few weeks the TV has attracted a number of Tatko's friends, four or five of them, who come in the morning and stay all day. By the time Dobrin gets home from school, they have nothing left to say to each other. They just sit there, flaking peanut skins into their chest hair and watching the TV. Distracted by the scratching and belching and crunching on nuts, Dobrin can hardly follow the program on the screen. At least Stassi talks, he finds himself thinking.

Today Stassi leans over and whispers, "Your dad's got boobs," eyeing Dobrin's father shirtless.

Dobrin tweaks Stassi's forearm until he says *ow,* but Stassi's right; Tatko does have boobs. Dobrin worries he will grow boobs too. He hopes this won't happen until he's married, or at least until he's twenty or eighteen.

In the meantime, he wishes his dad would stop walking around bare-chested all the time. At the pool, Tatko's boss makes him wear a shirt, though he doesn't mind if Tatko rolls up the sleeves to get an even tan across his biceps. Dobrin thinks he looks impressively strong when he does this. Tatko's arms are broad and flat and three times the circumference of Dobrin's.

Some of the other men are wearing shirts, but not all. Nudging Stassi, Dobrin nods at one of them with boobs as big as Tatko's. Immediately he is sorry to have drawn this comparison. They are not the same, his father and these men. *His* father has a job. *His* father has a satellite TV.

A barman at the pool café, Tatko works from May until September. Only from September to May does he sit on the couch, and even then, not all the time. Once or twice a year he manages to pick up a week here or there, waiting tables at a conference or tending to a private party. When that happens, there's a feast at home, with meat and yellow cheese and a bottle of perfume for Maika, presented with great flourish in front of friends, the price tag still on.

Back when they were talking, Maika used to plead with Tatko to find another job. She would come home with ideas for him. "Marietta says Nikolai has more work than he can handle." Or, "Stefan says they're looking for a repairman at the motel." But Tatko would get angry and say he made parties, not repairs. He was waiting on the couch for something good to come his way.

These days Dobrin would relish such an argument. He suspects Maika is not so angry about Tatko's joblessness as she is about the couch sitting and the satellite TV. Even Maika knows there are not enough jobs to go around this town. It's likely Tatko couldn't get another one even if he tried.

To make up for the rest of the year, when summer comes

around, Tatko works long hours. From dawn until dusk he serves *kebabcheta* and beer and keeps the shrill *chalga* music turned up high. He stands behind the grill and calls to his cluster of tables—a slab of cheese? some bread? a little Ruska salad?—his grin slathered on, thick and saucy. His customers buy it. "Boris!" they holler to him, ordering food and drink as they rarely do at restaurants, as though this is some great celebration. Every few minutes, Tatko raises his hands and snaps his fingers and rotates his hips. "Oho!" he calls, caught up in the swirl of his own good humor. Chef, waiter, bartender, no one takes better care of customers than he.

Tatko's bar is the only profitable part of a business that should do better than it does. The next pool being three villages away, there is little competition. This pool is clean and well kept and chlorinated enough to kill all the germs. What's more, nestled at the foot of the mountain, it gives the effect of swimming in a big green cavern. But Vulkov, Tatko's boss, keeps the prices high. People have to ration their trips to the pool, saving their *leva* for the most beautiful days. They come more frequently at the end of the summer, once they have given up hope of affording a trip to the Black Sea. But it is not enough to make up for the earlier months. When Vulkov pays Tatko at the end of the summer, his fifteen-hour days, his boundless energy, they do not matter. Vulkov says he can offer more if Tatko will accept electronics—*TV, stereo, VCR, you pick*—in lieu of cash. Tatko is pleased to make the deal.

Hearing Maika's key in the door, Dobrin wonders if Tatko is still pleased with the deal he made. A week ago he told the couch-sitters, "Next year, CD player," but he hasn't mentioned it again. As Maika passes through the room she deliberately steps in front of the TV. "Extravagances," she hisses, grabbing glasses and bowls off the table and out of hands. "Look at this mess." Dobrin wishes she wouldn't do this—it embarrasses everybody—but this, he suspects, is her aim.

The men leave, but not before Tatko retorts, "You have your extravagances, I have mine." He is talking partly about the Cadbury eggs Maika buys for Dobrin and the food she puts out on their first-floor balcony for stray dogs and cats. But mostly he is talking about the money Maika spends on migraine remedies. Once a month she goes to see a woman for treatments. Velichka claims to have extrasensory powers, which she uses to put spells on water and herbs and animal fats people buy to cure migraines and burns and other afflictions. She claims she can cure anything, and she has a great many followers who believe in her. Maika pays ten *leva* for the bus ride, thirty *leva* for the visit, and one hundred *leva* for ten gallons of water, which Dobrin has to help her carry back on the bus.

"If you're going to spend that kind of money, at least go to a doctor," Tatko says. It's not so much money, really, but it's been a long time since there's been store-bought wine on the table or a stick of dried meat to eat. Dobrin knows if Tatko ever saw Velichka, there would be no end to his fury. For as much as Dobrin wants to believe Velichka can help his mother, instinct tells him she's a fake. It's not that Velichka doesn't look the part; rather, she looks *too* much like the earthy, spiritual vessel of energy she claims to be. She wears long skirts and grows her hair down to her butt. She doesn't even wear a bra, which Dobrin finds terribly distracting when she's bending over the spigot in her yard, helping them fill the jugs. Her breasts are the largest he's ever seen, too big, if that's possible. He thinks if she were really serious about her work, she would at least wear a bra and roll her hair into a bun.

Once Tatko claimed he had poured Velichka's water out of the jug and replaced it with regular water and Maika didn't even notice. Maika cried when he said this.

Tonight, Maika endures her headache long enough to eat dinner. Afterward, she cooks rice in the fat left over from their meal, and Dobrin helps her carry it out to the balcony. Hearing the scrape of the metal bowls on the cement floor, the dogs and cats come running from all around, rib cages heaving, whimpering happiness. They lick Maika's hands, they are so grateful. When a dappled bitch with a freshly torn ear nuzzles its nose between Dobrin's legs, an embarrassing knot rises in his throat. He wonders about the difference, if one exists, between extravagance and need. Velichka's remedies, the way Maika suffers, isn't the cost trifling for the possibility of relieving her pain? Even the satellite TV doesn't seem like much of an extravagance when you consider how much use it gets. "Business," Tatko's friends call it, because this is what they have to do all day, and the fact of the big white satellite dish atop the building—doesn't that count for something?

Later on, Dobrin asks Tatko why the men never leave until after Maika gets home and gets angry about finding them there. Apparently this is funny. "You think it's better at their homes than at ours?"

A month of warp and confusion, a kaleidoscope of worries flickering through Dobrin's head. At night, he lies in bed and listens for sex noises, laughter, the opening and closing of the bathroom door. Granted these sounds have been missing before and they always, eventually, came back. Nevertheless he has noticed the spaces between them have grown longer and quieter, and he wonders about the time when they stop altogether and all they have left is the consoling chatter of the satellite TV.

Dobrin thinks if Tatko would apologize, Maika might accept what has already been done. It would make a difference if she knew he was sorry. But Tatko's jaw is set; his arms are crossed; his eyes are fixed on the TV. Who is he to apologize when he is not even sorry? How can he be sorry for this glorious TV?

Barking erupts outside Dobrin's window. The belated heat makes the dogs surly and tired. Ms. Kuneva says Americans call this Indian summer, this last burst of warm weather before it turns cold. To Dobrin it feels like a taunt—an aftertaste of the summer just past and a reminder the next summer is a long way off.

By his measure, it had been a good summer, perhaps even a great one. As in summers past, he spent most of his days at the pool, where Vulkov let him swim and eat for free. Staying home was not a good idea. When he stayed home, Maika got cross. She said she wanted to get *something* out of this arrangement. They couldn't eat a stereo, she would start in. Dobrin couldn't wear a VCR to school.

At the pool, Vulkov had Dobrin fill in when the lifeguard didn't show up. This made Dobrin nervous—he had not been trained to rescue people—but Vulkov said it didn't matter. People would feel safer and behave better with someone in the chair. Once his initial unease passed, Dobrin looked forward to the times Vulkov pushed his fat finger into Dobrin's bicep and pointed toward the seat. He was something of a celebrity on these days. Everyone wanted to talk to him and hang out by his chair. He suspected they were mainly interested in talking to a lifeguard and not so much to him. Nevertheless, he could not help but be pleased with how brown his feet looked against the light blue platform of the chair and with the girls' decorated toenails and pastel bikinis that turned almost see-through when they got wet.

On top of the sheets, wearing only his underwear, Dobrin can almost believe summer is still here. Just hours ago he was sitting in the lifeguard chair, staring down at the girls from his class, pondering the twin miracles of their breasts. As Dobrin slips his hand beneath the elastic band of his underpants, a man starts yelling at the dogs to shut up. A woman screams at the man. A chorus erupts on the street outside. Dobrin wants to yell too—aren't they supposed to be smarter than dogs?—but instead of adding to the noise, he gets up, leans out the window, and spits out the big glob of phlegm that has gathered in his throat.

"Dobrin? Dobrin Georgiev, was that you?" an angry voice yells. In Block 103, Vhod A, neighbors live close enough to recognize one another by the sound of their spit.

A month ago, Dobrin would have apologized for his crassness. Now, he lies back down and wraps a pillow around his ears.

"Ladies and gentlemen, take out your English workbooks." By the end of October, Dobrin's class has proven they are nothing of the sort. Still, Kuneva starts out every morning the same way, with hope and expectation they will have done their homework and come prepared to participate in class.

Likewise, Dobrin, at the end of October, still starts out eager to please, though lately he's been mesmerized by the satisfying symmetry of the elastic straps cutting across the back of

Tanya, who sits in front of him. He has noticed Tanya rotates among three different bras, and on one of these bras, the lower hook is broken. Dobrin thinks Lana from TV would never wear a bra with a broken hook, and yet he's realistic his possibilities for any type of contact are much greater with Tanya than they are with Lana. In this bra, Tanya is one step closer to being unclothed. Lately he's been devising strategies to increase their contact, the key strategy being to stand as close to Tanya's desk as possible while he stacks his books or puts on his coat. As of yet, she's only hit him with her elbow.

"Dobrin!" Kuneva is standing over his desk, looking at his half-finished homework.

Dobrin looks at it too, with more disappointment than guilt: he wishes it were done. The night before, he had sat down with his workbook in front of the TV. His goal was to have the homework finished by halftime. But the game wasn't so interesting because it was a replay of a game they'd seen before, and Dobrin got to thinking about other things, namely his father, who had not spoken to Dobrin in days. He started to wonder if maybe Tatko was angry at him, too, and once the thought got stuck in his mind, it became very important to say something, though he didn't know what. The goal became finding something to say by halftime, and this was all Dobrin could think about until moments before the buzzer, when he finally blurted out, "Who do you want to win?" Which was a stupid question of course, because they had seen the game, and they knew who would win.

After all that, Dobrin was relieved when Tatko ignored him.

In the corner of his mind, Dobrin registers Stassi talking, something about a date with Lana. On the homework sheet lying on his desk, he sees he quit writing in the middle of a word.

"Dobrin," Kuneva exhales in her weary way, "you have so much potential." For once, Dobrin is not fooled.

Maika wants to make one more trip to the garden to gather vegetables for the winter, and would anyone like to come? The way she says it, it's clear Dobrin is supposed to join her. Every spring, Maika plants *domati,* peppers, onions, garlic, potatoes, pumpkins, and zucchini—twice as much as she needs, because half will fail from slugs or neglect. Maika doesn't have time to care for the garden. The untended fruit rots on the ground. As it is, they have not been to the garden in more than a month, not since the day of the satellite TV. Dobrin is not eager to go. The slugs will be all over everything, and he will spend the entire time picking slimy gobs off leaves and stalks and collecting them in a jar. This late in the season, they will be the size of chili peppers.

But what Dobrin wants is irrelevant. His mother's migraine has subsided for the first time in a long while, reason enough for him to go. And then there's the incident from last night.

Maika had gone to bed. Stassi had stayed late watching TV and comparing every girl to his father's girlfriend. "You think *she's* got hooters," he said, using a word he'd learned from an American film. Stassi could pick things up just like that. "You haven't *seen* hooters until you've seen my father's girlfriend."

"Kakva e dumata?" Tatko said. "Hoo-ters?" Stassi sniggered at his strained pronunciation of the word. "Hoo-ters," Tatko said again, and Stassi clapped his hands.

They'd barely heard Maika's shuffling outside the door,

barely turned the channel in time, and when they did, they flipped to a news program Maika surely knew they had not been watching.

"What's so funny?" Maika said to Dobrin. Stassi was bent in half, shaking with laughter, and Tatko was smirking.

"*Nishto*," Dobrin scowled. Indeed, there was nothing funny about it: his father grinning like a schoolboy, his mother standing there in a nightgown too worn for company to see. Dobrin wished he could buy her a new robe and maybe a new haircut. He wondered if a new tube of lipstick could turn her lips into a smile.

The road to the garden is lined with houses. The first half of the walk is paved. As Maika begins her ascent in brisk, angry strides, Dobrin suspects this trip will be every bit as unpleasant as he is expecting. But soon they are joined by a familiar dog, and in spite of her anger, Maika cannot stop herself from kneeling by its side. "*Zdrasti*, Krastavitza," she says, her voice thick with affection for this creature with his milky eyes and jutting ribs. "Cucumber," the people of Old Mountain call this dog, who, almost entirely hairless, resembles nothing so much as a cucumber, right down to the mild acne rippling his skin. Owned by no one and cared for by all, the dog has his favorites: when Maika runs her hand over his ribs, his naked tail beats the pavement so hard, Dobrin fears either the dog's tail or his own heart will break from so much love.

"*Ela, maiche*," Maika says at last, rising to her feet and beckoning the dog to join them on their walk. But when the road gets steeper and turns to dirt, Maika tells the dog to stop. "You can't make it, Krastavitza," she says. "If you wait here, we'll be back in a little while." Obediently, the dog stops, and Dobrin's focus shifts to Maika, whose shoes slip on the wet ground and gather a thick rim of mud around the edges. Dobrin keeps his hand on her back to steady her. When he looks over his shoulder to see what has come of Krastavitza, he spots the dog curled in a patch of weeds exactly where they left him.

Upon reaching the garden, Dobrin takes the jar Maika hands him and starts collecting the slugs. It is cool enough the flies are gone, and the air is sweet with the rich ferment of composting fruit. Dobrin finds a sturdy twig about a foot long and starts picking the slugs off the pumpkins and zucchini that are still good. While Dobrin collects slugs, Maika rakes fiercely at the rotting tomatoes and cucumbers, combing them into a heap in a corner of the plot. Even though they are at opposite ends of the garden, he can feel the soft thud of her rake hitting the soil.

Dobrin tries to imagine Tanya working in the garden. Wondering what she'd wear, he keeps coming back to her snug green turtleneck, not only because it looks very nice on her, but also because of the green vegetation. He thinks it would be a good match. He imagines her picking strawberries and tomatoes and cucumbers in peak condition. He doubts Tanya has ever seen a slug.

Maika has finished raking and is coming up behind him, choosing the squashes to take home and wiping them with a dirty towel. "Dobrin," she says. "I want you to be a good boy, you hear?"

It has been a long time since Dobrin's mother reminded him to be a good boy. She used to tell him this all the time. "Be a good boy at school today," she'd say. "Be a good boy and clear off the table." If Tatko heard her say this, he would mock her. "That's right, Dobrin. You be a good boy," he would say, and Dobrin could tell he did not really mean it. Dobrin would not know what to do, who to please—usually his mother because he wanted to make her happy.

There in the garden, the words *Be a good boy* sound hollow as a rotted-out squash. Dobrin does not know what a good boy is, let alone how to be one.

They don't talk on the way back down. As they near the spot where they had left the dog, Dobrin hopes, even prays, Krastavitza will be there. But the weedy patch is empty. What remains is a matted circle where the dog had waited until he gave up and went away.

At two months, Stassi says there's still a chance. He says even if you don't like a person, if you share the same bed with them night after night, eventually you will have sex. It's just a matter of time.

Only yesterday Dobrin had thought his parents were on the verge of a breakthrough. The prices for central heat had finally been taped to the post office windows. They were impossibly high, higher than they had ever been. Maika figured they could afford to heat only two rooms, the living room and one other. She said it should be Dobrin's room; he was not the one who got them into this situation.

"*Gluposti,*" Tatko said, staring hard at the TV. "Dobrin's room is the smallest."

In the seconds Maika took to formulate her response, Dobrin had felt them on the edge of a conversation. Oh, this would be good. A fight, even one all the neighbors could hear, would be better than so much quiet.

But Maika had turned things in another direction. "Fine then," she said. To Dobrin she added, "You sleep with me, and your father will sleep on the couch."

A GOOD BOY 21

Tatko snorted. He has been on the couch ever since the satellite TV was installed.

"I like the cold," Dobrin said. He did not want to sleep with his mother. But Maika was clattering dishes in the cabinet; Tatko was turning up the volume on the TV. "I like the cold," he said again, louder and more insistent, but no one seemed to notice.

When the border is approached, eyed, retreated from, this is when Dobrin feels most discouraged. "There's still hope, bro," Stassi says. Dobrin hates it when Stassi calls him *bro*.

Cold is cumulative, Dobrin decides as he lies awake in bed. Two weeks of trying to beat the cold and he is losing the battle. It is only the end of November; he has at least four months of cold, freezing cold, ahead of him. He has taken to showering before he sleeps, starting the night out with groundless optimism: tonight he will be warm! But by two, three o'clock, any heat he started out with has escaped through the coarse plaid weave of the layered Rhodope blankets and dissolved into the air. Moment to moment, he tracks the steady creep of the chill as it penetrates his toes, feet, and ankles, loitering in his bones. He pulls the covers over his head to capture the warmth of his breath. It is a marvel to him that such warm air can come from such a cold body.

Even with his head beneath the blankets, he can hear the satellite TV. Listening to Tatko flip from the girls to a basketball match, he is tempted to go watch a quarter and warm up, but he doesn't feel like being with his father right now.

Earlier that evening, Maika had sent Tatko out on what should have been a quick errand—*Dobrin, tell your father to go buy bread*—and Tatko had not returned until long after dinner was finished. Dobrin and Maika had eaten alone, *gyuveche* with no bread, no satellite TV. Amid so much stillness, Dobrin felt small pinches of anger at the cat, who did none of his usual mewing for food from the table but curled up in a ball in the dent Tatko left in the couch; at the radiator, which did not hiss and pop as it so often did, but purred quietly without any punctuation whatsoever; and at his mother, whose bites slowed to a stop with her dinner half eaten. That was one thing about the satellite TV. Rarely did it pause between commercials and programs, and never, *never* did it stop.

Lately, Dobrin has started to wonder if they will go on forever like this, the quiet getting quieter, togetherness growing strained and unyielding, until things are impossibly hard, a fossilized existence. Beneath the layers of blankets, cold, anger, he lies still, like a body entombed. After a while, he bends a leg beneath the covers to make sure he can.

When Dobrin finally climbs into bed with his mother, he does it in the middle of the night, when his father is dozing in front of the TV, his face awash with electronic color. Dobrin's skin is chapped from the moisture of his breath beneath the covers. His nose is running. He opens and closes doors quietly. Once he has closed his mother's door behind him, he stands still, waiting for his eyes to adjust.

The room smells of Velichka's herbs, and the radiator crackles. Even though his mother is all the way over to one side of the bed—it's clear she's been expecting him—her heat is everywhere under the covers. Cold though he is, Dobrin finds this disgusting. He wonders how he was ever able to sleep with his mother when he was a child. He can hardly bring himself to get into the bed, and once he does, he lies stiffly on the edge.

He is awake and acutely aware of the thawing in his fingers and toes.

Stassi crosses a line when he claims his dad's girlfriend is even hotter than Lana. "She's from Germany," he says to Dobrin on a break between classes. Neither of them have pocket money to spend in the café, so they stay in the classroom, which stinks of damp chalk and body odor.

Dobrin leans against the radiator, pressing his fingers into its grooves. "So what?" He is tired of hearing about Stassi's father. Stassi's father lives in a huge apartment in Sofia. Stassi's father takes him to soccer matches. Stassi's father eats dinner at McDonald's almost every night. Dobrin thinks if Stassi's father is so great, he might visit once in a while.

"So she's pretty."

"Being German doesn't necessarily make you pretty," Dobrin says. There is a German teacher at school who isn't pretty at all.

"This one is. And she has real blond hair. My dad says she's blond *everywhere*."

Dobrin tries to imagine how this might come up in conversation between Stassi and his father. He doesn't think his own father would share such a detail. Besides, what about armpits? So many summers at the pool, and Dobrin has yet to see a blond pit. "You lie," he says, though he is not sure about this. He is not sure of anything Stassi says anymore.

He feels his mood deteriorating. The day started out well. He had done his homework and received a good mark. He asked Tanya for a pencil, and she turned around and offered him a choice of implements. Dobrin took his time deliberating and had gotten a good look at the rounded silhouette of her breast. For a small girl, she has big hooters.

The class is starting to file back in. Dobrin is glad the break is almost over and Stassi will have to return to his seat.

"Anyhow, tell your dad the answer is yes."

"Yes, what?"

"Yes on the German girlfriend. My dad can hook him up."

Stassi waits for Dobrin's face to turn hot before he breaks into one of his cackles. "I got you, bro," he screams, stomping his feet on the ground.

Dobrin has wanted to punch Stassi for a long time. Ms. Kuneva gets there just in time to see his fist land squarely in Stassi's eye.

A week of sleeping in Maika's bed and Dobrin has learned if he can distract himself from the intense heat under the covers and the smell of Velichka's herbs, he eventually will fall asleep. He strains to hear the score of the game, but all he can make out is the rush of the crowd, which, when filtered through the bedroom wall, sounds like running water.

In less than a month they will be into the new year and on the downhill slope toward summer. Dobrin has been thinking next summer he wants to be a real lifeguard, which means he will need training and a new bathing suit. When the winter is over and Maika is no longer paying for heat, he will ask her if she can afford these things. If everything works out, when Vulkov pays him at the end of the summer, Dobrin will be able to pay her back.

Payback. They are just now studying compound words. Cutthroat. Diehard. Kuneva makes the mistake of defining payback as *tit for tat*. Stassi has never heard anything so wonderful.

Tit for tat, he says about the punch. "Don't worry about it, bro," which makes Dobrin want to punch him again, if Stassi wouldn't like it so much. Stassi is infatuated with the ring of purple encircling his eye. He spends the whole class touching it. On breaks, he goes to the bathroom to see if it has changed. Kuneva has decided for as long as the bruise lasts, Dobrin must stay after school each day and write a one-page essay. The first day she made him write on the meaning of friendship. The second day he had to come up with different ways of working things out.

In bed next to him, Maika rolls from her back onto her side. When his mother lies this way, Dobrin thinks her torso looks like an angry violin. He can remember a time when things didn't always end in anger, when near arguments—those crackling moments when there's still a choice about which way things can go—ended with Tatko pulling Maika onto his lap and wrapping his arms around her waist, nuzzling her with his big, oily nose. Maika would laugh—*stiga be! that tickles!*—and Dobrin would laugh too. Tatko might find her breast with his hand and hold it for a moment before she pulled away. That was years ago, and still Dobrin can remember how he felt, at once joyous and bashful. Maika would extract herself from Tatko's grasp, and Tatko would stare after her—her chest or her retreating behind—the way he now stares at the girls on the satellite TV.

Love? Lust? Only now is Dobrin starting to suspect there is a difference. When he is watching the satellite TV, it is easy to believe he loves Lana and all her sprawling beauty. He loves the way she makes him feel. But during the daytime, he thinks what he feels for Lana is something less than love. He is not sure why he thinks this, only there must be something more to it than the sensations she ignites in his groin. He thinks of all the silly hearts he used to draw for Maika. *S lubov, Dobrin.* From Dobrin with love.

Earlier that day, Tanya paid him a compliment.

"I like your sweater," she said, not looking at him but playing with the zipper on her rucksack.

"*You do?*" Dobrin has only two sweaters, a blue one and a brown one, both knit by his *baba* and inherited from his father, both ugly and old and smelling of mothballs. What was there to like about such sweaters? Dobrin was wearing the brown one. He could see the ends of the yarn poking through the weave at the places where his grandma had finished one ball and started the next. He hated this sweater. Nevertheless, he wore it because the chill was still there—he could not get past it. This sweater is the warmest piece of clothing he has.

Tanya turned in her chair, and he could see he had embarrassed her. He scrambled for something to say to fix things. "Thank you." Or "It's old." Or "I like your sweater, too," which he actually did. Oh, God, he did. It was pink, starting to gray with age, and a little too small. Depending on the way she sat, the sweater rode up in the back, showing off an oval of bright white skin. It seemed terribly intimate to Dobrin to see this skin so low on her back, perfectly creased by the faint ridge of her spine. He wondered if she knew about this skin, if maybe she wanted him to see it.

Dobrin can hear the match on the satellite TV. After school,

Stassi had asked to come over to watch it, but Dobrin had told him no.

The exchange had taken place after Dobrin's detention, during which Kuneva had made him write an essay on ways to keep warm during the winter months. Of his own volition, Stassi had waited for Dobrin out in the hall, periodically kicking his soccer ball at the door to remind Dobrin he was still there. Dobrin had taken his time, hoping Kuneva would yell at Stassi and make him go home, but she just sat there, writing marks in the *dnevnik*. More than once Dobrin saw her pen skip when the ball slammed against the door, but surprisingly she held her temper.

"What do you mean, *no?*" Stassi said. "Barcelona, bro. Aren't you going to watch?"

Dobrin had planned on watching the match, but then he changed his mind. "My parents said they want a night with just our family."

"What do you mean?" Stassi said, fingering the mottled ring around his eye. "They're talking again?"

"A little." Dobrin had not intended to tell this lie, but he was happy with how it sounded. He wondered if it even was a lie or if it could be true. Maybe things *were* getting better, and he was just not seeing it.

"Didn't I tell you?" Stassi said, trying to maintain his cheer—but Dobrin could tell he was mad. "*Ami*, fine," he said, kicking the ball down the stairs and running after it. Dobrin followed at a slower pace. When he got outside, Stassi was nowhere in sight.

Now Dobrin can hear the satellite TV switch from the game back to the girls, the familiar music, always the same music, filtering through the wall. He slips his hand inside his underwear and inhales softly.

He had not said anything to Tanya after the sweater incident. She had not given him the chance. After class she had practically run from the room, leaving Dobrin to wonder if she was embarrassed or hurt or just in a hurry. Several times he's questioned if the moment really happened, if she said anything to him at all. Tomorrow he will redeem himself. He will say something to her whether or not he has a reason. He will find something. He will tell her he likes her rucksack or her nibbled pencils or the slope of her back when she leans forward over her desk. He will tell her he had noticed her tan lines at the pool and the way her bathing suit rode up over her hips. He will wear his brown sweater, and Tanya—oh, Tanya. He will ask her if she wants to come over and watch a show on the satellite TV. She can choose the program. She can. Oh. There in the darkness, it seems so easy. The million things he would like to tell her. Yes.

Next to him, Maika throws back her covers and rises from the bed. Dobrin uses his clean hand to cover his face and waits the humiliating stretch of time as she fumbles for her slippers, her sweater, the doorknob. He hears the kitchen door open and close, listens to the tick of the gas turning on, the oven door opening, the chair pulled up close.

This is how they will spend the night. Maika in front of the oven, Tatko in front of the satellite TV, and Dobrin in a puddle of his own misery, wondering if this is how it feels to be a man.

GALIA

Galia's parents were the kind who bought the bar of chocolate before she asked for it. Approaching middle age when they had her, they'd had time to anticipate her needs. They bought shoes before she could walk, a dictionary before she could talk, and a battery of pens, pencils, and paintbrushes when her fingers were still doughy and fat. They purchased her grades in batches at the start of the Bulgarian school year: they could get a whole semester of sixes with a side of pork or wool enough to knit two sweaters. They bought her ticket to University a year in advance. They bought her valedictory remarks from Petya Docheva, the smartest girl in class. For a ten-minute speech printed on note cards, Petya charged the amount she needed to cover the University entrance exam fee. Petya got a near-perfect score on the exam, and still the University couldn't find a place for her. When the word got out Petya would work in a café the next year and retake the entrance exam the following summer, Galia refused to leave the apartment even to buy bread. She didn't want to see anyone, least of all Petya. Galia's *tatko* said if Petya was really smart, she would have taken her tutoring money and lined the pocket of a University professor. "Petya hasn't learned the most important lesson," Tati said. "By now she should know, you get what you pay for."

Tati's most recent purchase, Vladi, is asleep on the bed. It's 2:15 in the morning, and the room is black, except for a sallow sphere of light from the bedside lamp. His smell is a combination of stale and sour, saturated as he is from a full day of drinking, the first shot of *rakiya* taken at 9:00 A.M. He looks peaceful—hair scalloping the top of his forehead, mouth open just enough for guttural sleep sounds to escape—except for the scar on his arm. It runs from his shoulder to his elbow, a centimeter thick, and round, like a rope stitched to his bicep, red, lumpy, and enraged. The doctors say it will never go away, which is good, she knows, for Vladi's sake. He needs that scar—that angry piece of evidence. Much more than he needs a wife or a father-in-law who buys him. Things.

They hardly spoke after Tati dropped them off at the hotel. The hour-long ride from Old Mountain to Sofia in Tati's police car had finished them off, with Tati talking the whole way about the disaster with Petya Docheva's mother and Stefan Nachev on the dance floor. How they had groped each other—"Like animals!" Tati yelled—and wouldn't stop, not even when first, Petya, then, Tati, suggested they sit down. How he'd known something bad was going to happen, the way they were humping and bumping so close to the band. How they were lucky no one had been killed when the equipment came crashing down, cords ripped out of the wall, speakers knocked off tripods. Galia could only assume the crash reverberated in Vladi's head the way it did in hers—a throbbing echo of the day's events that refused to subside.

After they checked in, Vladi spent fifty dollars on Marlboros from the hotel bar. He didn't look at Galia when he took the wad of wedding money out of his jacket pocket and peeled off the bills. He could have bought the cigarettes for a fraction of the price anywhere else. As he was counting out the money, he stopped and looked at Galia, his eyes yolk yellow and his skin peppered with blackened pores. He just stood there, fists filled with money, willing her to say something.

But Galia's mind was white—white dress with a row of buttons hard to undo, white sheets pulled taut across the bed, white skin never exposed to sun. She flushed, fish mouthed, desperate for words that would not come.

Up in the room, Vladi lit a cigarette and turned on the TV. This was how he was: he could not be in a room for one minute without needing the TV. "You drain me," he said, blowing smoke from his nose and staring at the soccer match on the screen. "When I'm with you, I feel like I'm with nobody."

Galia knew she should be hurt by this, but in truth, she was relieved. This was not so bad, she thought. This was not the worst thing to say. Vladi's words were not kind, but they also were not untrue. Vladi saw her for who she was—one of those fake Gucci purses that looks okay on the shelf but splits at the seams as soon as you put anything inside. In a way, she was grateful Vladi already understood this about her. There would be no surprises.

Tears seep from the corners of Galia's eyes. She is overcome with gratitude for this unexpected reprieve. Her nightdress is damp with steam, and her curly hair has frizzed into a thick wedge. She was in the bathroom too long, fretting about whether to lock the door, what to wear, the things they would do when they shared a bed. She had worried until her head hurt and her hands trembled and her gums bled from brushing her teeth. Even after so much brushing, she can still taste Vladi's smoky kisses—on the church altar, the municipality stairs, the dance floor—three of them in total, each one lasting a little longer than the one before. Looking at his lips now, she tries to remember how they felt, pressed against hers. Mostly, she recalls they tasted of cigarettes and, at the moment they kissed, Vladi had closed his eyes.

To her mother's chagrin, she had not followed suit. "*Ne taka, Galche*," Maika had said. "The next time, you close your eyes. You'll scare him if you keep your eyes open." Each time, Galia vowed she would close her eyes, but each time she failed her mother's command. "Why do you do that?" her *maika* hissed at her in the bathroom stall. But Galia could not explain the tenderness she found in the oily lines creasing Vladi's eyelids. Though she knew from the movies closing one's eyes was normal kissing behavior, she believed then, as she does now, with Vladi it was something more—something borne not out of habit, but intention; not out of disgust, but mercy.

With Vladi asleep, Galia is more alone than she's been all day. She was not allowed to dress herself or do her own hair. Once she was securely fettered by button, clasp, and pin, her mother had followed her everywhere, even to the bathroom, where she held the gown out of harm's way. Galia had been squeezed and kissed and hugged and carried—none of which was as difficult for her to bear as the fact of the purchase, the sale being celebrated.

That Vladi is sleeping through the final stages of the transaction by no means nullifies the deal; nevertheless, Galia feels more at peace than she has in months. There is comfort—

albeit small—in knowing moments like this will exist. They can share the same room and not be together. Several hours into her marriage, she is unchanged and untouched, safe and separate and alone.

Leaving the TV and lights as they are, Galia sinks into a chair, moving quietly to preserve Vladi's sleep. The room is too cold, but she does not mind. The flow of air from a vent in the wall gives her something to think about: how her goose pimpled arms look, thin and milky blue in the nightdress she has chosen, a thick, pink cotton, pleasingly opaque so as to reveal nothing. Only now does it strike her that the tiny embroidered flowers sprinkling the gown are suggestive of something— sweetness, purity. At once, the gown seems oddly out of tune with the night's intentions. The hotel bed is, after all, as long and wide as a trampoline.

Quickly, she is caught in a swirl of fear and regret. She knows where she is headed, down the well-trod path of *could haves, should haves,* and *if onlys,* her destination being the damning *how could she let this happen?*

When Galia was five, she watched the lady behind the counter rest her finger on the scale when she weighed cheese for the customer at the front of the line. The lady would not do this to Maika, but she would do it to a woman with a thin coat and scuffed purse. Galia knew what the shop lady was doing. She stared at the thick finger resting on the scale until the lady caught her watching.

The line leading up to the counter was long, and people looked cross. The lady looked cross, too. "Why don't you wait for your mother outside?" she said. "Here's a piece of *lokum.* You can eat this outside."

Galia understood she had done something wrong. The finger was large, and from where she stood, her head just below the counter, it was not difficult to see. But no one else noticed it. She shouldn't have noticed it either.

Maika transferred the powdered sweet from the shop lady's thick fingers to Galia's palm. "You wait right outside," she said, nudging her toward the door. "Don't go anywhere."

Outside, another girl was waiting for her mother, only she had moved beyond the door and was talking to a hairless dog standing in the square. "Can you see, Krastavitza? How many fingers am I holding up?"

Krastavitza could not count the fingers, but clearly he enjoyed the attention. His tail wagged and his whole body wagged with it.

Nibbling on her square of Turkish delight, Galia wondered if the dog was really named Krastavitza. *Cucumber* was just the right name for the tubular dog. She wondered if all dogs were so round beneath their fur.

"How many fingers, Krastavitza?" The girl was holding up three fingers. "Come on, Krastavitza. My fingers are getting tired." The girl was starting to sound angry. Krastavitza cowered on the ground. "I said, how many fingers?"

"Three," Galia blurted out.

The girl clapped her hands, and Krastavitza jumped up and barked. "Very good, Krastavitza. Now how many?"

Galia waited, giving Krastavitza a chance to answer on his own. "Two," she finally said.

"Good, Krastavitza," the girl said. "You are very smart."

At that moment, the woman with the thin coat emerged from the shop and passed Galia on the stair. "Petya," she called sharply. Galia wondered if she was poor because she spent so much money on cheese. "Are you talking to that sick dog?"

"No," Petya said, scrambling to her feet.

"Then who are you talking to?"

Petya looked at Galia, and even though they appeared to be close in age, Galia withered beneath her gaze. "I was talking to my imaginary friend," Petya said.

"That's not what I saw," the woman said. "*Haide,* Petya. It's time to go home."

The girl joined her mother, and they set off down the square. Though the girl had been very small, she loomed large in Galia's memory. For when she named the hairless creature who wandered the square "Krastavitza," she gave the dog an identity. And when she called Galia her imaginary friend, at once Galia understood her place in the world.

It was less a revelation than it was a recognizable fit, the way Krastavitza's naked skin sheathed his tubular body like a fine suit or the way her sneakers felt, so nice and light on her feet, that after a few minutes, Galia could almost forget them—the shoes, and even more, the feet inside them.

For, by the time Galia met Petya in the square, she'd already glimpsed her own irrelevance—in the chemistry set sitting on her shelf, the telescope poised at her window, the typewriter centered on her desk. When these things appeared in her bedroom, she did not know what to make of them. Maika and Tati expected her to put them to use. She filled the chemistry vials with buttons from her mother's sewing box and played the typewriter the way she'd seen a man in the square type on his accordion, though she could not lift it from the desk. She played and sang along to the taut, clicking noises she produced, until her mother got concerned and put the typewriter away.

It was a life arranged and planned for, requiring a careful squelching of unwanted tendencies and a perseverance in sculpting an ideal. As soon as Tatko announced her engagement, Maika put Galia on a diet. The dress was tailored not to the body as it was, but as it would be. Sure enough, by the day of the wedding, Galia was bony and angular—*kato model,* her mother admired—and the dress fit like a sleeve over Galia's perfected form.

Just the thought of so many months on skinless chicken and watermelon, tomatoes and cucumbers, has Galia famished. She hasn't eaten all day. There was a bite of cake, but little else, for she had been too nervous to eat. She looks around the hotel room and spots an array of chips and peanuts in tinsel packages she doesn't dare touch. Vladi shifts in his sleep, stretching out his short, muscular legs. Tatko speaks often of the athletic sons they will have: one will play soccer, and the other volleyball, he says, confident he will have his way.

In third grade, the girl from the square charged two pieces of pumpkin pastry for an hour of homework. Petya's mother set the price to make sure Petya ate something after school. She was the smallest girl in class, with thick, black-rimmed glasses, black hair down to her chin, parted in the middle and tucked behind her ears. Galia used to sit at the kitchen table and watch Petya work math problems and write sentences in a cursive that was even and fluid. Galia's pastries were gone in minutes, brown flakes scattered on the table, napkin crumpled in a ball. But Petya made her pastries last the entire hour, taking small bites between equations, careful not to get grease spots on the page. Galia liked the way Petya's pencil sounded as it moved across the paper. Sometimes, she pushed too hard and broke the tip off, and Galia would sharpen it over the garbage pail while Petya picked up a reserve and kept on writing.

In fact, Galia did not need help with her schoolwork. She followed along easily as Petya wrote the figures and letters— she could have done the work herself if given the chance. But Tati was unwilling to take chances with his only child. She would not have to work or worry in order to succeed.

At first, it took a certain restraint to watch and not do—to sit across the table and observe the tiny black-haired girl lick her fingers and gnaw on her pencil. Galia envied the gravity with which Petya etched the words and equations onto the paper. For a small girl, Petya carried a heavy weight. The kids at school said Petya had to clean the house and cook the dinner because her mother was busy and because she had no father. It seemed unfair to Galia that one small girl had so much responsibility and importance while she had none.

It was likely this thought had crossed Petya's mind as well, for while she was unfailingly accurate and thorough in the homework she wrote for Galia, at times she was impatient with her charge. "Did you see how I did that?" she might snap on completing an equation. "Next time, you do it yourself." At other times, Petya stared at Galia, as though puzzling over a problem she could not solve. It reminded Galia of sitting in the hairdresser's chair, while the *frizyorka* and Maika conferred on how best to manage Galia's thick nest of curls. But unlike the hairdresser, Galia sensed Petya never found a solution, and when she departed in the late afternoons, she left feeling her job was only half done.

After Petya went home, Galia would take the finished homework and chewed pencils and go into her bedroom and close the door. There, she would copy all the homework onto a separate piece of paper. She was pleased when she could get the pencil to make the same intelligent sounds Petya made, though her numbers and letters always looked different: while Petya's figures slanted neatly to the right, Galia's angled in all directions. Sometimes she got too bored to finish, but most of the time, she made it to the end, only to crumple up the page and throw it in the dumpster on the way to school the next morning. In the end, it did not matter if she turned in Petya's work or her work or no work at all. Any action or inaction could be remedied by a bushel of onions or potatoes or a bottle of Jim Beam.

It was a seemingly flawless system, giving to each party what it needed. Tati got the marks he wanted: Galia's record in the *dnevnik* displayed a satisfying row of pot-bellied sixes. The teachers looked forward to having Galia in class. That year, they would be able to buy a sheepskin slipcover for the living room sofa or a month in a cottage on the Black Sea coast.

Galia got ten *leva* for not talking in class. Maika said it would be better if she didn't show off, and like a good girl, she didn't say a word. Petya, on the other hand, answered all the teacher's questions. No one liked her—so skinny and smart and unfashionable in her home-sewn jeans.

Petya's mother increased the price for Petya's services each year and could be seen wearing a new coat, a new dress, a new *gadje* on her arm as she walked down the square. With each new boyfriend, Petya's mother looked younger and prettier and more in love. She dated them, one after the other, until she met Stefan, the best handyman in town. Him, she dated for years, but only when there was something in need of repair.

Perhaps Petya got the least from the deal: after a while, she tired of pumpkin pastry and stopped eating the squares on her plate. Maika started giving her money for snacks. This ended, however, when Maika learned Petya was using the money to buy hotdogs for the hairless dog in the square. The diseased creature, which many hoped would die, looked round and happy and was starting to grow fuzz.

This system carried on without so much as a pause or hiccup until Galia reached the tenth grade. That year, she had an American teacher who got angry with her for not speaking in class.

"I get these beautiful homework papers from you, but you won't say a word," Dean said to her early in the year. His name was Mr. Riley, but he told them to call him Dean. They were working through a chapter called "It's a Crime" in their English workbooks. "Can I hear you use *fraudulent* in a sentence?"

Galia opened her mouth but seemed to have forgotten how to make any sounds. It was impossible to think with all the classroom snickers and the boiling sounds in her stomach. She stared at the list of words she had been assigned to memorize. *Transgression, felony, misdemeanor, corruption.* She knew them all.

"Quiet, everyone," Dean said, pacing the front of the room, running his hand through his red hair until it stood on end. How everyone loved that hair! The rich blue-red nest—not a hint of blond or brown, but a pure redness, like a tomato just shy of ripe. Dean knew his hair fascinated the students, and he used it to hold the class's attention.

Out of the corner of her eye, Galia could see Petya frantically waving her hand. Like a propeller, the swinging arm lifted Petya from her seat and pulled her forward across her desk. The kids snickered at Petya's bony rear end, her pocketless jeans, her shirt tucked into the ragged waistband of her white underpants. "Mr. Riley," she grunted repeatedly, breathless with effort. Bits of paper and nubbins of eraser pelted her behind. Humiliation pooled in the roundness of Galia's cheeks. Petya knew as well as everyone else that Mr. Riley would not call on her until Galia had had ample time to answer the question. It was clear Petya was trying to save her.

Finally, Dean relented. "In my class, it's a crime to turn in *fraudulent* homework," he said. He wrote zeroes in the *dnevnik*, though the other teachers reminded him the lowest grade was two. Tati offered to buy Dean a television for his apartment, but Dean refused. "I'm trying to help her," Dean said in broken Bulgarian, the color of his skin deepening to match his hair. "You're not doing her any favors."

When Tati cursed Dean at the dinner table, Galia stared into her plate in silent dissent. For though she couldn't bear being at the center of this controversy, she found Dean terribly handsome with his brilliant hair and his pale skin, and after a while, the embarrassment she felt when he called on her in class evolved into something more like gratitude. In the beginning, he called on her every class, waiting two or three minutes for an answer buried beneath years of inertia—an answer that would never come. As the year drew on, the questions slowed. Some weeks he might call on her once or twice, others not at all. But he never gave up on her the way other teachers did. It was as if he knew she held the answer on the tip of her tongue, offering to her again and again the bittersweet lozenge of an opportunity on which she could not act. It was agonizing, how much she wanted to please him, to answer just one question. She thought if she could get herself to answer one, the next one might not be so difficult. Soon she would be answering all the questions for herself. But that first answer—the thought of words tumbling from her mouth and clattering to the linoleum like *contraband*—she couldn't do it. So they were stuck, looking at each other, the current of their wills passing between them.

As the zeroes multiplied like tiny gasps of horror next to Galia's name, it appeared Dean had won. For some, it was threatening to see a system disrupted this way. Who was this young American to come along and start shutting things down? But there were plenty of people who appreciated Dean and would invite him to dinner at their homes. They liked his tattered pants and untucked shirts; they were glad for his defiance. These were the people who warned Dean against having his girlfriend rent a car when she came to pick him up at the end of the year. They suggested a taxi. They offered to drive him in one of their cars, a Lada or Trabant. When the girlfriend arrived in a sporty, if battered, rental car, they warned Dean, "A Fiat is a Fiat. No matter the cracked windshield—it is not safe here." Dean hugged his friends good-bye and told them not to worry. His flight was early the next morning. He would be gone before dawn. When Dean and his girlfriend finished packing the car in the early hours of the morning, they parked it in front of the police station for safekeeping while they caught a few hours of sleep.

The next morning, Galia was in the kitchen making herself a cup of tea when Tati walked in, his uniform rumpled, looking exhausted but happy. He was a senior officer and did not work nights unless he chose to. Galia knew from the pale glow of peace across his forehead that a battle of some sort had taken place, and Tati had come out on top.

So much scrabbling to get by or get ahead (your ambition is determined by where you start). It's rumored one shop lady has a small piece of red tape marking the precise spot where she should rest her finger so it won't be visible from the other side of the counter. Whatever the trick, it must be working, because Galia has never seen a pinky, thumb, or any finger in between resting on the scale.

All these years, and still she is watching. Now, she watches the minutes on the digital alarm clock switch over one after the other. She imagines they are slowing down. At one point, it seems they have stopped, and she holds her breath that somehow she's been saved. But then they start up again, ticking over one by one, tracking the plodding march of time, along with the faint ebb and flow of Vladi's snore. All her life, time has been her unbudging companion; all her life, she has willed it to go away. Now, she pleads with it to return, *come back, let me try again.*

When Galia got to University in Sofia, Tati rented a nice room for her in the apartment of an older couple—the parents of a fellow officer. Galia had her meals prepared for her, and it was only a five-minute walk to school. She went to class and studied hard—she did well by her own right. But when her papers and exams were returned to her with neat red sixes and no other marks, she was certain they hadn't been read.

By the time Galia entered her last semester at University, Tati's plans for his next big purchase were already underway.

The negotiations began on a routine roadside stop just east of Sofia, where the road wound and curved around the Stara Planina. Several tunnels had been blasted through the mountains to offer a more direct passage to and from the capital. Just after one of these tunnels, Tati's partner was waving the cars over, and Tati was issuing tickets—the goal being not to enforce the law, so much as to elicit bribes. If the driver complained, Tati reminded him, "In America, they make you pay to drive on their highways," thumbs in belt loops, like he'd been there. Eventually, the driver would offer a portion of the ticket price. When Tati accepted, everyone went away happy.

Seeing Vladi's arm in a sling, Tati said, "A hundred *leva* for driving while disabled."

"Sorry," Vladi said, opening his wallet and showing Tati the empty insides. *"Nyamam nishto."*

Tati noticed Vladi's eyes, green as an onion shoot, and even though he could see Vladi's coat was made of real leather, he believed he didn't have any money. "Well, what have you got?" Tati said, peering in the window. *"Kakvo e tova?"* he nodded at a volleyball on the seat. His nephew had a birthday coming up in a month, and he could see the ball was of professional quality.

"I'm sorry," Vladi said. "I can't give you that."

"It's just a ball," Tati said. The line of cars was growing. Tati's partner looked over at them, shoulders raised in question.

"Prosto ne moga," Vladi said defensively. "It's not *just* a ball."

Tati had already decided the ball looked too used to give as a gift. The car, on the other hand, was a Ford—a burgundy two-door, not more than ten years old. The kind of car you didn't have unless you knew somebody.

Tati made Vladi wait for him by the side of the road until

he was finished with his shift. After he split the morning's earnings with his partner, he led Vladi to a nearby *mehana* and ordered two *rakiyas* and fillets with *garnitura*. They drank the *rakiyas* without touching their food and ordered two more. Vladi told Tati about the ball and the promising volleyball career that ended with a slip on a patch of sweat and a series of cracks in his humerus. There were four cracks, popping like the celebratory fireworks dispatched at the end of a match—in this case, a career. The National Sports Academy said he could keep the car and the clothes and the big-screen TV, but they terminated the lease on his Sofia apartment. He had to be out by the end of the month.

When they emptied their *rakiya* glasses for the fourth and final time, the negotiations were well underway. After Tati counted out the bills to cover lunch and laid them on the table, he considered his companion, then reached into his wallet for a few more. The fillet had been lean and tender, the *rakiya* smooth and fruity, the company outstanding.

The deal was finalized in front of two hundred friends. Sitting at the head table, Galia had the feeling she was at someone else's wedding. The way people came up to her and petted her—she could hardly recognize them, or herself for that matter. It was like some charade, with Galia and Vladi standing beside each other like two people in love. When the band broke for dinner, Tati took the microphone and presented Vladi with the keys to an apartment wrapped in a decorative foil sack and tied with curls of ribbon. Amid stamping and applause, Vladi hugged Tati. Then, chest out and chin high, he raised the metallic package over his head, gripping it with both hands and turning in a circle for everyone to see.

At that moment, Galia had to believe things could get no worse. Playing with the buckle of her shoe, she willed the clapping to stop, the meal to end, which in time it did, leaving her feeling depleted. She allowed the party to bubble up around her, dancing, drinking, here the chink of dropped glass, there a splash of laughter.

In time, she spotted Vladi out on the *balcon,* smoking a cigar. He stood in a ring of his former volleyball teammates, disrupting their handsome circle like a missing tooth. Were they really so tall? Galia had wondered. Or did Vladi look smaller than before? Or with so much night ahead of her, was Galia seeing things the way she wanted to see them, less daunting, more manageable than they really were? She'd been playing such games all day, trying to gauge the reality of what was happening to her. Watching Vladi's lips close around the shaft of the cigar, she recalled how they had felt when he pressed them to her own. How was it possible so hard a man could have lips so soft?

Sensing her gaze, Vladi looked inside. He beckoned her to join him.

"*Kakvo?*" Galia said, though through the closed windows, he could not hear. She looked around, hoping he was gesturing to somebody nearby, but for the first time all day, there was no one around. "Me?" she questioned. *Please no.*

Vladi beckoned again. He was laughing with the cigar clenched between his teeth and rolling up one sleeve of his shirt.

Galia rose slowly to her feet, feeling wilted from the heat and unsteady on her heels. Vladi had hardly looked at her all night; now he was eyeing her with a glee she did not trust. The yards of satin that had bustled around her at the start of this day hung heavy from her shoulders, cutting painful gashes in her flesh. She pushed open the door.

"Galche," he greeted her, wrapping his arm around her and kissing her on the cheek, the moist butt of his cigar poking her in the arm. "Galche," he said again. She had never seen him so drunk. "Touch this," he said, indicating the scar on his arm. "*Ela*, touch it," he said, grabbing her hand. "Tell the boys how you like it."

This was the lowest point, Galia can say for sure now that the day has passed. Just the thought of it, and her throat constricts. The cold hotel air feels even colder when her cheeks are wet. She tries to stifle the memory, but without success. She will never be able to rid herself of the incident, standing with her fingers jammed into Vladi's arm, Vladi laughing while his friends looked on, unsmiling, annoyed, ashamed. Rather, she will learn to live with that scar. She will touch it, caress it. During happier spells in their marriage—there will be several—she will even press her lips to it. The root of Vladi's moodiness and depression, it will darken many of their days, but not all of them, thanks to Tati, who will secure for Vladi a position at a firm doing business of the sort one does not talk about and from which Vladi will never feel satisfaction—though he will find small solace in his cell phone, his thick wallet, and the clean, slick sounds of silk rubbing between his thighs when he walks to work in the morning. On more than one occasion, he will tell her the swish of the pants makes him feel tall.

In part, she will remember those moments on the balcony for the event they precipitated later on. For the tears do not stop coming, the air does not stop blowing, and the sniffling— well, she *cannot* sniffle, inhale, exhale with Vladi lying right there in the bed. Indeed, she has little choice but to take up her sweater—beneath which her nightdress looks modest, even appropriate—and her silly bridal purse, to slip her feet into a pair of jelly sandals, and to leave her husband on their wedding night.

When I'm with you, I feel like I'm with nobody, he had said. Perhaps he won't even notice she's gone.

The hotel nightclub—Club Cosmos—is hardly Galia's desired destination. On the contrary, she only goes there after she has tried the restaurant and lobby. Finding the former closed and the latter empty, she hides in a public bathroom long enough for the tearstains to fade. She might have stayed there all night were it not for the lady who comes to clean. Thus expelled, she follows a faint trickle of music down a flight of stairs and through a pair of heavy brown doors.

She has been to nightclubs, of course. On certain nights, going to nightclubs has been impossible to avoid, particularly in high school, when her whole class would go on the eve of a holiday and her parents would not let her stay home. But this place is like no nightclub she has ever seen—no pounding music, no pulsing disco lights, no acned Russian girls taking off their clothes—none of the haze and frenzy you might expect. Rather, there are fat upholstered booths and small tables, and in the center of the room, a tiny stage, on which a single couple twirls beneath a rotating mirrored globe. Beside them is a quartet with a woman singing a ballad in thickly accented English.

Galia might have preferred the frenzy; she feels frightfully conspicuous in this strange place. Of the ten or fifteen people huddled around tables, several have turned their heads to look at her. Even the singer is watching Galia, the words to the song drifting involuntarily from her mouth. Just as Galia considers slipping away, a man in a dark suit asks, "Table for one?"

She has no choice but to allow him to seat her. As though sensing her need for escape, he does not give her one of the tables by the door. Rather he leads her—in her nightdress and sweater, her bridal purse shimmering in the globe's prismatic light—clear across the room to a table bordering the stage. When he pulls the chair out for her, she feels unbalanced; she is not inside her body as she tucks herself into the plush red velvet fold of the chair.

"Something to drink?" he asks.

She wants to say nothing—she does not want a *smetka*, a debt, even one she can pay—but she can see how strange it would be for her to sit here without a drink. She orders a Coke, and when he asks her if she wants ice, she says "no" before it occurs to her she is speaking English with this man, a *Bulgarin*. "No, thank you," she says, the words sounding strange, smooth, even nice.

By the time her Coke comes in a tall thin glass with a wedge of lemon perched on the edge, she is starting to feel more in control. She can be agreeably anonymous in this strange place. She has earned nothing more, nothing less from the day's hardships. Just a Coke and a lemon and a moment alone.

The spinning globe casts a soothing, silvery light. Vladi, Galia knows, does not mean to hurt her—not with his comments, not with the episode on the *balcon*. She, of all people, can understand his fury at the economics of tonight's transaction: the two-ended arrow connecting buying and selling. He has seen through the porous screen that divides thinking that you're taking from knowing what you're giving in return. She, better than anyone, knows how he feels. At this recognition, Galia experiences a strange spasm of hope that maybe . . . oh, she should not wish for so much.

"Excuse me." The man in the suit is handing her a glass of white wine. "Someone asked me to bring you this."

"Oh. I—" She's lost the words. "No order."

"No, miss," the man says, putting the glass down before her. "Someone has ordered it for you. Please. Enjoy."

"*Molya*—," Galia starts, but the man has left. She wonders if there's something she has misunderstood. She glances at the tables around her, over which people hunch in tight clusters of two and three. Aside from the woman on the dance floor and the singer in the band, there are no other women besides Galia. To her right is a table of thick, dark-skinned Bulgarians, smoking and looking around the room. The rest of the people look like foreign businessmen. They are mostly middle-aged and wear pastel sport shirts. Several booths down, three men are smiling at her.

Heat prickles Galia's scalp. She does not know what to do. Maybe she should get up and return the glass to them. That would be best. She will tell them she has a husband and cannot drink their wine, but thank you, it was very kind. Galia knows this is the thing to do, and yet, no one has ever bought her a drink. And though she knows it's wrong, and though she does not care to drink alcohol, she thinks on this night—in this pocket of borrowed time—she should drink this glass of wine.

The stem of the glass feels fragile in her hand. Sipping the chilled wine, Galia feels delicate and fine, even pretty. There is only one other time Galia can recall feeling this way. It was when Dean hired a bus to take their class to an American library in Sofia. On the way there, he passed out a fill-in-the-blank worksheet and played a song called "Piano Man" over and over. When they had the words, they sang along with the tape. It was a good song, and they sang at the tops of their voices, and it was so nice Galia was sorry when they reached the library. But then, getting off the bus, Dean had been standing there, and he took her hand and said, "Watch your step." She knew it was nothing—he did it for all the girls—but she can remember how special it felt to hold his hand.

So aglow is Galia with this memory that when a man in a light green sport shirt sits down and asks her name, she answers "Galia" without a twinge of nervousness. He asks her where in Bulgaria she's from, and she learns he's from Chicago. "Al Capone. Bang. Bang," he says, and she smiles at his joke. It seems he's been here for a while.

As much as Galia would prefer to be left alone, she cannot help but be flattered by the man's attention. Aside from the red in his eyes, he is not bad looking, and his cologne is dusky and tempting. She feels the queasy excitement she had so often felt in Dean's class, especially when he passed close by her desk. She has not experienced this feeling since he left. Not on the day he left—absolutely not then—but some days before his departure.

Dean's car was gone. So were his faded jeans, his rucksack with the clips and buckles, the cherry pulp *kaval* he had bought from a player in Plovdiv. The music teacher had been trying to teach him the difficult instrument for nearly a year, and still when he brought it to class to demonstrate what he had learned, he could produce little more than a hoarse whisper at three tuneless pitches.

That morning, Galia tried to quiet her wobbling hand as she wrestled her teacup into its saucer. Maika was offering *banitsa*, eggs, yogurt, bread, cheese, jam. Galia could feel the excitement swelling, the air in the room growing thick.

"*Vsichko e nared*," Tati said, sitting down at the table and unzipping his coat.

But everything was not okay. As her mother set some Turkish coffee on the stove to boil, Galia excused herself and left. Her parents waited until she closed the kitchen door behind her before they started talking. Through the pane of rippled glass, she could see their heads bent close and could hear the rapid rush of their voices—voices laden not with guilt or with shame, but with wonder. The midnight feats. Victory exceeding all hope. Dean had made it so easy, proving once and for all it was naïveté and not virtue that made the boy so stubborn and principled.

Galia spent the day walking the foothills of the mountain in the old part of town. There, the road ran steep, and the people—villagers who still wore their crocheted vests, their homemade shoes, long after their village had grown into a town—lived in the houses their fathers and grandfathers had built decades earlier. They did not have heat, these houses, and many of them still used wood stoves. Yet the people stayed in them even when the town erected new cinderblock apartments down below with radiators and heat and gas stoves and hot water straight from the tap.

No, the villagers stayed put right where they were on the steep mountain incline. Generation after generation plastered and replastered their houses in blues and pinks and yellows, some garish in hue, others sun-baked to near white. Many of the houses—even the bright, freshly plastered ones—bore bald patches where the plaster had crumbled away, exposing the underlying brick and mortar. Galia wondered if the owners hadn't left the holes uncovered on purpose, the toothy weave of bone and flesh a testimony to the foundation upon which each family was built.

On her way back down, Galia saw a crowd gathered at the bus stop. There were not so many reasons for crowds to gather in this town; she knew it was for Dean. By now, the whole town would know what had happened. She had taken her time up in the hills, trying to prepare herself for this new wave of shame, only to understand she would never be ready to face the people down below.

She would not have stopped at the bus stop had she not seen Petya. "Come on," Petya said to her in a way that did not invite so much as command. Galia and Petya added themselves to the back of the crowd. At the center, Dean was talking to two police officers. All year, people had been praising his noble attempts with the Bulgarian language, yet now as he spoke—*tova ne e kraya*, he said over and over again—the words sounded distorted, his American accent at once repugnant and dim. A collective embarrassment muffled the crowd as they listened to him argue, "This is not the end," with such earnestness, he almost convinced them it was true. But they could not believe him, because they knew the car was gone, and by now, they were eager for him to be gone too.

The girlfriend—Laura was her name—had brown hair and was plumper and more ordinary than Galia had imagined. She stood next to Dean and stared at the ground, deaf to Dean's Bulgarian conversation. By the curve in her shoulders, Galia could tell she, like everyone else, wanted Dean to give up. She waited, and he argued, and the officers chewed large pieces of gum. As Galia looked on, she felt her shame spreading out like a big wet puddle, seeping through the crowd to include the officers, friends, even Laura—all those who were wronging Dean yet again, without his even knowing it.

Minutes earlier, Galia had felt like an enormous pimple on the face of the crowd. She had been certain Dean would see her, would single her out, adding to a disgrace that was already complete. Now, things had shifted, and she began to fear he would miss her. As her disappointment grew—over Dean's ugliness, Laura's duplicity, the betrayal of friends—so too did her desperation grow to connect with him once more. She was standing on her toes, struggling to see him, willing him to see her, when Petya leaned over and whispered in her ear, "Do you think they have sex?"

Galia cannot think of Petya without remembering those words. How shocked she had been to feel Petya's breath on her ear and to hear the same words she had asked herself many times, yet always in the privacy of her own mind. At that moment, shared with Petya, the thought seemed unbearably vulgar. Yet one more violation of her beloved Dean. Galia had been furious with Petya. Though by now, fury has dissipated and evolved into another understanding about her friend.

Maika had invited Petya to the wedding, and by some act of providence, she had been able to come. This summer, she had received a scholarship to take courses in Japan; her flight was scheduled for the day after the wedding. Galia and Petya had not kept in touch, though Maika had updated Galia on Petya's doings. After a year working in a local café, Petya had retaken the University entrance exams and been accepted to study Japanese philology. She now had one year left to go. On the side, she translated interactions between Bulgarian and Japanese businessmen and escorted Japanese visitors traveling and working in Sofia.

There was a whiff of cynicism in this last detail: Petya, her mother's daughter, being chosen to accompany businessmen on their travels. For this reason, Galia felt no small triumph—for Petya, and not for herself—when she laid eyes on her at the wedding. Petya was small and unfashionable as ever, dressed in a skirt and blouse several sizes too large. Her hair and glasses were the same as they'd been in high school.

It was not until later in the evening—after the gifted keys, the poked scar—that they managed to greet each other. The seamstress had attached clear plastic teardrops to the torso of Galia's dress. Hugging Petya, she was shamed by the chatter of her movements.

But Petya was distracted by her mother and Stefan wrapped in tight embrace out on the dance floor. "I'm so sorry," she said, turning her back on them. "I don't know how to make them stop." Red freckles of misery sprinkled her cheeks, and her shoulders sagged. Looking at her, Galia understood one more chance she had not taken—a friendship she had failed to recognize in the warm breathy secret that passed by her ear.

It was not long before Petya's mother brought the celebration to an end. It seemed to have been a while since she'd last needed a repair, because she and Stefan were all buttocks, breasts, and crotches, grabbing flesh by the handful. Galia had never seen such a display. She worried Vladi would want to do the same—she could not imagine being handled that way.

She knew she shouldn't watch, but she couldn't take her eyes off them. She saw the whole thing happen, when they bumped into a speaker and sent the entire system crashing to the floor.

Do you think they have sex?

The man sitting across from her is telling her about his travels in Spain, the elongated hands of a man named El Greco, the cheerful mosaics of someone named Gaudi.

Gaudy. She remembers that word. It is the word for a dress like hers. So many yards of blue-white satin ruined from being dragged across pavement and dirt, and for what? To make her look beautiful? Virginal? Chaste?

"Your glass is empty. Let's get you some more wine."

Galia recognizes the irony in this wedding night, the little daisies on her bridal nightgown. The clean and the dirty, the lurid and the pure. She knows Maika and Tati are lying in bed next to each other, talking about the wedding and the fine husband they found for their daughter. Maika is thinking about the sex. All night, her mother had been giving her hints. Be sure you shower. Be sure to wash yourself down there. Be sure to use the scented soap in your bag. Try to relax. Have a glass of wine. Trust your Vladi. He will know what to do.

In the morning, Maika will ask her, *So?*

Dean did not see her at the bus station. He climbed the stairs of the bus and sat down next to Laura and looked straight ahead as they pulled out of the station. Since then, no one had heard from him.

But in Galia's dreams, it happens differently. Dean looks back from the top stair, spots her in the crowd, and in his authoritative, twenty-four-year-old voice, asks her the question she'd both feared and wanted: "What do you have to say for yourself, Galia?"

The answer changes from dream to dream. Sometimes it's as simple as, "I'm sorry" or "Thank you." One time she said, "Please come again." Another time, she said, "You look nice in blue." In one particularly galling dream, she said, "It would be *fraudulent* to pretend I won't miss you."

With one hand, the American has intertwined his thick fingers with her own. The other is stroking her arm. Watching him work his way toward her elbow, she hears herself say, "Good-bye."

"Good-bye," she says, pushing her chair back. Tottering slightly as she stands, she leaves without paying for her Coke.

Over the course of her marriage, she will replay this ending time after time, until it warps and twists and bends in her mind. She will remember the yellow glow from the wine and the man who held her hand. She will never once doubt the decision she made that night—not even when Vladi's black mood touches the horizon. Rather, she will find satisfaction in her memories of her wedding night, not for the transaction that would be finalized when she returned to the room, but for the deal she saw coming, and so, got up and walked away.

SATISFACTORY PROOF

The night before graduation, Plamen's mother called to confirm their meeting in front of the Bulgarian Technical University at 1:00 P.M. sharp. *"Chuvash li?"* she said. "With your black shoes. Don't forget them." To Plamen's mother, completing a master's degree in number theory was a feat dwarfed by the difficulty of remembering one's own shoes. "And please, lots of people will be there. Stand up straight so we can see you."

Plamen had not stood up straight since his third year in high school, when he grew until his hair brushed the ceiling. He was the tallest person he knew. In the beginning, he had enjoyed the astonished faces of family and friends. His towering physique garnered him a good deal of attention, which he occasionally fueled with a casual elbow propped on short shoulder or head. But by the time he got to University, he was tired of the incessant requests from schoolboys who begged him to play basketball. He was sore from the bruises he incurred at doorways and in public conveyances designed for more normal-sized people. The slumping, which had started as a semipermanent ducking posture, became something more, something akin to a folding or repackaging of his ungainly form. Each time they visited, his parents pestered him to stand up straight, but Plamen, quietly, refused to comply. His parents were short and could not understand the difficulties of his formidable height.

Press your shirt. Eat a big breakfast. Plamen sank lower into his landlady's balding velvet sofa. This was not how he had pictured the completion of his degree. Finally: to be finished with Professor Mateev and his arduous master's proof! For three years, Plamen had imagined lightness, a lifting of the great pressure that bowed his shoulder blades like the wings of a stork. But there was no such euphoria. Instead, badgered, beleaguered, and just plain tired, on his graduation eve, Plamen felt his burdens not alleviated, so much as redistributed, as his mother pelted him with instructions. *Get a good night's sleep. Wear clean socks.* Would the phone call never end?

By the time he hung up, there was another voice crowding his head—of Nikki, his landlady's son, talking to his own mother just a few meters away.

"Plastic bottles, Maika," Nikki was saying, blowing a curl of smoke through his nose. "That's all people want these days." Plamen's *hazaika* nodded obligingly, even though she did not like people smoking in her house. Even though, she'd admitted to Plamen, she had not been much of a bottled beverage drinker before Nikki'd gone into the business.

"Glass bottles—" Nikki took a swig of yellow pineapple soda. "Glass bottles are out, Maika. There'll be no more walking home from market with a bag of glass bottles clinking against your leg. No more gashes cutting across your fingers from carrying bags of those heavy bottles. No more breaking and chipping—yes chipping, Maika! Have you ever considered how lucky you are never to have gotten a shard of bottle stuck in your throat?"

By Plamen's measure, the only thing lucky about this scene was that it was the last of its kind. After graduation, he would never have to drink sugary sodas and listen to Nikki talk about bottles. Gratifying as this thought was, Plamen knew if he were *really* lucky, he would have been spared this final encounter altogether. Nikki was not due for a visit: in the eight years Plamen had boarded with his *hazaika,* Nikki had come once each year for his mother's birthday. According to this progression, they had several months before Nikki should arrive.

To what did they owe this visit? Plamen's focus drifted to Nikki's rumpled suit and the single eyebrow running the width of his forehead. "Ahhh, Maika," Nikki exhaled after gulping the better part of a glass of soda. He slammed his glass down on the table and belched. "Worry-free soda," he said, swallowing an unruly chain of burps. "You don't know it yet, but it's going to change your life."

Plamen's *hazaika* smiled softly but did not look up from the pair of Plamen's shoes she was polishing. From the sad slope of her neck, the tears seeping from her eyes, the interminable polishing, it was obvious, to Plamen at least, she was not thinking about a soda-induced life change, so much as she was another one: the loss of a second son. After graduation, Plamen would return home for a summer in Old Mountain and a couple of months to calculate whatever came next.

This business with the shoes had been going on for days. She began by wiping them with a cloth and checking the laces weren't frayed. Then she pulled out a dented tin of wax and made a big deal of polishing them. "Only for special occasions," she said, spreading the polish with a tender, circular motion, her hand balled up in the shoe to flatten the creases. She applied the polish generously, going over scuffed patches two and three times. Apparently, she did not believe she had many special occasions left.

It angered Plamen to watch her work on the shoes, tears running down her nose and getting massaged into the leather. Eight years. He'd given her eight years, living in Nikki's tiny bedroom with its dank wallpaper and threadbare rug. He had paid his rent on the first of every month. Kept his room neat. Come and gone quietly. Eaten breakfast with her and dinner sometimes if he didn't have a study session or a meeting with a friend. If she turned off the TV, he would study with his door open, but then she wanted him to study at the dining room table, where the light was better and where there was room for plates of cookies and sticky bottles of cherry liqueur.

It was not his fault Nikki came back only once a year. It was not his fault, even with Nikki sitting in her living room— *a special occasion,* if only to her—she could barely look at her son for the attention she was giving a pair of shoes.

Yet could he blame her? At the moment, Nikki was pouring himself more soda and furrowing his mighty brow. "Ever wonder where the bubbles come from, Maika? Ever think about that?"

Bozhe Gospodi. It was time to call it a night. But as Plamen contemplated slipping quietly out of the *hol,* he heard Nikki say, "Isn't that right, Plame?"

"*Molya?*" Plamen said. He hated it when Nikki called him *Plame.*

"I bet you can tell us how they get the bubbles in the soda,"

Nikki said. "You're a smart guy. You would know a thing like that."

Plamen's face grew hot. He stared hard at *you're-a-smart-guy* Nikki. Was that a potshot? He had no idea how they put the bubbles in soda.

"Hey, Plame, are you okay?"

Plamen was not okay. He had not been okay for months, years even—not since Mateev had entered his life and ravaged his ambitions. And now this.

"*Ela* Plame," Nikki said, pushing back a chair at the table. "You look like you need a drink. What'll it be?"

Plamen eyed the scene with distaste, his *hazaika* caressing his shoes as if life depended on it. Drained though he was, he had to at least *try* to ease her despair. Reluctantly, he rejoined the party. His choices were pineapple, blueberry, and strawberry soda. He chose blueberry, though it hardly mattered. The sodas all tasted the same—very much like plastic.

No amount of soda could measure up to the hardship Plamen had suffered for his master's proof. At the end, it got even harder. Exponentially, irreparably so.

Though thirty days had passed since his thesis defense, the event still singed his awareness, failure branded on his every nerve. He had presented his work before a panel of five University professors. To guide the conversation, he had assembled a slide presentation outlining his proof. He had spent his birthday money from his grandparents on a laser pointer the size of a pen that produced an exhilaratingly sharp red dot, which he moved about the screen to highlight his findings. He had been correct in assuming the panel would not have read more than the first page or two of his thesis; thus, the presentation enabled an interested conversation, after which the panel applauded him. When they asked him to leave the room so they could confer, he had little doubt about the significance of his accomplishment.

There, in the cool of the tiled foyer, Plamen basked in a moment of satisfaction—the first and only such moment to come from his master's project. As an undergraduate, he had relished the prospect of advanced studies in number theory and the chance to work with Todor Mateev, Bulgaria's leading number theorist. He could not have guessed theirs would be an unhappy union. Whether it was a void of chemistry, or—as Plamen believed—an inability on Mateev's part to value an intellect divergent from his own, adviser and advisee had maintained a civil, peevish relationship of the sort no one can enjoy.

Through a narrow window in the door, Plamen could see the men smiling and laughing as they ate the cookies his *hazaika* had baked. He could not help but indulge in thoughts of the things being said about him—an extraordinary talent! one of their own! He knew the satisfaction of spending time with a good proof. The validity of his proof was indisputable; Mateev had challenged it with every conceivable case to make sure it held up under all conditions. The proof was also eloquent and concise; Plamen could not tolerate shoddy workmanship. He believed a proof should be no less elegant than the truth it purported. His, he was certain, was just that.

The panel spent only five minutes deliberating his fate as they devoured the cookies. Mateev delivered the news: Plamen's proof was deemed of limited import, but still fine work—the work of a gifted mathematician. "Congratulations," he concluded with robust collegiality.

If Plamen could be grateful for any one thing, it was being spared a hug or handshake. He was not deceived by Mateev's cheer. He stared at the frames of the professor's glasses, thick and obdurate as the man himself. Finally he managed, "Of limited import?"

The words tasted foreign on his tongue. What was this degree, if not a sour surprise? Though Plamen planned to spend the summer in Old Mountain, he had assumed he would be back, contributing to the circles of mathematical thought that revolved around Sofia, quiet and constant as the trolley lines that buzzed down city streets.

Of limited import?

"Well, of course," Professor Mateev said. "But what did you expect? You are at the beginning of your career. Greater things will come."

The urge to stand up straight or otherwise defend himself against Mateev's damaging appraisal was a reflex born out of three years of desperation. But when he attempted to shrug his shoulders back and lift his head high, he found a great weight lay across his back. He couldn't stand up straight even if he tried.

"You've really done it this time," Nikki was saying. "It's not every day a guy gets his master's. Isn't that right, Maika? Maika, is that an empty glass I see?"

Plamen winced as his *hazaika* accepted a refill. How much longer would this go on? By his calculations, they had each imbibed more than a liter, which should have been enough to satisfy even the most obsessive beverage salesman.

Still, Nikki pressured them to drink. "Plenty more where this came from," he said with a hint of bitterness Plamen found refreshing. Nikki was referring to the stash he'd discovered in the closet that afternoon. Every month, he sent his mother a carton of sodas; every month, she consumed at a slow, but steady pace, drinking the soda from one of the small copper espresso cups Nikki had given her for her birthday. It agonized Plamen to watch her. Tiny cup. Pained expression. Evidently, she'd lost some ground, and Nikki had found an entire carton of undrunk soda—a backlog he could not digest. "Say, Plame, think your parents might like some soda?" Nikki's brow arched optimistically. "What if I give it to them at half price?"

"*Ami,* they're not much into soda." Plamen couldn't remember the last time he saw his parents indulge in a store-bought beverage.

"*Haide.* Half-price soda. You can't beat that."

But Plamen was not in the mood to bargain.

What amazed Plamen was not the fact of his family teetering on the brink of collapse, so much as how quickly they had reached this point. His grandparents had tended the same modest patch of land for half a century, and then in the space of a year, everything had been disrupted. All spring, his father had phoned to report his grandparents' struggles: the goats were hungry; the onion and garlic had yet to be planted. His grandfather was losing weight, and his grandmother couldn't remember if he'd eaten or not. All spring, his father fretted into his ear, until finally, Plamen snapped at him for encumbering him with knowledge he could do nothing about, busy as he was with his studies.

"I'm not asking you to do anything but listen," his father had said. But even listening made Plamen angry, for listening didn't end when his father stopped talking. Like the swinging balls of Newton's cradle, this transfer of information set off a push-and-pull he couldn't abide. Listening turned into knowing his grandparents were aging and his parents were working too hard—a knowledge that promised to grow heavier with each tomato, each pepper, each zucchini Plamen ate, kilos and kilos plucked by their stiff, arthritic hands.

After this conversation, Plamen expected his father to stop calling. But he called the very next evening to report Plamen's grandfather had been in the mountains that day and had not yet returned. It was not unusual for him to run late: on days when Dyado took the goats out to graze, the village had gotten used to the animals making their way home in an obedient pack, udders bulging between their legs, and Dyado following an hour or so behind, unable to say how he had passed the time. But on this evening, hour after lost hour had passed. By 11:00 P.M., when Plamen's father summoned him for a search, worry had escalated into full-blown fear.

Plamen caught the midnight bus for Varna, and, after an hour's ride, had the driver drop him as they passed Old Mountain. His father was there to take him the rest of the way. All night, they traversed the mountain, stumbling over root and stone, with only the tepid light of a dying flashlight and a sliver of moon. They found Dyado just before dawn curled at the base of a tree, several kilometers beyond the usual grazing spot. His clothes were wet, and his cheek was scraped from a fall.

"Tati," his father yelled when they found him. But even as they knelt beside him, Dyado showed no signs of recognition. He lay on his side, clutching his empty *rakiya* bottle. His eyes were wide, and he was smiling strangely.

Once they had gotten him back to the house, Plamen and

his father loaded the car with tins of goat cheese, heads of young lettuce, and a flat of spring berries, all picked and prepared by his grandmother. Plamen's father drove him back to the city and dropped him at his apartment with just enough time to grab his books and get to class.

Everything had changed in a single night. The aftermath of Dyado's accident was both widespread and profound. The village rotated the responsibility of tending the goats. When there had been fifteen healthy men, each man had tended the goats once every fifteen days. But the village was aging. Without Dyado, they were down to five able-bodied shepherds.

Meanwhile, Plamen and his father would carry their own share of the burden. The implications were clear: Plamen's grandparents would become increasingly incapable of tending the garden. Plamen's parents would start going every weekend, every Tuesday and Thursday night. In another five years, they would be pensioners themselves and would move up the mountain to the village house, where they would nurse their parents, work the garden, and provide for Plamen, who, even if he had great success with his mathematics, would still find it expensive to buy food.

This was the typical arrangement. Nearly everyone Plamen knew had grandparents and a village to supply the family with food. All his life, Plamen had been suspended by this system, without considering its precarious equilibrium. As he slipped to the bottom of their family pyramid, he felt foolish at having failed to see the complexities of this arrangement—and at having missed an instability that had always been there.

It was past midnight when Plamen managed to extract himself from Nikki and the sodas, his *hazaika* and the shoes.

He could not have been more grateful for the quiet of his room, the closed door. Plamen had a full thirteen hours before he had to meet his parents; after tomorrow, he would be finished with Mateev once and for all. These truths were indisputable.

Or were they? As this last idea crossed his mind, he knew it was anything but true. Mateev was at the center of Bulgarian mathematics: if Plamen were to have a career in the field, it would be impossible to elude him. It was a menacing situation—one that threatened his entire profession. But he was too tired to think about it now. For one night, he would take respite from the truth and find solace in eight years lived in a steady state, this bed, this pillow, this room.

When he emerged the next morning, his shoes were packaged in a brown paper sack and placed by the door. The table was set with plates of cheese pastry and bowls of yogurt for three. Plamen was momentarily pleased to see Nikki was not at the table. But as soon as he took his place, his *hazaika* went to wake her son, who'd spent the night in his mother's bed, his mother on the couch.

"*Ostavi go,*" Plamen tried to stop her. "Let him sleep."

But she would not be dissuaded. "Nikki wouldn't want to miss your graduation breakfast," she said, which was absurd. Nikki had missed eight years of breakfasts with Plamen. How could anyone believe theirs was a friendship of consequence?

Nikki emerged, still in his suit, now wrinkled. "Morning, Plame," he said, showing the sluggish signs of a soda hangover as he took a seat at the table.

At least Nikki was not cheerful, Plamen thought. But there were other offenses: the crust stuck to his eyes, not to mention the smells—breath and body odor to make your eyes water. Nikki assailed Plamen with questions about the day, his plans, details that were none of his business. Meanwhile, Plamen's *hazaika* fluttered around her boarder, refilling his espresso cup and straightening his collar. Upon finishing his pastry, Plamen told them he had to go. He wore his old brown loafers and carried his good shoes so they wouldn't get dirty.

A soft morning fog rested on the city like a sweaty, gray cap. Coffee vendors doled out plastic cups of espresso and croissants. Plamen passed a pensioner sitting on a stool selling *gevretzi* from a burlap sack, the warm bagels smelling sweet with sesame. Seeing the old man's homemade shoes and crocheted vest over his tank undershirt, Plamen envied the simple, unburdened existence that came with poverty. He, himself, did not have much money—he was always scraping together *leva* to buy sandwiches and bus tickets—but he had enough to make choices. Add that to his list of burdens: the choices he had made and had yet to make.

He had, after all, *chosen* to work with Todor Mateev, rather than the other way around. Of course, there had been an interview, and Mateev had accepted Plamen as his advisee. But Plamen had been the one to seek out this relationship—which, after three years of jousting around a single proof, was as layered and adverse as the truth they'd set out to demonstrate. Plamen knew Mateev would never be his advocate.

It was not good for Plamen to think and walk at the same time. He was constantly losing himself in odd pockets of Sofia. Now, he asked a woman where he was in relation to Eagle Bridge and discovered that in twenty minutes' time, he'd traveled only a few blocks from his boardinghouse. He set off again, determined to keep his mind clear. But on this ponderous morning, thoughts crowded his mind, and he soon found himself wondering if he really did have choices, or if his fate—soldered to that of his country—was predetermined. Some weeks earlier, he'd heard an American journalist speak at the University. "The seeds of democracy have been planted in Bulgaria," the silver-haired man had said. "You're the gardeners now. Get out there and help it grow." While other students had clapped and cheered and wiped their eyes, Plamen had fumed silently in his seat. Why should this be his responsibility? Why had he been born into a country that needed so much from its people and gave so little in return?

At Eagle Bridge he started out fresh. But with his gaze tilted skyward, he did not see the little old lady, the rickety table, the tidy newspaper cones of sunflower seeds. After the collision, he helped right the table and offered her *leva*. She took his money and spat at him, *"Mahai se, be,"* until he heeded her request and left her huddled on the ground trying to salvage the day's wares.

Plamen scurried down one street, then another, trying to escape the memory of the angry lady, which trailed him like a stray dog looking for a handout. Always, there was someone looking for something, an entire pack of someones nudging him with their cold wet noses. There were days when Plamen could put them out of his mind, like a proof's many lemmas to be verified at a later time. But this day, at once grim and glorious, was not one of them, and without thinking, Plamen wound around lamppost and street corner until he found himself in a place that snapped him out of his trance. A street where he had been before—and where he should not be now.

Todor Mateev lived in a spacious, third-floor unit on one of the tree-lined streets bordering the University. He had a pretty, petite wife—herself a professor of economics—and two children, a boy and a girl, who played with their toys at one end of the *hol* while their parents entertained company at the other. Plamen had been to Mateev's home several times. Each fall, the professor had his graduate advisees over for a social affair—*rakiya* and salad, maybe some meat. Each fall, Plamen had been reluctant to attend and to pretend, even for an afternoon, that they were on better footing. The tenor of their relationship had been clear from the first stages of the master's proof, when Plamen's ideas were still rough. Even then, Mateev had grilled him on his work, challenging him to defend his most basic assumptions. While Plamen knew he should be grateful for the professor's rigors, he couldn't ignore the discomfiting possibility that Mateev's commitment was not to proving a numerical truth so much as it was to proving him wrong. Once this notion had entered his mind, he became convinced of it, and he was wracked with confusion about why, *why* Mateev should resent him. And who were these other students who laughed and chatted and drank with such ease while Plamen suffered a relationship that had never—not for one day—been easy?

Now he was mortified to find himself standing across the street from Mateev's home, in full view of his apartment. It was not far from his *hazaika's* house, but he had no reason to be there. Someone was bound to take exception to such a tall, awkward man loitering on this pristine block. Yet he lingered, curious about what was going on inside. It was a temperate day, and the balcony doors stood open. From between the billowing white sheers, shouts and cries emerged. Plamen could distinguish girlish shrieks, likely from Mateev's daughter, and shouts from Mateev himself. And splashing. A great deal of splashing, and what, possibly, could so much splashing be about?

Then he heard an unmistakable child's laugh, followed by a scream—"Tatko!" A naked, soapy little girl appeared on the balcony. Inside, Mateev was calling, "Eva! Eva! *Molya ti se!* Come back here, you scoundrel!"

The little girl pulled the white sheer around her so only her backside was visible from the street. A clump of soap bubbles slid down between her shoulder blades and paused in a dimple in her lower back.

Mateev was close behind. Wearing sweatpants and a T-shirt and with soap to his elbows, he was hardly recognizable but for his stocky form and heavy black-rimmed glasses. "Where did she go?" he hollered, turning his head from side to side, looking everywhere but at the girl. "Where is my *hooliganka*? She rolled out the door like a head of cabbage, and now she's disappeared!" To his right, the curtain twisted and pulled and emitted yelps of delight.

At first, the professor did not see Plamen. When he did, he fairly shouted with surprise. "Plamen! What are you doing here?"

Plamen did not answer. A Trabant with a burned-out muffler roared down the street between them. The sound, captured between the tight rows of buildings flanking the road, was slow to dissipate. By the time things quieted down, the chance to answer had passed. It was as though the bellow of the engine had been his response. Plamen thought it more appropriate than anything he could have said. With the little girl staring at him through her thin veil of curtain, the only thing Plamen could think to do was walk away.

Humiliation could be as tall as a mountain, dense as a forest on a moonless night. The night they had looked for his grandfather, it had rained a warm, melting rain. Plamen's mind's eye placed Dyado beneath a tree, not unlike the way they found him, only he was sitting up, alert and at peace. When they asked him what he was doing, he said, "Waiting for the rain to pass." A reason to be grateful for this rain: his grandfather's only excuse.

But when they actually found him, the rain offered little defense for his condition. Panning him with the flashlight to see if he was hurt, their dim circle of light illuminated a bloody cheek, shirt ripped at the sleeve, pants fly open and penis hanging out. Despite being drenched from rain, he smelled richly of urine.

With the sureness of a nurse, Plamen's father tucked his grandfather back in and zipped him up as if it was the only reaction a son could have. They walked the nine or so kilometers back to the house with Dyado limping along between them, barely capable of walking.

It was not until after his father had bathed his grandfather and gotten him in bed . . . after his father had calmed his grandmother and emptied his wallet into her kitchen drawer . . . after they themselves had climbed back into the car and started for home . . . after they had taken a few deep breaths, his father had said, "I hope I die before you see me like that."

Plamen had silently concurred. He could not imagine doing the things his father had done that night. He did not think, even in his most desperate hour, he would be able to cradle his urine-soaked father or touch his nakedness without so much as a flicker of disgust.

Immediately, he was ashamed for thinking this. A man was not supposed to refuse his parents the generosity they had shown him. As pattern dictated, a man should care for his parents when they could no longer care for themselves. This sequence of things was as rigid and ceaseless as the arithmetical patterns Plamen most loved. To disrupt the pattern, even in silent thought, was egotistical and irresponsible. Plamen's father was a sensitive man. Surely he had felt Plamen's disgust at the sight and stench of his grandfather and recognized in his son's silence his betrayal.

As Plamen took the blocks back to Eagle Bridge in blistering strides, he could feel the weight of the little girl's gaze. He was gravely embarrassed. He wished he had said he was getting a sandwich at the shop on the corner. His silence regarding the matter only added to its strangeness, and he wondered how he could possibly appear at his graduation. Graduate with what? What exactly had he earned?

By late morning, the fog had burned away, and the powerful June sun baked the concrete a chalky white. Plamen was sweating through his shirt. He sought the shady relief of an underground bookstall, where he fondled a fat cat asleep atop the books. But real relief eluded him. His parents were already en route. He hadn't talked to his father since his grandfather's accident. Once the villagers had relieved Dyado of his shepherding duties, the months had passed without incident. Still, Plamen could only assume his father was angry with him. He *should* be angry with such a son.

His mother, on the other hand, had had a tailor make her a new *complekt,* a skirt and blouse, for this very day, even though Plamen had told her not to spend the money. "You cannot deny me this," she'd said in a way that made it unclear what she cherished more: the outfit or the degree.

And what did it matter? If he failed to show up at his own

graduation, he would rob her of both. But to face Mateev, his father—impossible! There in the bookstall, with the cat purring and nuzzling his hand, he knew he could not attend the ceremony. Not with this pain in his neck, these tears in his eyes.

Plamen crouched down until he was eye-to-eye with the cat. Up close, the cat was filthy, snaggletoothed. Oh, the day had been ugly from the start. "Where are you going so early?" Nikki had pried over breakfast as he smeared a slab of butter on his pastry. "You coming back here before the main event?" If Nikki seemed irritated, Plamen couldn't blame him. There was no need for Nikki to be up this early.

But Plamen was irritated, too. What business was it of Nikki's where Plamen was going? Who was Nikki to pry into Plamen's affairs? It was preposterous. "I've got some documents to take care of," Plamen had finally said, hurrying out the door to avoid further questions. As proof, he stuffed a sheaf of papers into his pocket—which was a lie, of course. Who processed documents on graduation day?

He was still crouched, his chin resting on a pile of books, when he felt a presence at his side. Plamen turned his head to see a gypsy girl, who had picked up a book and was reading the back cover. With Plamen down on the ground, the kid's head was level with his own, and Plamen was surprised to see her reading with such interest. He wondered if she was really reading or if she was just pretending to read, and if he would soon feel a small hand in his pocket. It appeared the bookseller was ignoring the girl. Plamen tried to ignore her, too, but couldn't, given what was bound to happen—his pocket picked and then yet another request of his parents. Maika, Tatko, can I borrow some *leva*?

Hand on his wallet, Plamen rose to his feet and gave the cat one last pat before he turned to leave. Only then did the girl look at him, and he saw her eye had been poked out and crudely sealed shut. Plamen flinched; the girl turned back to her book. Plamen stood, frozen for a moment, before he dug into his pocket for whatever *leva* he had. When the bills landed on the books in front of her, the girl swept them into her pocket, put the book down, and walked away.

Plamen did not need two eyes to see how he'd been played. He watched the gypsy girl's back, enviably straight, as she pushed through the crowd, the faces coming toward her first registering her disfigurement, then averting their eyes. The girl, with her head up, soldiered on.

"You remembered your shoes!" his mother said. He was ten minutes late, and his shirt was rumpled. If his mother noticed these things, she did not mention them.

As for his father, there was not a trace of resentment in the warm hand that lay on Plamen's shoulder. "It's good to see you," he said.

Plamen did not know how to respond. To what did he owe this queer generosity? How could it possibly be good to see him with his wrinkled shirt? There was no way to explain this, nothing to say to these incomprehensible people, except to point them to the matter at hand. "Should we find a seat?"

He did not stand up straight for the graduation ceremony, nor did he stand tall when he introduced his parents to Mateev, who was as phony and demure as ever, and who, mortifyingly, had brought his daughter along.

"*Priyatno mi e,*" Mateev greeted them. "Meet my daughter, Eva."

"How old are you, Eva?" Plamen's mother asked.

Eva held up five fingers.

Head down, Plamen waited for his professor to mention their earlier encounter. But Mateev steered the conversation in a different direction, asking about his parents' trip and how long they would stay and did they leave any children back at home? In turn, his parents asked about Mateev's family and where was his wife today and were there other children?

"A girl and a boy, that's perfect," Plamen's mother said, making Plamen feel inadequate. He was appalled they should discuss such dull things with so brilliant a man.

The reception hall was brimming with people. Standing head and shoulders above the crowd, Plamen made out a couple of his friends and professors, as well as a table where women were selling sodas—red, yellow, blue. In the slanting afternoon light, among the swarm of black robes and muted costumes, the colors shone brilliantly. As much as Plamen hated the way Nikki carried on about his sodas, he wished Nikki could see them looking so splendid. Even from a distance, Plamen could fairly taste the sugary blue soda. *Worry-free soda* was what Nikki had called it. Plamen could use a cup.

He intended to leave his parents and Mateev only for as long as it would take him to buy soda—blue for himself and red for the little girl. But as he walked away, he could feel them watching him: Eva with her penetrating gaze; Mateev with his big black glasses; and his parents. He could feel himself drifting, getting lost in the crowd. *It's good to see you,* his father had said. There was no logic in his forgiveness, and yet Plamen felt it to be true.

The night they'd been out looking for his grandfather,

Plamen had been in a terrible mood. He kept checking his watch. Two, three o'clock. He had been up for twenty hours straight. Twenty hours, and there he was tromping through the mud and rain, trying to keep up with his father, who was scaling one ridge after the other with no regard for how far they were going or how long it would take them to walk back. There was no logic in searching all night in the dark and the rain, when daylight and dryness were a few hours away. And later, upon returning to his grandparents' house, there was no sense in his father's insistence that Plamen scramble eggs when clearly no one wanted to eat. Once in the car, there was no reason they should turn back because his father had forgotten the hundred *leva* he kept in the lining of his wallet. His grandparents would not spend the money his father had given them already. What good was one more bill?

That morning, Plamen had come home to his *hazaika* sitting at the table with a bottle of soda. There was no point in that either—the way she tortured herself when Nikki wasn't even there to see her drink it. "You don't have to drink that soda," he'd tried to tell her. "It's not even good for you." Which apparently was the wrong thing to say, because it made her cry.

Recalling this now in the crowded hall and craving a cup of blue soda, Plamen wondered if his *hazaika* might not like the soda. Was it possible she drank Nikki's drinks not because she had to but because she wanted to? She was probably drinking them now, whiling away the hours of his graduation—to which she should have been invited.

"So what time's the big show?" Nikki had asked at breakfast, ripping a second pastry in half and attacking it with more butter. Any signs of the obnoxious Nikki from the night before were gone, and now he was just plain cross. "Aren't you going to at least tell us about it?"

Plamen had balked at an answer. "*Ami,* I'm not sure," he'd said. "1:30? 2:00?" He had rushed through breakfast, hurrying to escape Nikki's increasingly direct questions. As he choked down the pastry, he was becoming progressively aware there was something purposeful about this—Nikki present at his graduation breakfast, his *hazaika*'s bloodshot eyes.

Nikki choked on a swig of his espresso, nearly dropping the cup into its saucer. "The graduation's today," he sputtered. "How can you not be sure?"

That was why Nikki was there, wasn't it? To escort his mother to the graduation. Lousy, monkey-browed Nikki had traveled clear across the country to partake in his mother's pride, to help her celebrate Plamen's achievement.

Now, they were clinking glasses on their own, Nikki bubbly and bitter as he wiped the tears from his mother's cheeks. "This is as good a celebration as any. Isn't that right, Maika? Isn't that right?"

But it was not right. It was not right at all. Plamen's conscience was enflamed. Standing in the orange afternoon light, suffering the scorch of comprehension, he discovered he had barely moved. The soda table was a long way off. There were Mateev and his parents clustered as a family. Mateev had hoisted Eva onto his shoulders, and she was mussing his hair into something disheveled and grotesque.

So much inane and inexplicable lightness. At once, Plamen knew he could not make it to the soda table. Nor could he bear the intensity of his embarrassment before Mateev and his parents, all three of whom understood too much already. Setting his sights on the door, he leaned forward and let his toppling weight propel his tall, conspicuous way through the thinning crowd until he pushed through the door and out into the late afternoon sun.

Finding a spot on a bench, Plamen sat down and rested his elbows on his knees. For once he did not think about the pain across his shoulders. He was not mindful of Mateev or the scalding insignificance of this degree or the staggering weight of an empty future. The penetrating sun, the strangeness of his folded figure in his graduation gown were lost on him, as he tasted the grit of sugar on his tongue, and cradling his head in his hands, nursed the swollen tenderness in his soul.

NEVER TRUST
A MAN WHO—

n the sopping wet spring of 1995, Sylvia rode the bus to and from Old Mountain more times than she cared to count. Her twin brother, Drago, was in Kyustendil, fulfilling his military service, and she felt obliged to visit her mother twice as often as usual. When she was a student, she'd catch any bus she could, usually from Poduene Station, which was a filthy place—thick with fumes and overrun by dogs and stalls hawking cheap underwear and overripe vegetables. Time and again, she suffered Poduene, because it offered the most buses to Old Mountain; if she missed one, she shouldn't have to wait too long for another. But lately she'd been catching the 1:00 bus from Nevski Cathedral, where there was no backup bus if she was late, but also none of the scrabble and mayhem of Poduene. It was cleaner, more convenient—things that, in the eight months she'd been out of school, had started to matter in a way that worried her. For even as she waited for that more civilized bus, she had a sense she was already getting older, already starting to set in her ways, like a tart, bacterial yogurt fermenting in a pot.

"Not *older*," Lazar had tried to reassure her the night before, when they were smoking in his room. As he lay on his side in the middle of the bed, propped on one elbow, the fluorescent light pooled in the dent in his forehead. "More *mature*," he said, ashing carefully into a chipped clay dish. "More *cultured*."

But Sylvia had just found out that Lazar was leaving, and how dare he belittle her cares! "Like a yogurt," Sylvia snapped from her perch on the chair. "Exactly like a yogurt." That Lazar did not know what to make of this—she was pleased she could be so opaque.

That year, Sylvia was working at a hotel in Bankya, a town outside Sofia known for its mineral baths and sanitoriums. She had taken her degree in tourism, which she had hoped would land her a job on the Black Sea coast or at the very least at one of the nicer hotels in Sofia. But there were not many jobs to be found. The tourists were not so eager to come to Bulgaria. After a short search, she had accepted a position at a provincial hotel where one of her University instructors had a connection. She was one of three girls who sat behind the front desk, each working a twenty-four-hour shift with two days in between to do as she pleased.

In the summer, the streets were bustling with people on holiday, and it was easy for Sylvia to feel satisfied with how she'd done. She passed her free time trolling the market, planning the ways she would spend her next paycheck. Though her monthly pay was little more than the stipend she'd received as a student, there was something about it—the fact of having earned it, perhaps—that made the money feel like a great amount. She would comb the market with utmost care for high-heeled shoes, faux leather handbags, and perfumed soap cakes, never making a purchase. Her biggest splurge was the occasional Zagorka at the local beer garden, where the summer staff gathered in the evenings. But even that was rare, because with Sylvia's pale skin and high forehead and spray of freckles across the bridge of her nose, there was almost always someone who wanted to buy her a beer.

Back in June, when Sylvia had gone looking for a room, she'd taken the cheapest she could find. It was a plain room on the second floor of a house with a small balcony and a bathroom across the hall, which she shared with two other boarders. The landlord and his family lived below in a separate apartment. She rarely saw them, thought little of them, except when she smelled the cooking from downstairs, and then she could think of nothing else but how nice it would be to be a guest at their table. There were times when the smell of frying meat drove her from the house, so hungry was she for a home-cooked meal.

But by late fall, the hotels and restaurants had emptied out. The market closed down, save a few stalls that carried toilet paper, sanitary napkins, toothpaste. Sylvia's hotel was big enough to keep her on year-round, though they seldom hosted more than a handful of guests. While the hours behind the front desk passed slowly, the hours back at the house passed slower still. The other boarders had left, and she suffered alone, the warped passage of time playing tricks on her, speeding up, slowing down, speeding up again, until the clock became an object of treachery and mistrust, and her resentment for the family downstairs—another night, another meal!—collected in every rut and dimple of the cold linoleum floor.

In retrospect, and even in the moment, she was aware she was going a little bit crazy. So much time! So much quiet! What was she doing there? She thought about quitting and going home, only home was quiet, too, what with Drago gone and Maika working more these days, her small dentistry practice filling every empty moment. Sylvia considered checking herself into a sanitorium before it was too late and they found her in bed, catatonic, hairbrush melted to the hotplate. But then Lazar moved in across the hall with his cigarettes and salamis and capped tooth. Most nights, she was so happy to see him—to see *somebody,* for that matter, but especially him—that she could forget her worries altogether and be kind and light, cute and cajoling.

For it was impossible to compare his troubles and hers. He told her just enough. Something about his wife's hair falling out in clumps. Something to do with her bladder. After spending all day with his wife in the sanitorium, he did not want to talk about it.

Indeed, he had said so little, there was no way Sylvia could have seen this coming: that his wife's condition would improve so quickly, that after just a month, the time would come for them to leave. He would be gone by the time she got back from the weekend in Old Mountain.

"That's great," she had managed. "That's really great." Though clearly it was not great. The news sank in like a big red stain, impossible to hide. Impossible to be pert and perky. Impossible to be anything but difficult. "Exactly like a yogurt," she snapped, which meant nothing, really, except that she hated yogurt.

The bucketing March rain that poured down on Sylvia might have been manageable (at least it wasn't snow) were it not for the wind that whipped around the Nevski, buffeting her from behind. Forget the umbrella. Back, side, everything from the thigh on down—she was wet, soaking wet, not to mention cold, for they were just barely inching into spring. A person could drown in this kind of rain, she thought. That was the other thing about this bus: there was no station or shelter, and the cathedral was too far away to wait inside. There were no good options. Sylvia blamed Drago for this. She was still irritated he hadn't made more of an effort to get leave so he could be with their mother on Women's Day. "At least try," she had pushed him over the phone. But when she called back, she'd gotten the sense he wasn't trying too hard, and when, Drago, did you become such a ninny?

Lazar said she was being too hard on him. "You don't know what it's like," he said, and perhaps she didn't. But she was tiring of the visits home, of so much sitting at the kitchen table with her mother, who said over and over how proud she was of Sylvia, oblivious of how much this sounded like she was trying to talk herself into it. Rather than take offense, Sylvia had grown increasingly concerned, for it was unlike her mother to be so diffuse and unaware. These muted movements, these tepid smiles, this maddening fixation on pride were cause for worry.

But try explaining that to Drago, who wanted something concrete—a limp, a lump, a cough—rather than an essence. "I don't really get it," he said to her on the phone. "I think I'd have to see her to know what you're talking about." Which was precisely Sylvia's point about going home for Women's Day, but clearly he didn't get that either.

The bus arrived at 1:00 on the dot. By then, the glue of her right shoe had dissolved, and the sole flopped beneath her foot as she lifted it to the stair. Still, Sylvia was cheered by the roof over her head, the rush of warm air, cheered more than she thought possible. "*Zdrasti,*" she said to the driver, happy to see it was the regular guy. Over the course of so many rides home, she'd developed a fondness for him—for keeping his bus so clean and for always being on time. She imagined him a family man, with a wife who dressed in the latest fashions and two children waiting for him at the end of the line. Fishing her coin purse from her coat, she exchanged damp *leva* for a bus ticket, taking note of the smell of detergent on his shirt and the papery dryness of his palm, which was coarse as a canvas glove.

"Be good to yourself," Lazar had said in parting. "Buy a magazine for the ride." As though they were parting for just a few days, instead of forever, and a quick flip through a magazine could make her good as new.

It was just like Lazar to suggest such a thing: on the few occasions Sylvia had shared her concerns with him, he had brushed them off as paltry, childish. "Bring a book," he'd said when she told him how bored she was at work. "Turn on the radio," he advised when she fretted about the possible numbing of the eardrums she imagined might come from so little stimulation.

Her mother did the same thing. "You have a hot plate," she said, when Sylvia complained about the delicious smells coming from downstairs. During the day, Sylvia would predict what the family would eat that evening—meatballs and potatoes, stuffed peppers, *perzhola*. Five times out of ten, she got it right. "Why don't you make something on the hot plate?" her mother urged. And though hers was the only voice Sylvia had heard all day, and though she could be certain that her mother, for her part, was eating nothing more tempting than a bowl of beans and broth or else an egg, scrambled and salted, a slice of bread, it was all she could do to fend off tears until she got off the phone. "Yes, Mamo. No, Mamo. Yes, Mamo. Love you, too."

No, she had not appreciated Lazar's instruction, and yet she had followed it. As the bus eased forward, the heat blowing up from beneath her seat, sodden magazine spread across her lap, she felt transported from her cares. The driver flipped on the *chalga* music—the winding minor chords, the gypsy pulse were a part of this ride—and Sylvia could fairly feel the well-being coursing through her veins, at once palpable and precarious. A stolen glance at her seatmate nosing in on her magazine was all it would take to ruin it, and so she stared straight down at the pages in front of her, which offered articles on flirty hair colors and ways to make him happy in bed.

So fixated was she on preserving this rare moment of satisfaction, Sylvia might not have discerned the bus pulling over and stopping on the side of the road. But for the thrashing sounds of rain, she might not have noticed the doors open, the fragile figure appear on the stair. She might not have recognized this creature—boy, girl, man, woman, it was hard to tell. Stringy hair plastered to head. Complexion puckered and spongy. She might not have known this person at all were it not for the voice—*Kolko?*—the raspy nasal tone she would know anywhere.

The driver did not even look at her when he brushed her money away. This stop-off was a deed of decency, not an activity for profit. Sylvia wished he had taken the *leva*. Petrol prices were high; he should have taken them and treated her like anyone else. Once they were back on the *magistrala,* he should have left her alone, so the incident would pass, and she could be just like everyone else. Instead, he broke the standard no smoking policy and handed back a cigarette, already lit, which Kuneva could barely hold between her stiff fingers.

When Sylvia was in ninth grade, Ms. Kuneva had told their class, "Never trust a man who carries a kerchief in his pocket." "K-e-r-c-h-i-e-f." She said each letter as she wrote the word on the board. Then she dug into her purse and produced a small lace-trimmed square into which she blew her nose with great gusto. "Kerchief," she said, holding out the balled-up cloth for all of them to see. "Hanky," she carried on. "*Hanky* is a synonym for *kerchief.*" She wrote this word up on the board, too. "H-a-n-k-y. Hanky."

A flit of giggles made its way around the classroom. *Hanky*—the silly sound of it—was just the sort of word they loved. From then on, they would look for every excuse to use it. As in, "*Gospozha,* can I go to the bathroom? I think I left my *hanky* at home." Or, in the event of blood drawn from a paper cut or picked scab, a forcefully whispered, "Let me wipe this with my *hanky,*" which, if Kuneva heard, she could not get angry about, because at least they were speaking in English.

"Tissue," she continued with yet another blow of the nose, and dutifully, they wrote this in their notebooks, entry number 584. That year, they would add 1,463 words to their English vocabularies, many of them having to do with things that were on Kuneva's mind. That fall, when Kuneva had taken up mushrooming, they learned forty-three different kinds of edible and inedible mushrooms, including *boletos, morels,* and the most ominous of mushrooms, *the angel of death.* And when she'd mistaken a *jack-o'-lantern* for a *chanterelle,* they learned words having to do with nausea, including *vomit* and *queasy* and the delightfully noxious-sounding *puke,* which they practiced in mock dialogues in front of the class.

"I'm not feeling well today."
"You're looking a bit *green around the gills.*"
"Well, I just *puked* in the trash can."
"You don't say. Did you catch that nasty *bug* that's going 'round?"
"No. I ate a *jack-o'-lantern.*"
"Blimey!"

The dialogues blended vocabulary words from Kuneva and polite British expressions from their English workbooks and curses the sharper-eared students had managed to pick up from Arnold Schwarzenegger and Jackie Chan films. Though the conversations could be about anything having to do with the words at hand, to the great merriment of the class, pair after pair chose to replay Kuneva's misfortunes. And though Kuneva would argue against this—"No, no! Tell your own story!"—she couldn't suppress a smile, and they could see she liked to be at the center of things.

After *tissue,* Kuneva had gone on to teach *jilted, dumped, spurned, forsaken*—grown-up words, words that were sobering for a ninth-grade class. For the first filaments of love were already forming among them, Vanina and Stoyan, Olya and Misho. If you weren't one of the lucky couples, you were watching closely the oily machinations of love: the sweaty hand-holding, the slippery kisses, the gifts of greasy snacks from the school café—pastry with marmalade or a bag of crisps—displayed on the corner of the desk and eaten slowly, appreciatively, throughout the day. So public were these romances that the thought of being *dumped* was at once terrifying and delicious, and whose side would you be on when it was over?

Indeed, while there was always the choice to revel in the fun that could be had at Kuneva's expense, there were moments, long moments, when the only sounds were those of Kuneva writing on the board, the wheeze of air through her oversized nostrils in sync with the motion of the chalk. The class would take notes in perfect silence, aware that Kuneva was telling them something no other adult in their lives would tell them, that they would otherwise have to learn on their own—from TV or movies or from each other. If someone were to open the door during these moments—"*Gospozha,* can Mrs. Georgieva borrow some chalk?"—the unwitting outsider might look at his or her fellow students strangely, sensing the pall that had come over the room, and what was going on? After class, they would report how Ms. Kuneva had been *spurned, jilted, shunned,* and *forsaken,* and wasn't that funny? For it would have been impossible to explain how giddiness had turned into sobriety, which had turned into respect, even awe, for one who had been through so much and lived to tell the tale.

Just barely, Sylvia thought grimly, as the bus tunneled through a mountain pass, emerging into more rain on the other side. Smoke wafted back from the front of the bus, carried on a stream of hot air from the dashboard blower. From where Sylvia sat, she could see a puddle had formed at Kuneva's feet, but by now the dripping had started to slow. The small towel the bus driver had handed back for mopping face, head, and shoulders lay crumpled in her lap. As Kuneva stared vacantly out the windshield, cigarette fixed loosely between her lips, it appeared wetness was the least of her problems.

More than five years had passed since Sylvia had last seen Kuneva. Aside from her current waterlogged condition, it seemed little had changed. She still wore the same mauve coat, mauve dress, and matching shoes, the same mauve stockings. It was Kuneva's special occasion outfit, worn on days when spirits were high, the first and last days of school, days when they had special programs in the auditorium. It was the outfit she wore on her birthday and on trips to Sofia or out on a date. Today, the occasion was Women's Day—a holiday that, to Sylvia's knowledge, had never panned out well for her English teacher. She didn't want to imagine the spat that had left Kuneva stranded in this storm, a piece of roadside flotsam, and what kept her hoping? *Never trust a man who—*, she had taught them. Yet, time and again, she disregarded her own advice.

Of course, if Sylvia was being honest with herself, she would admit this was exactly what had happened with Lazar. Staring at the soggy hollow of Kuneva's cheek, Sylvia could only blame herself for having trusted him so much. She had recognized the intention behind this distance they kept, her on the chair, him on the bed, the physical boundary of their relationship. She had known he was married, known that there were properties in Balchik and Albena on the Black Sea coast that needed to be maintained, and he could not possibly stay away too long. He had shared with her all of these things, and still Sylvia had given herself over to him in a way she could not explain— in a way she had not entirely realized until he told her he was leaving.

Yes, if she was being true to herself, she would admit that, without specific thought or intention, a discreet backdrop of belief had formed—one that had her living at the seaside and putting her tourism degree to good use. Spending her free time strolling the sandy boardwalk, her extra *leva* going to fruit-filled *palachinki* and bicycle rentals. Laughing and sunny nearly all the time, so full was her life, her head, her heart. And before all that, a belief this relationship was about to take a turn—from cigarettes and smoky companionship to something more.

Instead, she'd been *dumped, jilted, spurned, forsaken.* Blimey! She hadn't expected that at all.

An ache in her throat, her chest, her heart. She could not afford to indulge in injury just now. Another thirty minutes, and she would be in Old Mountain with nothing planned for Women's Day. She would be able to spot Block 103—the building with not one, but *two* enormous satellite dishes on top—before they even reached town. She would have to put on a smile, turn the key in the door, and *Chestito, Mamo! I'm home!* She would have to figure something out—her mother had offered no leads. "Is there something you would like, Mamo?" she'd asked the last time she'd been home. "What meal are *you* hungry for?" she had inquired over the phone. But they were fruitless questions. Her mother never asked for presents or special treatment. She never bestowed on Sylvia and Drago the pressures that, in a normal family, might have been shouldered by a husband or father: it was not their fault their father had left her before they were born.

Only what Maika failed to understand (what Sylvia could never have told her) was that it would be easier if she made requests, rather than leaving it up to them to figure something out on their own. That was why she and Drago were never ready when Women's Day rolled around. The pressure of wanting to make a big deal, but never knowing what to do. Finally, the day would arrive, and no longer able to delay, they would embark on a meal, something complicated and ambitious they would start on after school. When Maika came home from her office, Drago would greet her at the door, take her coat, and usher her into the kitchen, where Sylvia would be wearing her apron and cooking something she did not know how to make—stuffed grape leaves or moussaka. Once, they had attempted chicken and rice and paid for the chicken with their own money. But choosing the meal and buying the chicken had taken so long, they had just begun cleaning the rice when their mother got home. And even though Maika ended up doing all the work, and even though chicken and rice was really Drago's favorite meal, she was happy to accept the warm beer he poured for her. She was happy to sort through the rice for rocks, her dentist hands making quick work of the project, happy to sit and wait for more than an hour for the chicken to cook. Drago refilled her glass with a bottle he'd stuck in the freezer, and she laughed more and more as the night went on, because she did not usually drink, and because this slapdash celebration was just the right thing.

To replicate such an evening without Drago—Sylvia should not even try. She had sent him half of her meager savings for their birthday—*spend it on something you want*, she'd written—though in her mind, she was already anticipating Women's Day, and she had trusted he was doing the same.

By now, Kuneva had set to resurrecting herself. She dried her hair with the towel and ran a comb through it, clipping it at the temple with a plastic barrette. Rifling through her purse, she produced a damp hanky, which she took to the mascara smudges that ringed her eyes. Slowly, she was starting to look more like herself—not pretty, exactly. No, Sylvia had never considered her teacher the least bit good looking. But where appearances were concerned, Kuneva had always made a great effort, and for this effort, there were moments when she did not look bad. Now was one of them, Sylvia thought. For the warmth of the bus had brought a blush to her cheeks, and a wisp of hair danced at her brow. As the driver joined Kuneva in having a cigarette, Sylvia felt a trickle of tenderness that a day so ugly could proffer such kindness—no matter the smoky air that filtered back and hung heavily in the closed cabin of the bus.

At first, Lazar's smoking had bothered her. She, herself, was not a smoker. She did not mind anything else: his alarm in the morning, the scrape of his chair, the impossibly loud bolting and unbolting of the door. Even the bathroom noises were welcome after so much quiet. The splash of water, the grunts and sighs, this evidence of life, however crass, was just what she needed. But the smoke that curled beneath her door within minutes of his homecoming and continued into the early morning hours was more than she could handle. Within days of his arrival, smoke had penetrated her nose, her pores, every fiber of her bedsheets and clothing. She'd taken to stuffing a towel under the door, but then the room felt noxious and tight, and gasping for oxygen, she'd had to remove it.

Finally, she'd decided to say something. She was there first. As she approached his door, she was not sure what she would ask. "*Molya ti se . . . ,*" she would begin sweetly. Do you think you could you keep it to one cigarette an hour?

That was how they'd first met. Her standing in the hallway,

wringing her hands about what to say. Him swinging open the door on his way to the bathroom. Disarming her completely. "*Bozhe Gospodi!*" he said. "You scared me."

"I'm so sorry," she said, a flush in the face. "*Ami*—do you think—could I have a cigarette?"

Since then, she'd had plenty of time to analyze this changed course. That she'd been unnerved—this was not so unusual for Sylvia, who had never been one for public speaking or confrontation. Harder to explain her attraction to the man who answered the door: Lazar wore a striped robe, parted to reveal a stocky middle covered by a worn white tank top, dark chest hair poking out at the neck. One of his two front teeth bore a dull silver cap, and an indentation the size of a one *lev* coin pocked the upper right corner of his forehead.

But his face was round, his skin was clear, and his eyes were sympathetic. He did not think twice about fetching for her not one, but two of his cigarettes.

"Thank you," she'd said.

"*Niama zashto,*" he said, waving her off, and that might have been it—a cigarette and nothing else, if she hadn't gone back the following night and asked for another. And even though Sylvia was aware of her own fragile state, and even though she knew that any living being—a cat, a dog, a rat—would be welcomed amid so much loneliness, she also knew there was something about this guy that appealed to her. Forget the hot plate. Another cigarette was just the thing. Another and another.

Just over halfway to Old Mountain, the tape of *chalga* ran its course. The driver flipped it over, and the music began anew. He turned up the volume, the lively Roma banter bringing spirit to the bus. Smiling appreciatively, Kuneva leaned in to say something to him, which Sylvia could not hear above the music that whined over the speakers.

"Never trust a man who doesn't wear a wristwatch," Kuneva taught them. "W-r-i-s-t-w-a-t-c-h." Tempting as it was to find comedy in the way her chalk pounded the blackboard like a jackhammer, the rest of Kuneva looked clammy and vulnerable, and it was impossible not to feel a little bit sorry for her. "'Wrist' and 'watch.' *Wristwatch*," Kuneva said, calling on Drago to show off his watch.

By the middle of the ninth grade, Sylvia's class was starting to feel as if they knew something about the rules of love. Vanina and Stoyan had split and reunited on a weekly basis, and everyone was keeping track. Meanwhile, Olya and Misho had become increasingly entrenched, so that they were never apart. Only most of the time, they did not look like they were enjoying each other's company. Indeed, as love was tested among their members, it was proving harder than it had originally seemed. Yet the status of being in love—and thus, being lovable—was nonetheless desirable, even coveted, and the pressure to pair up was more intense than ever.

Late. Tardy. Delayed. Overdue. Stood up. Kuneva taught them, and Sylvia pictured her sitting alone at a café table, *standing up* after the second coffee to order a Scotch. *Let down,* Kuneva explained, and each student resolved not to disappoint their English teacher, who, crabby as she was, had been *let down* plenty enough already.

Heartless. Ruthless. Merciless. Sylvia was amazed by the endless string of words Kuneva could reel off, many more or less the same, with just the slightest change in meaning to differentiate one word from another. *Heartache. Heartsick. Heartbreak.* She found herself wondering how all these words had come into being, that the range of feelings should be articulated with such precision.

When it came time for dialogues, they tried to be extra clever to cheer Kuneva up.

"Are you okay? You're looking a bit *down in the dumps.*"

"As a matter of fact, I'm *heartbroken.* My boyfriend is three hours *late* for our date."

"You don't say. Do you think he's been *delayed?*"

"*Ruthless* bloke. He *stood me up!*"

"I'm sorry to hear that. Can I offer you a *hanky?*"

"Bloody hell! I don't need a *hanky.* I need a drink!"

"You've got that right," Ms. Kuneva said, and even though there was sadness in her eyes, they managed to make her smile.

Pair after pair repeated this scenario, making minor substitutions—*heartsick* for *heartbroken, tissue* for *hanky.* When it was Sylvia's turn, she used *heartless* for *heartbroken, napkin* for *hanky,* mistakes that were enough to jar Kuneva from her trance. "Sylvia, you have no sense of nuance," she said sharply. "The shades of meaning are lost on you."

At the time, Sylvia managed to make a joke of it. A lack of nuance, coming from Kuneva, was almost a compliment. "*Cranky* is a synonym for *Kuneva,*" she said in the corridor and after school, pleased with her clever, nuanced comeback, and clearly Kuneva did not know what she was talking about.

But Kuneva's observation, delivered on a day when she was baring her heart, stuck with Sylvia, not as a wound or scar, so much as an explanation, surfacing only every now and then when she was feeling particularly low. For it was not as though Kuneva'd told her that her sentences were simple or her articles were wrong. Rather, her accusation seemed to have broader application, and Sylvia was stricken with the idea that hers was a general insensitivity—one that extended beyond vocabulary to an all-purpose bluntness, and here she was going through life, missing subtleties left and right.

By standard measures, the evidence—kissing, touching, and whatnot—was not there. But there were other things Sylvia had taken to be just as important. Mostly, there were comments. "You're a nice girl," Lazar had said early on. "Isn't there somewhere else you should be? Something else you should be doing?" Which struck a note so resonant in Sylvia's tormented soul, she'd almost cried out, "Thank you! Thank you for noticing!"

Then there had been the questions about a boyfriend and why she didn't have one.

Sylvia's face had turned red, then purple. "It's not so simple."

"What do you mean, 'it's not so simple'? You're a pretty girl. Why should it be more complicated for you than for anyone else?"

"Well, I'm here, aren't I?" she retorted. Surely, it was indisputable that a suburb of Sofia was not the best place to be meeting guys her own age. In the summer, possibly, but not now.

And yet, location was something that would never stop Drago, who had had a string of girlfriends starting in high school and never letting up, not even when he left for his military service. Now, it was some girl, Natalia, sending him packages and calling every other night to make sure he was okay. Her mother hadn't objected to Drago's activities: the disco on school nights, the requests for *leva—Maika*, could you spare . . . ?— and always she could. At some point, she had decided Drago needed his own room. For the last couple years of high school, Sylvia had shared a bed with her mother, and Drago had kept the room by the front door, so he could come and go as he pleased.

It was not that Sylvia didn't go out: she and Drago shared the same group of friends, and it was not so unusual for her to join them, especially on weekends. There was Pavel, her date for the ball, who was always asking her to go to the café and who liked to slip his hand in her back pocket whenever he had the chance. But Sylvia was not particularly taken with Pavel, who had full lips and heavy thighs and a propensity for things sentimental. Nor had she been taken by Yordan, or Mikhail, or Kamen, or the scene in general. For there was something about these pairings and unpairings, these agonizing contortions she didn't entirely relish, where an object as simple as a wristwatch should be an instrument of injury and where people's hearts got sore or sick or broken, and for what? Time spent in the unmowed field behind the disco doing God knows what. "Where did all these grass stains come from?" her mother had once asked Drago. Perhaps Maika didn't have a sense of nuance either.

Even when she got to college, Sylvia chose safer routes, preferring small gatherings and close friendships to intoxicated crowds and lusty couplings. In fact, she was not ill at ease with a beer in her hand or a strong arm wrapped around her waist, and there were relationships—albeit not so many of them and none of any length or weight or consequence. For the patterns of distrust and avoidance that had been born in her high school years perpetuated—worn subtly and disguised in affability and *I'm sorry, but I'm busy tonight. Perhaps another time?*

"You know, you're cute when you blush," Lazar had said. Sylvia had been both embarrassed and pleased, and this had made her blush even more.

"Now you're doing it on purpose," he had said, at which point, Sylvia had excused herself. By then, her face was flooded with heat, and there was no way to make the blushing stop.

This was the way so many of their nights ended, Sylvia returning to her room aglow with so much attention. After a few weeks, a cheap bottle of red wine and a greasy stick of *lukanka* appeared on the table, the tough meat served on butcher paper. Lazar would start the evening seated at the table, slicing the salami in neat little disks and chewing thoughtfully, often quiet about his day at the sanitorium. But eventually he lost interest in the food, and the wine took effect. Retiring, wine and ashtray in hand, to the middle of the bed, he left Sylvia alone at the table to blush and giggle, and to watch, as the night drew on, the white fat of the salami grow soft and yellow.

As they closed in on Old Mountain, the rain had abated to a comforting patter. Meanwhile, relations between Kuneva and the driver were advancing, with Kuneva standing up every minute or so to whisper something in his ear. She appeared to be fully recovered. Sylvia thought if this was the first she had noticed of her English teacher, she would think things were fine, perhaps finer than usual, and she would be happy to see Kuneva in such a fine state.

But there was nothing fine about being picked up on the

side of the road in a perilous downpour. When they got to Old Mountain, there would be no ignoring Kuneva and the circumstances of her roadside recovery. Most of the passengers would be traveling beyond Old Mountain to Berkovitza, Varshetz, or Vratza. Only a few of them would get off in Old Mountain, and Sylvia would be forced to greet Kuneva. She would not ask for an explanation: she could extrapolate a scenario well enough from so many years of Kuneva's love-torn chronicles. On the contrary, it was Sylvia who would be called on to do some explaining. *No, Gospozha. Yes, Gospozha. No, Gospozha, I don't have a boyfriend.* What had Sylvia taken from her lessons? This was what Kuneva would want to know.

The irony was, when it came time for dinner with her mother—Women's Day and nothing planned—this same inescapable topic would be untouchable. How many times over the last month had she wanted to mention Lazar to Maika. How many times had the words slipped away, because she wouldn't—she *couldn't*—say them. There was even the open invitation: "I haven't heard you this happy in months," Maika had said, an edge of curiosity in her voice bidding Sylvia to say more. But this, by her mother's own determination, was not part of their repertoire. There were things Maika did not talk about, and as a result, questions Sylvia and Drago did not ask, things they did not tell her. And if, at twenty-two, there was a whole half of Sylvia's history Sylvia herself knew nothing about, this bothered her not nearly so much as present-day topics that could not be discussed: Drago skulking around like a tomcat, Sylvia enduring her first broken heart, Maika wasting away in her apartment. If there was one thing Sylvia had learned this past winter, it was the toll of loneliness. Even as she'd argued with Drago, she'd suspected there was nothing really wrong with Maika, but also nothing really right. And the strategy that had worked for Maika for the better part of two decades, burying herself in the job of raising twins, wasn't working so well anymore with both of them away, one of them not even making it home for Women's Day.

At first, she'd been so angry at Drago, she'd considered skipping the trip home herself. Let him carry some responsibility for a change. But Lazar did not think this was a good idea. "You'd better go," he'd said, rubbing the dent in his forehead, which was what he did when he was being most thoughtful. "Especially if Drago's not going to be there."

He was right, of course: she had to go. How quickly her anger toward Drago had morphed into something altogether different—an amazement, really, at how inside her life Lazar was. Though she'd only known him for a few weeks at that point, she'd felt like she'd known him for a very long time.

Now, staring at the seam that angled up the back of Kuneva's stringy calf, she understood he was probably trying to get rid of her, so he wouldn't have to pack with her around and so there would be no chance of her running into Elena. Sylvia had never met Lazar's wife: in Sylvia's mind, she always had a bandage wrapped around her head, looking pale, sickly, pathetic—but how could Sylvia know? She had never seen a picture. There was so little that had ever been confirmed . . . really, she hardly knew her—or him—at all. Could *thinking you knew* be a synonym for *not knowing*? She felt utterly duped.

As the bus barreled on through the persistent drizzle, she was ashamed of herself. And of the driver, who could hardly keep his eyes on the road for all the attention he was giving

Kuneva. And of Kuneva in her mauve getup, to whom knowing or not knowing clearly didn't matter.

"Never trust a man who can't hold his liquor," Kuneva taught Sylvia's tenth-grade class.

Sylvia remembered the lesson well. She remembered Kuneva had been out sick for several days—a thing memorable for the sheer glory of three, four days without Kuneva.

There was no substitute teacher to take Kuneva's classes, and the class spent the extra hour in the school café, drinking Fanta or coffee made syrupy with sugar. On these occasions, Pavel would squeeze in next to her with a soda or juice for her that she did not want to drink, both for the message it would send to her classmates—that this was an affair worthy of their attention—and because she did not like sweet drinks. And so she sat, drink untouched, the suggestion of a beverage awakening her thirst and leaving her with no option but the fountain, which was located just outside the boys' bathroom, where the floor was always wet and where water did not even taste like water, so strong was the smell all the way out into the hall. Better to go thirsty.

Sylvia would never have admitted, not even to her closest friends, she was glad when Kuneva returned and there was not so much time to spend in the café. That first day back, Kuneva seemed slightly shaky, nervous even, and after the initial glee—one of *those* lessons—the class quieted down. It was hard to pinpoint what was different about Kuneva, except she was wearing noticeably more makeup than usual. Sylvia'd wondered if she'd gone a little bit crazy, what with the makeup caked onto her cheeks. Who in their right mind could think that looked good? But then, it seemed even Kuneva knew she did not look good, and she would not look at them, not even when Vanina started coughing and couldn't stop and had to excuse herself to take a drink from the fountain.

"Drunk," Kuneva said, "Drink, drank, drunk, only in this case, I'm using *drunk* as a noun, as in, 'Stay away from that man. He is a *drunk.*'"

That day, Kuneva seemed to have crossed a line from sobering to downright sad. *"Alcoholic,"* she said. *Lush. Boozer. Sot.* The words had a woozy, saturated feel, not unlike the sensation most of them had experienced at one time or another, New Year's with their parents or behind the disco with bottles of beer or a homemade *rakiya* pilfered from a pantry. But these occasions, even the ones that had ended in *puking,* had been largely silly and fun. Kuneva was referring to the noun form—the unemployed father, the wasted neighbor, the man who staggered down the square petitioning for a *lev*—people you didn't laugh about.

Eventually the lesson veered into familiar territory, and they could feel Ms. Kuneva's strength returning to her. *Heartache. Heartsick. Heartbreak.* No one told her she was repeating herself. They were coming to understand these were not words you learned once, but over and over again.

That day, the dialogues had little to do with Kuneva's story.

"Stay away from that man. He is a *drunk.*"
"You don't say."
"They say he's suffering from a terrible *heartache.*"
"Is that so. Was he *forsaken?*"
"You could say that. His dog died."

"Look out! Here he comes!"
"Bugger off, you bastard!"

"Bugger off, you bastard!" Even as Kuneva clapped her hands with delight, there were tears in her eyes. So successful was this dialogue, pair after pair repeated it verbatim. "Bugger off, you bastard," Kuneva repeated each time, until the tears were rolling down her cheeks, so that by the end of class, she had wiped away enough tears, and along with them, enough makeup, to reveal a swatch of purple skin splashed across her cheek.

In the end, Lazar had treated their relationship like it was nothing at all. "*Ami,* why don't you come for a visit?" he said, his lips and teeth stained from the wine. Usually, a bottle of wine could last them two, three, four nights. But that night, they'd finished the entire bottle, and Sylvia could feel the wine—dry on her tongue, pink in her cheeks, loose in her legs, which she feared might not even be able to carry her from the room. The way Lazar was sprawled, messy on the bed, she could tell he was feeling it too.

"That's ridiculous," she said. Even as a *lush,* she was committed to being sour. "What would you tell your wife?"

Lazar shrugged. "What should I tell her? That you kept me company during these days. That you were a good friend. What's wrong with that?"

And of course, there was nothing wrong with that. But it felt wrong to Sylvia, the comments he made, the bottle of wine, the greasy *lukanka* getting oilier as the night drew on.

"Every year, Elena spends the month of August in the vil-

lage with her parents. You could come then," he offered, snuff-
ing out one cigarette and lighting another. "August would be
the perfect month for you to come."

Always, with Lazar, the solutions were easy. There was still
the matter of her job at the hotel, which would be filled to capacity in August. There was her mother, who would not understand this visit, and where will you stay, Sylvia? Who else will
be there? Sylvia inhaled and blew the smoke through her nose.
"And do what?"

"Go to the beach," Lazar said. "Isn't that what people do at
the seaside in the summer?"

Sylvia could not stop the tears that sprang to her eyes.
Kakvo? What's wrong with the beach? She could not respond.
At once, she felt tremendously foolish sitting in this chair, this
room, smoking these cheap cigarettes like they were all the
sustenance she needed. *Molya ti se, most girls love the beach.*
How could she and Lazar have spent so much time together,
shared the same conversations, the same bottles of wine, the
same cigarettes, and ended up in two totally different places?
She did not know how.

By the time they reached Old Mountain, Sylvia needed a
hanky more than she needed a cigarette. Kuneva was caressing the driver's neck and running her fingers through his hair.
The station was deserted: people did not wait out in a rain that
could sweep you away, and by midafternoon on a holiday, trav-
elers had gotten to where they were going or were already well
on their way.

Sylvia was gathering her things when the driver turned
around. "Everybody off," he said. "This bus is stopping here.
Another bus should be coming along shortly."

The grumbling that followed was lost on the driver, who was

already off the bus with Kuneva. *"Bozhe Gospodi,"* the woman next to Sylvia said, heaving herself from the seat. "Can you believe this?" And though Sylvia was as taken aback as anyone, and though the woman was not looking for a response, the answer that sprang to Sylvia's mind was yes, yes, she could.

As Sylvia climbed the steps of Block 103, Vhod A, she could smell the chicken and rice. Drago had not called. Later, he would admit he'd caught the bus to Sofia to see Natalia, who had her own room in the Student Village and who had managed to sneak him into the canteen for free. "I can't remember the last time I had a meal like that." The way he said it, so fully sated, disgusted her: if food had been the object of Drago's longing, how had he managed to pass up their mother's chicken and rice?

As it was, Sylvia and Maika ate the meal without him—largely in silence. Though Sylvia could fairly taste her mother's disappointment in the forkfuls of food she lifted to her mouth, she ate heartily—making up for Drago, who couldn't manage to pick up a phone . . . for Lazar, who would be having the last of the greasy *lukanka* for his supper as he packed his suitcase . . . for the family downstairs, who had never once invited her to dinner, and *no, Mamo, I'm not trying to diet.*

When she was finished, her *heartsick* mother chirped, "This was nice, wasn't it?" and "There will be plenty of leftovers for you to take back with you."

Afterward, Sylvia excused herself to go out on the *balcon.* "I'm going out for a smoke," she said, as though this was a long-time habit her mother should accept. In fact, Maika had pleaded with them not to smoke: she had seen too much gum disease, cleaned too many nicotine-stained teeth to bear it. This hadn't stopped Drago, who had been smoking covertly since he got to college. That Sylvia should pull out the cigarettes now ... it was either that or say something she didn't want to say.

It was hard to tell if it was still raining or just dripping. Above her, the satellite dishes hovered like large white umbrellas, shielding her from whatever weather remained; below her, the sounds of television and smells of cooking filtered up. Women's Day or no, the roles of men and women remained the same.

As Sylvia fumbled for a cigarette, she saw a large yellow dog jump out of a dumpster and start lapping from a puddle. Whether it was the cold or the urgency, her fingers were not working properly, and it took her several moments to get a cigarette lit. Of course, the cigarettes were Lazar's, the pack placed on her doorstep during the night. "Take some cigarettes with you," he'd written on a note he'd slipped inside. It occurred to her now these cigarettes were an admission of sorts: sometimes there was no solution.

Sylvia inhaled once, twice. In the distance, an engine turned over three times before it started up. There was the bus, making its way past her mother's apartment, angling for the main road it would take the rest of the way home. And when it got there? Sylvia could imagine the story that would be told: a breakdown by the side of the road. Or a flat tire that kept them waylaid for hours. The water on the road—he didn't even see what had punctured the tire. She could imagine the response: *eto, skypi.* Here's a little *rakiya*, a little salad, the meatballs are back in the oven, *mili.* You must be hungry. Beneath the tenderness, the tang of resignation: *trust* is a synonym for a callused heart. His wife had learned that lesson long ago.

Meanwhile, Kuneva would be home in her flat, brandy

perched on the edge of the bath—whatever she did to relax. Sylvia did not want to picture it, and yet there were things only Kuneva could illuminate for her, things she could learn even now. Oh, to be back in that damp classroom, notebooks open, pencils out. These are the questions she needed her to answer: Did she consider the day salvaged? Had she already forgotten the events of that afternoon? Did one *ever* forget? And this, most important: was there fulfillment now, in this long, hot soak, or was the loneliness only more profound?

Even as she asked it, Sylvia knew this was a question to which she should have her own answer by now—only she didn't. Not yet. Just a numbness that, on this chilly night, left her unable to feel heart, fingers, nose.

The night before, when she'd finally gotten up to leave, she felt wobbly and weak. "Here," she said, handing her half-smoked cigarette to Lazar, who had just lit one for himself. She stood by the side of the bed for what was intended to be only a moment, but in her *alcoholic* state was probably more than that. Looking down at him, a cigarette in each hand, she willed him to put them down and say good-bye properly. But he would not even look at her—and no wonder. The least he could have done . . . well, she would have appreciated a little warning.

Perhaps it was the proximity from which she was viewing him, hair thinning on crown of head, pock in forehead deeper than previously noticed, and what had put it here? Perhaps it was the back of his neck, creased in two places, old tan lines the proof of summers worked hard and honest in the sun. Perhaps it was the stiffness of his pose, which looked strained from this angle and not at all comfortable. Finally, Sylvia managed to pick up on a tension, a *nuance*, she'd been too angry to notice: this was not nothing, this *was* something, and he was choosing the difficult path, the hair falling out in clumps, the sanitorium.

Sylvia had long finished her cigarette, impossible to light another. Here was her mother beckoning her inside. "Sylvia? Come." The affection in her voice was more than Sylvia deserved. Behind her mother, the golden glow of the kitchen, the whistle of tea water on the stove, a cake on the table—a celebration to finish. And so Sylvia followed her mother inside, where they would pour their tea and knock their mugs and drink to their fidelity.

I GUESS THAT COUNTS
FOR SOMETHING

Three months after Lubo was laid to rest in the cemetery behind the old church, Neddy makes coffee for both of them, just as she has for fifty-four years. *"Malko cafense?"* she says, pouring the thick espresso into a pair of cups they had been given for their wedding. By now, the cups are webbed with tiny brown cracks and chipped at the rim, their taste and texture as much a part of drinking coffee as the liquid they hold. "Does this coffee taste right to you?" Lubo would have asked if he was there. Toward the end, nothing had tasted or smelled or sounded or felt right by Lubo's measure, and she was constantly reassuring him. "Yes, Lubo," she says this morning in the same weary way she had responded when he was alive. "It tastes just fine."

Neddy drinks her coffee in a few swift gulps; the cup is emptied almost as quickly as it is poured. Soon, Radka will be over for Lubo's cup. From her window across the street, she will have watched Neddy trundle down the steps of her house and make her way down the dirt path to the shed out back. She will have calculated the minutes Neddy has needed to bring the coffee to a boil three times, to stir in four heaping teaspoons of sugar and boil once more, so that the liquid is thick and sweet as syrup. She will have waited until the coffee is poured and Neddy has finished her own cup, because the way Neddy inhales her coffee in great, scalding swallows makes Radka nervous. She will have waited until Lubo's cup has cooled just enough, and then she will join Neddy in the shed to discuss the heat wave that's settled on Old Mountain, the inexorable baking of the flesh, and look how puffy you've gotten, Nedyalka. You've started to rise.

By the fourth day of the heat wave, Neddy has come to see it as more of a slow roasting. It is still early, and already sweat bastes her brow, traces her spine, and blanches her breasts and buttocks. The two black dresses she made when Lubo died are not intended for this weather: constructed of sturdy polyester, they are designed more for endurance than comfort. Fanning herself with a flattened carton from Lubo's cigarettes, scratchy fabric chafing her thighs, she insists, "Really, Lubo, it tastes just fine." How many times before he believes her?

A door whines on its hinges. "Dancho," Margarita calls for her grandson. "*Kade si, be?* Breakfast is getting cold." The edge in her voice slices clean and sharp through the early morning quiet.

Neddy tries to imagine how breakfast can get cold on a day like today. But then, this is not about breakfast, is it? Next door, Margarita's grandson has come for the summer, because his parents are having problems and need to sort things out. The whole of June, Margarita had gloated about Dancho's visit. "Where is *your* grandson, Nedyalka? I haven't seen him since the funeral." (No matter that Neddy's grandson is twenty years Dancho's senior and a busy mathematician.) Alas, the gloating has taken care of itself now that the boy is here with laundry and a poor appetite and a soccer ball that ricochets off the side of the house.

Two weeks have passed since the boy's arrival. Next door, Neddy hears a steady stream of *Bozhe Gospodi*'s and where-is-he's and that's-enough-television-for-you's. She hears Margarita sighing as she beats the rugs, loud, heavy sighs intended for Neddy to hear, but Neddy does not budge from her seat in the shed. Since the funeral, she can spend hours like this without so much as a blink or quiver, only shifting on her haunches every now and then to ease a bit of stiffness.

Radka pokes her bony nose into the shed, the once-coarse beams of the doorframe worn smooth with age. "Did you hear that?" she hisses. "*At this hour?*" She flounces into Lubo's chair with an indignation honed to perfection during thirty years of teaching Bulgarian history at the high school down the hill. Over the years, Radka enjoyed hourly excuses to lose her temper. Now in retirement, she must look for reasons to work up a head of steam. "I don't know how you stand it," she says, yanking her knitting from her bag. "The ruckus that comes from that house. Doesn't it bother you?"

Neddy sweeps a few stray sugar crystals into a pile on the plastic tablecloth. Licking her finger, she presses it to the granules and lifts them to her mouth, nibbling the grains of sugar with her teeth. Meanwhile, Radka turns her attention to the sweater she's working on—a complicated project that will take all summer. She jabs her fingers at the previous day's work, examining her stitching, then pauses to take a swig of coffee. "We are a civilized society, Nedyalka," Radka says, relishing her own sense of righteousness. "One of the oldest civilizations in the Western world, and still *some of us* have yet to embrace it."

This is not the time for Neddy to tell Radka how much she

enjoys the sounds coming from next door. The slamming and scampering and scrabbling around, interspersed with silences that, Neddy knows from experience, are not to be trusted. If she sits still enough, listens hard enough, she can almost believe she is back at the beginning and not at the end. And Lubo is out with the goats instead of fermenting in the hot, steamy loam across from the church. And this boy in the yard is hers, dribbling his soccer ball among the neatly tended rows of zucchini, cucumbers, and peppers. When she finds the smashed vegetables, he will deflect blame with hugs and kisses and *I love you, Mamo's,* knowing she won't, she *can't* get angry.

No. These are not thoughts for sharing with Radka, who has never had so much as a cat, let alone a boy or a man or anyone else. Mostly, Radka has Neddy, who, at the moment, offers little satisfaction. "Five hundred years under the Turkish yoke and now this," she carries on. "How can you just sit there? *Bozhe Gospodi,* Nedyalka, what is the matter with you?"

For decades, Neddy has absorbed the fury that spills out of Radka over every last thing. Like a sponge she soaks it up—often going through her whole day feeling heavy and wet. On this sweltering day, as anger seeps into her pores, Neddy is aware she is already moist, nearly saturated, and still she soaks it in. She knows if she sits like this long enough, Radka will leave, and predictably, she does. As she crosses the road, Neddy can see a large damp spot on her dress where her back touched the chair.

Given the mild winter they've had, the villagers have been anticipating the heat wave for months. And still its oppressiveness has caught Neddy off guard. As her breathing takes on a silent pant, she feels duped, not so much by the extraordinary heat as by the surprise of it all. The last three months have taught her a thing or two about surprise—namely, that expecting, even *knowing* something is going to happen can't spare you the blow. That even if you can see a train coming down the track, sometimes all you can do is stand there and let it hit you.

Neddy did not cry at the funeral. In the days leading up to it, she had expected, even hoped, she would cry. Till then, she had not shed a tear, not even when she awoke to find Lubo had left her in the night. Though Neddy was not one for crying, it bothered her she could not weep over the death of her own husband. What kind of marriage could they have had, that she should not cry when it was over?

The morning of the funeral, she felt the tears behind her eyes. Sure as the darkening sky, she could feel them building up as she put on her mourning dress for the first time and discovered it snug across the bosom and behind—a thing that was not the least bit unusual for Neddy, and yet on that fragile morning, it was just enough to stir her sense of defeat, and what, really, did she have left?

But then there was Nasko urging her up the ruddy mountain road. *Haide, Mamo, it's almost time.* And then there was the road itself, so steep she wondered if it hadn't gotten steeper since she'd last climbed it. Indeed, it was all she could do to shuffle one foot in front of the other—*Ela, Mamo, give me your hand*—and breathe at the same time. And then there were the scabby stucco houses lining the road one after the other like a row of decaying teeth, and when had their houses gotten so old? Turning to look down the mountain at the cinderblock apartments that had stacked up in the valley below, Neddy felt out of step with the rundown houses that staggered up the road, with the modern apartments, with Nasko, who insisted she keep walking, and what could possibly be the rush? *Ela, Mamo, watch your step,* he said when she stumbled on a stone. As pain shot through her ankle, and she was finally, mercifully ready to cry, she discovered the tears had slipped away.

Standing before the *popa,* she tried to recall the tears. She imagined her eyes growing wet, the way characters' eyes glistened on *Dallas.* But it was cold and damp inside the church, and the smoky incense streaming from a copper burner on the floor choked her nose and throat. The church looked ragged. Holes pocked the plaster walls where gold leaf had been chipped off by greedy visitors, and water stains rendered images of the Holy Family brown and blotchy. Before Lubo had taken ill, Neddy had cleaned the candles once a week, digging out the waxy remains and taking the red glass containers home to scrub away carbon smudges. But more than a year had passed since she'd last made it to the church. When she went to light a candle for her husband, she found an empty candle box and holders spilling over with hardened wax.

As the *popa* extended his arms over Lubo's coffin and softly chanted a prayer, Neddy hoped Lubo was not watching this tepid send-off. The prayer that filled the church was recited by rote, the *popa* checking his watch every now and then to make sure he was going neither too fast nor too slow. Neddy's resentment mounted as she recalled how she had waited for the *popa* to visit Lubo after they'd stopped being able to make it to church, certain that Radka, and Margarita, too, were keeping him apprised of Lubo's condition. But he had never come. Now, Lubo was lying in a box, his final blessings late and lethargic. At last, a tear slid down her cheek, shed not for her husband, but for the fraud in which she took part as she placed six red roses on the coffin over the spot where she envisioned Lubo's heart.

Afterward, they had gone back to her house, and who knew where the plates of cookies had come from? Platters of *sladki* and *banichki* and even a syrupy plate of baklava. Bottles of liquors and homemade *rakiyas* and other unidentifiable brews. Neddy sat in Lubo's chair pulled up close to the fire, heedless of her obligation to her guests—guests who said they were sorry, but who were they kidding? As dementia had dawned on Lubo, he had gotten lost often, requiring regular search parties to find him and bring him back, sobbing and wet with his own urine, or else smiling as though nothing was the matter. First, they had relieved Lubo of his shepherding duties. "Give someone else a turn," they'd said; despite their kindness, Lubo had wept. Then, as things progressed, Margarita had suggested Neddy not leave him alone, and others had agreed. "You let us know what you need, and we'll get it for you." Sure, there were those who came to sit with Lubo, enduring his tears over nothing—the bitterness of his beer—and trying to ignore the crumbs on his face. But no one liked to see a man like that. The last year had been hard on all of them.

That day, between toasts, the conversation had rarely even touched on Lubo. Sitting with her back to the party, Neddy listened to talk of who'd planted what and how many sheep had been birthed that spring. In hushed tones, the same men and women who'd gone to grade school with Lubo in the tiny schoolhouse down the hill grieved not the loss of their friend so much as the mild winter just past that they would pay for come summer. A heat wave. The mere thought of it caused the party to break out in a sweat. In the pauses and gaps and collective silences, Neddy heard not reminiscences, but the counting and calculating of crops. Better to redouble their efforts now than to be short come autumn.

Oh, Neddy was in a mood—a thing so rare for her, not even Radka, not even her own son, knew what to do. *"Dobre li si?"* Nasko had asked her, his eyes like commas turned down at the corners. And Neddy, still cloudy with incense, resentment, and unshed tears, saw not her son, but her deceased husband. "Yes, Lubo," she said with a sigh, "you can have another drink."

After the funeral, rumors of the heat wave circled Old Mountain like a stray dog making its rounds, ugly and persistent. As spring drew on, villagers quizzed one another on their preparations. How many melons did *you* plant? How many cucumbers? Freezers were stocked with slabs of pork thick enough to withstand hours in the heat. And when the days grew longer, curtains were drawn across open windows to keep houses dark and cool.

Neddy has not been so ambitious. Back in May, Radka advised her to put wet towels in the icebox, but Neddy couldn't be bothered. Now, as sun pours through the swirled yellow plastic that forms the eastern wall of the shed and all but melts the tablecloth on which she rests her elbows, she thinks of those frozen towels. It is not too late. She could put a towel in the freezer this morning and enjoy it this afternoon. She *could*. But she won't. Maybe tomorrow, she tells herself, only tomorrow will be no different from today.

Since the funeral, she has not picked up a shovel, spade, or hoe. Swept up in a tidal wave of inertia, she cannot imagine another summer spent on her hands and knees in the garden.

She can imagine neither doing it now nor ever having done it. *How* had she worked her way up and down the rows of peppers, zucchini, and squash, planting and weeding and picking, filling her days with work as though this was the only way to manage? Somewhere inside her, a switch has turned off. She cannot live that way any longer. Though the land continues to produce: eggplants large as cats going to waste right under her nose. Lubo, for one, is mad with worry. "I know, Lubo," she says wearily. "The next time Nasko visits, he will take his pick."

Lost in her musings, Neddy has failed to notice Dancho standing in her doorway. "Pick of what?" he says, looking curiously at Neddy hunkered in the shed.

"*Ami*—," Neddy stammers, embarrassed the boy has found her like this. How long has he been watching?

"Pick of what?" the boy says again, making clear whatever it is, he would like a pick, too.

"*Ami*—," Neddy tries again, noticing the boy's stained tank top, shorts a size too small, and broken plastic flip-flops. *For goodness sake, Lubo, it's only a boy.* "Nothing," she says. What has she got for the boy to pick from? She cannot think of a single thing.

By now, the boy's gaze has moved past Neddy and is taking in the shed. There is plenty to look at: decades of accumulation, Lubo's things mostly, oily rag and tool, length of rope and torn shoelace, old boot and broken cowbell—packed together on shelves that run the length of the wall. For years, Neddy anticipated cleaning the shed when Lubo was no longer around. But these days, the idea of undoing this precious ecosystem is unimaginable. What would this shed be without the thin layer of grease and trace smell of gasoline? The sticky plastic *pokrivka* ringed with espresso circles and the stale mouse droppings swept into the corners?

Dancho is intrigued. "What are you doing?" he asks. Leaning against the doorframe, he pulls the shoulder strap of his tank top into his mouth and chews.

Never in Neddy's life has she been without an answer to this question. Always, she has been planting or cooking or washing or canning. Add to that caring for Lubo, which had become all-consuming in the final months. Now, with the boy waiting intently, it occurs to her she is resting. *"Pochivam sega,"* she offers, pleased with this idea. Lubo is resting now. She is resting too.

But Dancho is not at all satisfied. "It's only morning," he says, kicking at a pair of Lubo's slippers, which still wait for him beside the door.

Neddy shifts uncomfortably in her chair. The heavy black dress is wretchedly hot, and her face is flushed. Reaching up to lift her hair off her neck, she discovers her whole head is damp. So is the boy's. The boy needs a rest, too. "Would you like a drink of water?" she asks.

The boy consents, and Neddy gives him water from the garden tap. So deep had Lubo buried the pipe that to this day, however warm the ground gets, the water is icy cool. She serves it in Lubo's dented aluminum bowl that still rests atop the spigot. He drinks greedily, holding the cup with both hands. By the time he is finished, he is out of breath.

"Would you like some more?" She refills the cup three times before the boy has had his fill. When they are finished at the spigot, Neddy returns to the shed, and the boy leaves her. She wonders if he'll have a stomachache from drinking so much cold water so quickly. Perhaps she should have stopped him. But she enjoyed watching him gulp it down. As she settles back into her seat, she feels like she has done something with her day.

For nearly a month, heat swaddles Old Mountain like a scratchy woolen blanket. During this spell, Dancho drinks from the spigot in Neddy's garden nearly every day. At first, he asks for the water. But soon, he starts helping himself. Water lops over the sides of the cup as he brings it into the shed, which in midafternoon is several degrees cooler than the garden. Neddy watches the boy take great gulping swallows of water. When he is finished, she too is strangely sated. Soon, she finds the small cup of yogurt that has been her supper since Lubo died is too much for her, so large and round is the satisfaction in her chest.

It is the same feeling she had when she watched Lubo take his meals, his eyes fixed on his plate, wholly engaged in the business of eating. Early in their marriage, Neddy was embarrassed to look up from her own empty dish and find Lubo's plate still filled with salad, meat, and fried potatoes; as she watched Lubo eat, she was shamefully aware of her backside spilling over the edges of her seat. But the more she watched, the more she enjoyed watching—the muscles in his face that clenched as he chewed and the knot in his throat that marked each swallow. In time, she found that her own intake of food meant little to her. Rather, the grunts, the belches, the sighs— these were the substance of her meals. She guessed he understood this, the way he took his time alternating bites of meat and hot pepper, a nip of raw onion, a swallow of beer to wash it all down. So intent was he on the food before him he took

little notice of Neddy refilling his glass or slicing another piece
of bread, another wedge of onion and slipping it onto his plate.
When he finally finished eating, he would watch the *televisor* and drink another beer while Neddy cleaned up around
him, then rejoined him at the table, not so much as a word between them, not even when they brushed their teeth and Lubo
reached for her beneath the covers.

Oh, it has been a long time since Neddy has savored such
fulfillment in someone else. Long enough that by the time the
boy is finished drinking, her own stomach feels so pregnant,
so heavy with water, she is glad to see him stop.

Radka, for her part, is not at all satisfied with this situation.
"Why are you letting that boy drink all your water?" she scolds
Neddy one morning. For weeks, she has been watching this
from her window. "Lubo would not like it," she says. "Lubo
would not have you giving all your water away to any old creature who shows up in your garden."

But of course Lubo would have wanted the boy to drink his
water. Margarita's door whines on its hinges, then slams shut,
which is just the thing to stir Radka's agitation. "Would you
listen to that?" she says, craning her head to look at Margarita
hanging out the laundry.

Neddy does not need to look to see her neighbor pinning
clothing on the line, arranging socks, underwear, and T-shirts
according to size, her own hearty undergarments anchoring
the row. From the shed, she can hear Margarita huff and sigh
with every bend and stretch, the clothing tripled with the boy
here.

"Would it be so much to fix that door so we wouldn't have
to listen to it day in and day out?" Radka prattles on, a swallow
of coffee to fuel her fire.

Neddy has listened to Margarita's huffing and sighing for years—ever since Margarita's husband died and Margarita needed someone to hear. Only on this spiritless morning, the huffs, the sighs linger in the air, piling up like puffs of exhaust from a tailpipe until they form a thick black cloud.

"It's an agony for the ears," Radka sputters.

But this comment is lost on Neddy, who is experiencing her first brackish taste of the problems Margarita is negotiating next door. Though she and Margarita have never been close, there is something in this huff and sigh, something in the boy's tremendous thirst, that tells her things are not going well for his parents, and this strained summer arrangement is futile indeed.

Sometime after Radka has left, she hears a soft thudding coming from the yard. Rousing from her chair, she peers out the door and sees Dancho throwing rocks at the sun-bleached clothing. She watches the boy choose his rock, wind up, and take aim at one of Margarita's brassieres. Missing, he aims again, hurling rocks with such intensity, such meanness even, that he cannot pause when one of the rocks strikes Margarita's aluminum watering can, and another a squirrel, which freezes in place before it limps away. He doesn't stop until a rock finally lodges in one of the cups. Then, he pauses to empty the brassiere and begin again.

That afternoon, the boy stays even after the water is gone, sitting on the cool, packed dirt floor of the shed with his back against the doorframe. When he sits like this, it looks like a big weight is pushing him down to the ground. "Baba, why do you sit out here all day?"

It is a fair question—one Lubo asked *how many times* when

the shed was first built and again in the year before he died. In the beginning, it had something to do with moving out of Lubo's parents' house, being alone with Lubo and the baby for the first time. What would happen when he discovered she was every bit as plump and quiet as she seemed? At least the quake and shiver of the garden lent some semblance of life and animation. In the later years, long after Lubo had accepted her for all her shortcomings, it was habit, for certain, that she continued to spend her time in the shed, but also something more. A knowledge, she supposed, that when Lubo passed, this garden, these chipmunks and squirrels, these spiders and snails would remain. "I like it here," she says.

"It's just a dirty old shed."

"You don't like it?"

The boy shrugs. "It's not as good as my house in Sofia. You don't even have a bicycle."

Neddy has never ridden a bicycle, nor has she ever much wanted one. But there's an edge in his voice that gets to her. "You don't have goats," she says.

The boy looks surprised. "Neither do you."

"Yes, but I used to," Neddy says, feeling the sting of yet another loss. Six months before Lubo died, she'd had to give up the four white goats she'd kept. She'd sold them to Pesho down the hill for a pittance; the money meant nothing to her.

"It doesn't count if you don't have them now," the boy says.

Neddy has to agree. She tries to think of something else she might have, but searching the walls of the shed, she finds nothing of interest. The boy looks around, too. "At least you have that," he finally says, flicking his toe at a shiny cylindrical machine on one of the lower shelves. "What is it anyhow?"

"That?" The boy has chosen a thing that looks more interesting than it is. "That's a *chushkopek*." A pepper roaster, Neddy concedes, and not even a nice one.

"Oh." The boy waits another minute before getting up to leave. "Well, I guess that counts for something."

The following day, Dancho begins where he left off. After he finishes his third serving of water, he sets the cup down on the floor of the shed and squares his shoulders against the doorframe. "You don't have a basketball hoop," he starts. "You don't even have a basketball."

Neddy shifts uncomfortably in her chair. She had not expected to play this game again. "I have a soccer ball," she says, recalling an old *topka* of Nasko's.

"That's not as good," the boy says. "Unless it has an autograph. Does it have an autograph?"

"I can't imagine how it would," Neddy says truthfully. She wonders if this boy isn't a bit spoiled that he can make such demands.

"Well then that's no good." The boy sounds disgusted. "You've got to have something better than that."

Neddy thinks for a moment. "I've got a grandson who plays basketball."

"Is he professional?"

"No, but he is very tall."

Dancho is not impressed. "If he was that tall, he'd be professional," he says.

But Neddy will not allow her grandson to be so easily dismissed. That evening, she finds a photo of Plamen on his graduation day. "See?" she says, the following day, after Dancho has finished his water. In the picture, Plamen is hunched, and still he is almost as tall as the lamppost. "See how tall he is?"

Dancho takes the photo in his hands and stares at it for several minutes. When he gives it back to her, he is stingy with his approval. "When's he coming to visit?"

"I don't know." Plamen hasn't visited since the funeral, though he calls every now and then. The last time he called, he was about to leave for a mathematics conference, and he planned to be there for several days. "He has to go to Macedonia," Neddy says, imbued with a sense of importance. Dancho is standing so close, his leg hairs are touching her own. It is nice to feel the boy this close.

Dancho thinks about this for a moment, then shrugs. "I guess it doesn't matter," he says. "If he's that tall, that's pretty good."

Most days, Neddy is on the losing end. They agree the mole on her arm, even with two hairs poking out of it, cannot compete with the brilliant red strawberry that brands the blade of Dancho's shoulder. When the boy's report card with all sixes easily bests Plamen's postcard from Macedonia, Neddy begins to lose hope. *"Ah taka,"* she says with greater satisfaction than she feels. "Bravo, Dani," she says with a strange solemnity that, long after the boy has left, she cannot shake—not even when she reminds herself her own son was a fine student and her grandson is a master's level mathematician. Not even then. For they have their own lives now, and she cannot dwell on their marks forever.

In the final days of the heat wave, Neddy turns up a winner when she produces mating frogs, stuck one on top of the other, she found by the spigot in the garden. *"Vizh,"* she says holding them out to the boy.

Dancho takes the frogs gingerly in his hands. "What's wrong with them?"

"Nothing," Neddy says. She does not want to explain.

"Nothing?" he says skeptically, but then he is distracted by the frogs, turning them over in his hands. Growing bolder, he gives the upper frog a doglike scratch on the top of its head, the lower frog a tender rub on the belly. Soon, he settles into prying the pair apart, pokey fingers trying to wedge themselves between back and belly. Though Neddy is pleased with the boy's fascination, she is sorry for the frogs, one of which urinates on the boy's hand, and still he continues his machinations. As she watches this heroic struggle, an empathy swells within her for the tenacious frogs, which she herself placed in this predicament and which now cling to each other not out of pleasure or purpose, but out of fear.

By the time Dancho gives the terrorized frogs a rest, they appear to be frozen. He stares at them for a while, then wraps his small arm around Neddy's shoulder. "Baba, are there any more like that?"

By early August, the worst of the heat has passed. Slowly, the village comes to life. Down the road, Zhivka's granddaughter comes for a visit, as do Pesho's grandsons. Soon, Dancho has playmates from dawn till dusk. Sometimes he brings the other kids to drink from Neddy's tap. "See how cold it is?" she hears him say. "It's this cold even when it's fifty degrees out. It's this cold no matter what."

When not with the kids, Dancho spends most of his time kicking his soccer ball against the side of the house. "*Ela, Dani,*" Margarita calls in a voice that grows sweeter by the day.

It is the same singsongy voice Margarita had used on Neddy near the end. *"Eto go,"* she'd sing when she'd stop by to drop off a bottle of milk, averting her eyes from Lubo, who likely had drool on his chin or lint in his stubble. *"Haide,* Dani," she sings beseechingly, her tone bittersweet for the boy who slams his soccer ball against the side of the house over and over again.

Even Neddy can hardly stand the sound, which throbs like a headache throughout her day. But for once, Radka takes little notice. Sipping her coffee, she counts the stitches under her breath—*edno, dve, tree, cheteree*—before settling into a rapid rhythm of stitching. It is an extraordinary sweater, the only pattern for which is Radka's vivid imagination. When finished, it will be too beautiful to wear. The same can be said for all the knitting projects Radka undertakes, which are nothing like the mundane socks, booties, and knobby sweaters everyone else produces, warm pieces with destinations—husbands, children, and grandchildren. When Margarita or Ilonka or the others come over to watch Radka work, invariably someone will suggest that this sweater can only be worn on *Dallas* anyway, and though it is meant for a joke, Radka doesn't laugh. From the look on her face, Neddy knows she is imaging her life as a knitter for *Dallas,* already planning the next sweater with even more colors and even more extraordinary designs.

This morning, Radka works without an audience, except for Neddy, whose mind is elsewhere. Though the boy isn't coming around so often anymore, she finds herself thinking ahead, wanting to be ready for the next time he does. So far, the best thing she has found is a tomato the size of a melon growing in the garden. *"Ah, taka,"* she said to Lubo, releasing the heavy red fruit from its strained stem. She caught it just in time—there are no bruises or bad spots or signs of splitting.

Washing it and centering it on her table, she thinks if she were still feeding Lubo, she would have chopped it up for a salad without a second thought.

But several days have passed since Neddy picked the tomato, and now it is going soft. Flies land on the puckered fruit, and juice has seeped onto the table. Next door, Dancho is kicking his ball again. Neddy wishes he would take a break and come see her tomato.

Radka reads her mind. "*Bozhe,* Neddy, what are you doing with that rotten tomato? Look at these flies," she says, jabbing her needle at the air.

Neddy shifts in her seat. She feels stupid about the tomato, impatient with her friend who carries on with her knitting—*edno, dve, tree, cheteree*—while the soccer ball slams against Margarita's house and the flies buzz in her ear.

"*Ah taka,*" Radka says, resuming her focus on the project at hand, and Neddy can see how pleased she is with this fine sweater and the fact that Dancho is out there kicking his ball instead of drinking all of Neddy's water.

"*Ah taka,*" Radka said the evening after the funeral when the guests had cleared. Nasko had finally gone home, and they were alone, Neddy glued to her chair before the fire. Radka had pulled up a chair next to her and, pouring them each another plum brandy, settled down to share the fire with her friend. By then Neddy had come to see the flames as small flickers of anger she was feeling for every last thing. The guests had cleaned up after themselves. But a quick look around and there was Lubo's ashtray on the table, his shoes on the floor, his half-drunk *rakiya* bottle on the windowsill. There was Radka fidgeting in the chair next to her, every now and then grunting contentedly, as if to say, isn't it nice to have that behind us?

Usually, Neddy can tune out the driving click of Radka's needles, but this morning it taps on her last nerve. This relentless friend, these buzzing flies, this rotting tomato—she cannot look at any of them for one more minute. "Just get rid of the tomato," she snaps at Radka, who jumps in her seat, nearly tipping over her coffee.

Neddy, too, is startled. She has behaved badly, and yet this was her intent. Let Radka be the one to sit and suffer in her chair. Let Radka be the one to soak up all the anger.

But Radka does nothing of the sort. Rather, as though by matter of course, she picks up the soggy tomato by the stem and carries it back out to the garden, settling it there with a distinct tenderness. On her way back, she runs a towel under the spigot, which she uses to wipe up the mess. During all this, Neddy remains rooted to her chair, feeling heavy and foolish and oddly entitled to this moment. Her eyes follow Radka, swishing the tomato juice on the table, wringing out the towel, and swishing it again. When she is finished, Radka packs up her knitting and takes leave of her friend, carrying the extraordinary sweater in one hand, the dirty towel discreetly, dutifully in the other.

Toward the end of the summer, a colicky rain takes hold of Old Mountain, settling in each day in the late afternoon and continuing through *Dallas*. Dancho spends these hours with Neddy in the shed. Mostly they sit in silence and listen to the rain spatter the yellow plastic pane. The boy sits on the floor with his shoulders pressed against the doorframe, sighing every now and then—a habit he's picked up from his grandmother.

The day before Dancho leaves, he sits for nearly an hour in one of these moods. At last, he gets up and comes over to her. "Baba, when's that tall guy coming for a visit?" He leans against her, reaching up and twisting a strand of her hair. Neddy is ashamed she has let her hair go like this. She hasn't had it cut or dyed since Lubo passed away; by now, it is gray and frizzy and coarse. But Dancho doesn't notice. When he twists the strand of hair, she feels a tug at her scalp that is more pleasant than painful. She puts her hand on his back and holds him to her. With his body pressed against hers, she can feel his warmth through the fabric of her dress. With his face so close, she can almost taste the sweetness of his breath.

"You mean Plamen?" she asks, hardly aware of her own words. How long has it been since someone has pressed his body against hers? There were hugs when Lubo died, bosoms and arms and bodies that clung to one another in perfunctory embrace. But this was different, this casual commingling of the flesh. She can feel his hips pressing into her thigh. She wonders if it is indecent, the way she loves this boy.

The last time Lubo touched her had been about six months before he died. It happened during a cold snap in October. She had not yet put the heavy blankets on the bed, and he had pulled up close to her for warmth, his breath tickling the back of her neck. She was never able to sleep when he was breathing on her neck, but that night, she lay still and let Lubo warm his shivering self against her body. Her nightgown had ridden up to her hips, so there was little separating their bodies save the awkward ring of fabric around her middle. His body cradled her ample buttocks and the underside of her thighs; eventually, he wedged his frozen fingers between her legs for heat.

At first, she'd been embarrassed. For decades, their intimacies had been functional—a matter of meeting Lubo's needs, and this in itself had brought her pleasure. But quickly her embarrassment gave way to amazement at how cold and bony he was. She wondered how much life he had left in him. She'd known it would not be long.

Once his fingers had thawed, she'd felt his hands grow restless, caressing her hips, thighs, the girth of her behind. Soon she would no longer be able to feign sleep. She waited as long as she could, realizing she was dreading this, knowing it would be the last time, wondering if he was aware of what he was doing. "Lubo?" she asked.

"*Da?*" he said, and in a single word, she could hear how alert he was. He was the old Lubo, the Lubo she hadn't known in more than a year. Neddy gasped at the sound of his voice, so present and alive, it was as though he'd never left. In the silence that followed, his hands paused, tense, as he waited for her to accept his offer.

"Baba?" Dancho says, still waiting for an answer.

Neddy strokes the boy's backside, letting her hand rest on the back of his tanned leg. She could hold this boy for a very long time.

"Will he come for a visit before I leave?"

Will who come? Neddy doesn't know what the boy is talking about. That night, when they were finished, it was she who had clung to Lubo in the hope he might still be there in the morning.

But come dawn, it was the other Lubo who sat across from her in the shed. "Does this coffee taste all right to you?" he had asked with the anxiety of a child.

Neddy could not look at him. "Yes, Lubo," she says, staring

into the bottom of her cup, the leftover grounds swept into a dizzying swirl of disappointment. "It tastes just fine."

"*Kakvo?*" the boy says. From the scowl in his voice, Neddy understands she has stirred his impatience—and he hers. How many times must she say it? *It tastes just fine.*

"Oh forget it," he says, pulling away. Though Neddy can discern a cooling against her leg where he had pushed up against her, it is not until she hears the last few drops of rain spatter the shed and inhales the sweet smell of the garden composting all around her that she is aware he is gone.

The next day, it is dark when Neddy rises. She makes the coffee and drinks it hot, then sits and waits for the day to begin. Beyond the shed, there is a general stirring, chickens strutting, cavalier tomcats staggering home for a drink of water and a place to sleep. As the dew drops away, even the plants prick and tremble. This morning, the quiver is everywhere around her, inside her. A pang of impatience—was the coffee too strong? But all she can recall is its scalding heat, which smarts like a burn inside her chest.

In a few hours, the boy will leave. During the night, the fact of his departure settled on her like cooling ash, the ground beneath still smoldering, too hot to touch. At last, Neddy had gotten up and placed a wet towel in the freezer, but even the icy compress applied to forehead, neck, and back-of-knees was not enough, and she never managed to sleep. All summer, she had understood Dancho's was not a permanent arrangement; for months she has known this day would come. Still, she is no more ready for the boy's departure than she was for Lubo's death. That she realizes this—that she can feel the ground vibrating beneath her, yesterday's faint rumble growing louder and more insistent—counts for something, she thinks. But not good enough, the boy would say, and for the hundredth time, he would be right.

Neddy's eyes skim the shed—a half-hearted perusal, though it is hard to see, the sun not yet up. Whatever she is looking for (she does not know what) is not on these shelves. By now, she has memorized every last item, and the best she has produced—certainly the frogs—weren't in the shed but in the garden, which has gone to ruin, and Nasko never did take his pick.

Oh, on this shaky morning, even the frogs can inspire doubt. Neddy is at once wracked with guilt . . . for the little fingers that, under her watch, pried so mercilessly at the committed pair . . . for hungry hand left to linger on innocent backside, soft and delicious and wrong.

"*Bozhe Gospodi,* Neddy," Radka hisses. "What are you doing up at this hour?" Plunking down in Lubo's chair, she pulls out the sweater, which is finished, but for a few stitches needed to attach cuffs and arms and collar. "The last thing I need is for you to start sneaking around in the middle of the night."

Neddy does not have the strength to argue it is *not* the middle of the night, *already* the darkness is starting to lift, and *soon,* frightfully soon, the boy will be gone. Besides, it appears Radka has been up plenty of hours herself in her race to finish the sweater. Bloodshot eyes. Fingers rubbed raw. This is how Radka gets at the end of a sweater: overcome with panic that soon the sweater will be done, and at the same time, unable to stop herself from pearling those last, most delectable stitches.

"I can't even see what I'm doing here," she says, craning in her chair to catch the dim rays of dawn. But she hardly needs to see, so well does she know these stitches. Within moments, she is knitting. "*Edno, dve, tree, cheteree. Edno, dve, tree, cheteree*," she whispers over and over until Neddy finds herself drumming the table, *edno, dve, tree, cheteree*, her anxiety on the rise.

Next door, the screen door slams. Everyone is up early this morning. Dancho's mother arrived by herself the night before. "Did you bring my bicycle?" Dancho had called down from the upstairs window. His mother's response was followed by a strained silence, during which Neddy could fairly hear the boy's calculations. "Is my bicycle still there?"

Edno, dve, tree, cheteree. In her frenzy, Radka has not even touched Lubo's coffee, which has developed a film across the top, a tiny fruit fly flailing on its surface.

Then the footsteps are pounding up and down the stairs. Then the car doors are slamming. Then the shouts are escalating. "Did you pack your soccer ball?" "Did you eat your breakfast?" "Is my bicycle still there?" Then the good-byes are being said. "You be good to your mother, you hear?"

"Good-bye, Baba," the boy calls, and in Neddy's besotted mind, this is intended for her. She chokes on the knot in her throat, coughing until Radka looks up from her knitting just long enough to see the damp in Neddy's eyes.

There is a pause in the stitching, a blip of betrayal, but then the knitting resumes. For already, the next sweater is taking shape in her mind, with colors and patterns more vivid and consoling than they can ever be in real life. In the quiet that follows—one last honk of the car horn, a dropped stitch, and not so much as a huff from Radka—Neddy recognizes the hurt of one who has tried so valiantly to claim another as her own. Funny that in this moment of estrangement, she should feel closer to her friend than she's felt in a long, long time.

Neddy's gaze fixes on Radka's fingers, which fly across the sweater. Through her wet eyes, the colors are a blur, like yarn woven through the spokes of bicycle wheels. The boy will be back, she tells herself. If not next summer (surely Margarita will not allow it), then maybe the summer following, or the summer after that. By then, Lubo will have been gone not three months, but three years. Dancho's parents, independently of one another, will have loved and lost and loved again; meanwhile he will have cycled through bicycle, basketball, and cell phone as the objects of his affection. *Dallas* will be replaced by *The Bold and the Beautiful,* and a dozen more sweaters will have been knitted and abandoned in Radka's cellar. Neddy will have goats again, first two, then four, then eight, and she will be really good at this game they play, these fictions they knit to keep them warm.

COLD SNAP

DAY ONE: THE DAWN OF (IM)POSSIBILITY

Dobrin didn't see his mother fall, but he heard about it afterward.

Stassi said she toppled down headfirst and you could see her underwear. *Panties,* he said, with all the relish of one who loved underwear of any variety. All the way down, you could see them, and then when she landed, there they were. He said it was a little disgusting how much you could see. He said he would never be able to look at Dobrin's mother the same way again.

Dobrin's father said that was the way it was with Maika. Tatko said if it wasn't her head, it was her shoulder. If it wasn't her shoulder, it was her ankle. He said unless there was blood, he wasn't going to worry about it.

Marina from upstairs said you could hear it crack. She said she had just stepped out of her office to get a breath of fresh air when Maika fell. While she hadn't actually seen it, she'd heard the crack clear across the schoolyard. At first she'd thought a tree branch had broken, but then she realized someone was hurt, and there was Maika at the bottom of the stairs. She said you couldn't even see the ice. She said invisible ice was the worst kind.

She said this in a hushed voice so Maika wouldn't hear, even though she was in the other room with the door closed, and Tatko had turned on the TV. They had just gotten her settled on the sofa with her leg resting on two pillows, and Marina, making to leave, had asked Dobrin to put water on for tea.

It was cold in the apartment—cold enough that you could see your breath. All the apartments in Old Mountain were attached to a single switch for central heat; because heat was expensive, the town had set a rule that the temperatures had to remain below freezing for four days before it was turned on. For Dobrin, these days were a torture even worse than school. Even worse than Stassi seeing his mother's *panties.*

That day, Dobrin had stayed home sick and had spent the entire day in the *hol,* where they had set up the space heater until the central heat was turned on. They'd bought this heater the year before, when they could not afford central heat for Dobrin's room: at least this would keep him warm at night. Now Dobrin regarded the small, portable radiator with the kind of fondness he usually reserved for stray dogs and pretty girls. And sometimes for his mother.

But the space heater was doing nothing to help him in the corridor, where Marina was zipping up her boots. "You look cold, Dobrin," she said. "Why aren't you wearing a sweater?"

Dobrin did not know why. Only now he was too cold to go into his unheated bedroom to retrieve one.

"Don't forget the tea, Dobrin. *Chuvash li?*" she said, and the way she looked at him, he knew she was trying to decide if she could trust him.

Dobrin did not particularly want to be trusted. He was not really sick. But it was so cold, he had not slept well. And he had not done his homework for English class. In fact, he had not done it for several days. So, he had lied to Maika and told her he was not feeling well. He had vowed to himself to do all his homework, even to do extra work in his English workbook, so he would be set for the next week or two. But then Tatko had turned on the TV, first one match, then another, and the next thing he knew, here was Maika home from the hospital with her broken ankle and it was dark outside and he still hadn't done a thing for school.

And when he thought about the crack heard clear across the schoolyard, he felt sick for real. There was no chance he'd do the homework now.

"Dobrin, the tea?" Marina pressed.

"*Da,*" he said, even though the thought of one more minute away from the space heater was unbearable.

Dobrin put the water on to boil, then went back to the *hol,* where his mother was stretched out on the couch with her eyes closed. He tried to avoid looking at her—she did not look good—but it was hard not to look at the purple circles that ringed her eyes. Somehow, in the tumble, she had managed to bang her face. He was no stranger to black eyes, but these were the worst he had ever seen.

As if sensing his gaze, his mother spoke. "It was a bad fall," Maika said, her eyes still closed. "The doctor said I'm not going to be able to do much for a couple weeks."

Silence, except for the TV and the sound of Tatko breathing through his nose. Dobrin did not like to hear his mother talk this way. He wished the tea would boil faster. He wished there was something he could do.

"I don't know what this is going to mean," she said, and then another silence for this to sink in. Dobrin did not know either—only he did know, at least in part. For if Maika could not teach extra classes at the Technikum and private lessons at home, it would be difficult, if not impossible, for them to afford heat. Dobrin's heart sank at the thought of it: he could not imagine living in this cold all winter long.

That night, Tatko made pork and onions for dinner, a dish Dobrin liked well enough when his mother made it. But Tatko had added too much salt, and Dobrin could barely eat it. Maika on the couch. Tatko sipping slowly on his *rakiya*. Silence and more silence, because the TV hurt Maika's head. As Dobrin picked at the food on his plate, he thought he could not possibly be more miserable.

Finally, Tatko took a bite of the pork. "Plah!" he said, spitting out a half-chewed chunk of meat. "Plah! Plah! Plah!" he said, until they were all laughing, even Maika. "Plah! Plah! Plah!" Tatko said as he poured them each a *rakiya*, one for Tatko and one for Maika, a swallow for Dobrin to erase the taste. Dobrin drank it too quickly and felt the burn in his chest for the rest of the night.

Later, when he took the leftovers out to feed the stray dogs that rushed their ground-floor *balcon*, not even they would touch the pork and onions. Still, they whimpered and nuzzled Dobrin: even without his mother, who they loved more than anyone, they were happy to see him, and Dobrin felt a sob rising in his throat. They always did this to him, only usually Maika was there, and he couldn't show he was crying.

But tonight he was alone, and his mother was inside with purple eyes and a broken ankle. And the kisses of so many cold wet noses were too much. Under this wriggling mass of gratitude that would refuse the ruined pork but lap eagerly at the salt of his tears, he was not sure what was wrong with him, if he was happy or sad. Or if the two weren't one and the same.

The crack heard clear across the schoolyard. It was a clean, solid sound. A definitive snap, not unlike an impacted tooth that breaks from the root. As a dentist, it was a sound Marina would not want to hear.

It turned out, the crack was that of a human ankle bone, the ankle belonging to her first-floor neighbor, Pavletta Georgieva. Marina's office stood on the edge of the town square, close to the school, but with a large marbled schoolyard in between; in such cold that made all things quiet, the crack might have been her very own bone, so loud and clear did it ring between her ears. She was having a hard time getting past it. This was a thing Marina had tried to disguise (after all, she *was* a medical professional), and for the most part, she had managed to be a soothing, authoritative presence during the taxi rides to and from the hospital, the X-rays, the doctors' visits, the waiting, waiting, waiting. It wasn't until they were back from the hospital, with Pavletta situated comfortably on the couch, that Marina had let down her guard and described the crack, the sickening sound of it, to Pavletta's son, Dobrin, who was fine at first, then started to turn green.

As the day drew on, Marina could feel the crack becoming something internal, something akin to the pulse she heard in her temples after a brisk walk. When she got to her apartment, she closed herself in the kitchen, oven on, door open. The room would warm quickly. In the meantime, she retrieved a bottle of wine from atop her cabinet, wiped off a thick film of dust, and poured herself a glass. One sip, and she was looking for her cookbook, the chapter on baking. This glass of wine, this urge to bake: something had snapped. Marina was as sure of this as she was of the cold holding them all frozen in time.

Always, this was a difficult time, waiting for the heat to come on and watching the thermometer's mercury bounce with all the spit and whimsy of a child at play, while so many lives hung in the balance. Back when the children were home, Marina had boiled big pots of beans and bought a game of Scrabble so Sylvia and Drago could practice their English. During these weeks, the twins spent hours at the kitchen table playing that game: though Marina did not know English, she would mimic them—*boy, toy, hat*—to make them laugh. But a few hours of distraction didn't change the fact that the bathroom was cold, the floors were cold, their beds were cold. It was the kind of cold that left a scar, which you covered up with scarves and hats and sweaters all winter long. No matter that when the heat finally came on the apartments were hot, so hot, that shorts and a tank top might suffice.

It wasn't until the first winter the twins were away at college that Marina uncovered another scar of sorts: for if she missed her children (and she *did* miss them—as much as she might her hand, her heart, her head were these to be so brutally extracted from her and packed off to Sofia), at no time was the pain of their absence more acute than during these cold, captive days when they had once been so intensely together. Difficult as these days were, she'd come to cherish them—which made them all the more difficult to cope with on her own. The first year she was alone, she found herself bending over the steaming pot of beans with tears in her eyes, then decided crying into a pot of beans would not do. The next day, she purchased the biggest, most powerful space heater money could buy and put it in her office. What was at once both indulgent and necessary to ease her suffering, quickly became a boon of the sort she could not have anticipated. Word of the heater spread overnight, and her roster of appointments filled with those wanting an hour to roast. That year, and every year since, she'd worked twelve-hour days and six-day weeks in the month or so that preceded winter. In a single month, she could clean the teeth of half the people in town (nearly all the people with teeth to clean). And though she grew hot and dry from so much heat, she realized a level of professional success she could never have imagined. At the end of the month, she changed the money into dollars and deposited it into a bank account for the grandchildren she hoped to have one day.

The cookbook asked for flour, sugar, egg, vanilla, which Marina measured into the bowl. The wine, a treat so rare, made her uncharacteristically sloppy. Soon, flour dusted the countertops and sugar granules crunched underfoot. Rather than clean these messes before they could spread, Marina removed her slippers and stepped squarely onto the spilled sugar so she could savor its grit beneath her sole.

Yes, the crack had been as sharp as a clap of thunder, as decisive as a tree branch felled on a rooftop. To dull the sound, Marina churned the batter with a wooden spoon until her hand hurt. She drank the wine until her tongue was dry with tannin. She stood over the open oven door until her face was red, and she was so hot she could barely stand it.

Marina had just put her first tray of cookies in the oven when she heard a familiar yell from downstairs. "Fuck!" the voice hollered. "Fuck! Fuck! Fuck!" She had heard Sylvia and Drago say this word, *fuck,* while they were playing Scrabble. She'd known from their giggles it was a word they should not be saying, and she could presume, not for the first time, things were unhappy downstairs. Sipping at her wine, she wondered, amid these sharp snaps, cracks, explosions, if things were really so impossible as they seemed.

Vladi decided to name the baby Vladi. "Vladislav if it's a boy, Vladislava if it's a girl," he said, plucking a potato from the platter that sat on the counter.

This was how he greeted her when he got home from work. Not *Zdrasti, skupa.* Not *Sorry I'm late.* Not *How was your day?* Not *It smells good in here,* even though it always did. That there was no such chatter—Galia had always counted this as one of the blessings of their union. You said what needed to be said. You skipped the small talk. In this one, fundamental way, they were a good match.

Which was why she had not brought up the issue of the name herself. What did Vladi care about the name? Vladi, who had said nothing, or the equivalent of nothing—*Pass me the salt*—when she told him she was pregnant. Vladi, who had neglected to comment on the vomiting that had lasted for four months. Or the crib that had appeared in the second bedroom. Or her changing body, until the day she caught him watching her get dressed. Then he told her she looked plump.

Now he had laid claim to a thing as precious to her as the baby itself. "A little Vladi," he said, taking another potato from the platter and swiping at the drippings in the bottom of the roasting pan before popping it into his mouth.

Galia used the corner of her apron to wipe the tear from her eye, the sweat from her lip. One would never know they were without heat from the temperature in this apartment, a space heater in each room. Her parents had left them behind when they'd given them the apartment, taking a smaller unit on the other side of the square. "You'll need the space," her mother had said, and then camped out to watch the lights go on and off from her new apartment across the courtyard. And to wait, impatiently, for the space to fill.

Fill it did, with bears and blankets and a frilly bassinet. For two years, her mother had waited for this baby, stockpiling things the baby would need. Just that day, Galia had decided it was too much and had packed some of the things away. For even as her mother was filling the room, there was another space being filled—a space Galia hadn't even known existed until it started to bulge with fluid and flesh and a sense of fullness she could not have imagined. With this swell, this new dimension, Galia had concluded some things were hers to decide. And she felt ready to take these decisions on her child's behalf, as she had never been able to do for herself.

One of those decisions was the baby's name. "Miroslava." The name meant *peace* and *glory*. They would call her "Mira," for Galia was certain she was a girl. The name and gender were as fixed in her mind as the very fact of this baby.

And so it was in defense of this peaceful life she resolved to say something before Vladi had a chance to get used to his idea. She would tell him no, the name was Mira. She would say it in a way he would know it was not negotiable. She would. She would. She would.

But first, she would ply Vladi with chicken and potatoes and a glass of *rakiya*. "*Molya ti se,*" she said briskly, brushing past him to put the platter on the table. He grabbed three more potatoes as she went by, which he proceeded to dip into the fat and slide into his mouth, grease collecting in the crease of his chin.

The only thing left to do was to pour the *rakiya*. As Galia reached for the bottle, she felt reassured by the belly that pressed against the counter's edge: her very condition as the carrier of this child made her not just emboldened, but obliged.

Then, the eruption.

"Fuck!" Vladi shouted, and Galia knew without looking that grease had landed on his tie. "Fuck, fuck, fuck!" he carried on until Galia thought her ears would explode.

On a regular night, she would have tried to protect the baby, who had to listen to her father scream like this. She would have draped a dishtowel over her belly in the most casual, offhand way in an attempt to muffle the sounds that reached her daughter's embryonic ears.

On a regular night, she would have been embarrassed for her neighbors in Block 103, Vhod A, who most certainly could hear Vladi through the floor, ceiling, and walls. After several of these episodes, it was a wonder they still said hello to her in the hall. But they did, in the same way they managed to maintain their general regard for one another despite the noises and smells that traveled through the bathroom vents, the cockroaches that scuttled the stairs, and the lightbulb that had repeatedly disappeared from the elevator fixture until they had reached a tacit agreement to suffer the elevator in darkness.

But tonight, Vladi carried on so long, Galia wondered if this might be about more than just a tie, or an entire wardrobe of ties ruined exactly like this, and how could he do this to himself night after night? There was a general clumsiness Vladi could not transcend. Despite his smart wardrobe, his powerful connections, the clumsiness was always there. She wondered if he carried on because he knew she, too, was screaming inside, and he needed to scream for both of them.

Whatever the reason, he finally stopped and left the kitchen, returning minutes later in a sweatsuit. But by then, Galia had already retired to the baby's room with a chocolate bar. She had heard that mothers who ate chocolate while they were pregnant had happy babies.

Anyone else, and there might have been a swagger in the step, an ease of the shoulders, a lift in the chin of a problem solved. The woman had walked into Nasko's office in broad daylight. She had presented herself with clarity, dignity. Nasko had liked her instantly, and the decision had been made even before she had spoken.

Or had it? During these trying times, he knew he should be grateful that one task—arguably the most difficult of the season—had taken care of itself. And he *was* grateful. Of course he was. But only to the extent he would allow himself to believe any decision could be so easy. And so it was as Nasko closed the Office of Central Heat for the night, he felt very much the same way he had felt that morning. It was not in his nature to rest easy when there was still a job to be done, a switch to flip, a town to heat.

As he began the steep climb up the rugged mountain road to visit his mother, he took off at a good clip and soon found himself breathless, sweating with exertion. The difficulty of the climb was exacerbated by the food he carried, too much food, but what else was there to do with the gifts that, for weeks, had been arriving on their doorstep?

Darkness draped the rugged village road. As he approached

his childhood home, Nasko could savor a dab of anonymity. On either side of the street, windows flickered with firelight. The village houses that clung to the mountain above the town did not have central heat, and thus, did not have to wait for a switch to be flipped. Gathered around their fires, the villagers did not think much of chopping and hauling enormous amounts of wood. They had never had it any other way.

Meanwhile, the townspeople at the mountain's flat foot suffered modern inconvenience. These days, all eyes were fixed on Nasko. Either you were cold, desperately cold, and wanted, *needed,* the heat. Or you did not know how you would pay your bill, so you wanted to delay the heat as long as you could.

Or you could not afford heat at all, as was the case with the woman who'd come that day. "We will not be taking heat this winter," she'd said, simple as that. A thin, raised vein ran from hairline to brow—of course, it was not so simple. Nasko's ledger indicated four occupants, and hadn't he seen her in the square toting a baby, another youngster in tow? Not exactly pretty, she was nonetheless a striking woman, tall and skinny with white teeth, a straight back, and a worn coat pressed to perfection. When she spoke, she bore the quiet confidence of one who knew what she had to do to manage her affairs, of one who, by virtue of her dark gypsy skin, her wiry build, the thin flesh of her nostrils, had never received a favor.

There was no ask, no plea. Until she had presented herself, Nasko had not understood *this* was what he wanted. He wanted to give this gift unsolicited, with nothing given in return. None of these offerings that landed on his doorstep, pastries and pickled vegetables, food to last his family the entire year. None of these saccharine appeals, coughing baby in arms, as though he were in some position of power. As though he controlled the weather as well as the heat, and sure, no problem, he would see what he could do.

Occupied by these musings, he almost passed his mother's house. On the door, a sign with a black bow announced the death of his father eight months earlier. By now, the bow had faded to gray, and the sign had weathered crisp and frail as his father had been in his last months of life. The way it had aged, you would have thought his father had been gone for a very long time.

Nasko knocked on the door. "*Vlez*, Nasko," a spirited Radka hailed him. They had been waiting. He hesitated, arrested by the pressure of expectation, of two more people who wanted something from him, even if it was what he wanted, too. He wanted to see his mother and to make her happy. He had to remind himself of this in order to push forward into the room.

He was greeted by a heat so fierce it stung the senses. And wood everywhere, piled in neat stacks all over the room. "*Ami—*," he sputtered. At once, the bags of food were too heavy to hold. He rested them atop one of the piles and peeled off his coat.

"Isn't it great?" Radka said, a brief pause in her clicking needles. The pelt of knitting on her lap was an array of electric colors circling an odd black patch—a sweater no one would ever wear. "Have you ever seen anything so wonderful?" Beside her, his mother glowed with the rosy contentment of one who was complicit in this affair. And how was it her hair had turned a surprising shade of magenta since he'd last visited?

"But there was plenty for both of you," Nasko said, nursing a spike of anger that he had unwittingly abetted these activities. In recent years, he had paid a neighbor to chop and stack the wood for his parents; this year, he had done the same for

Radka to thank her for the care she'd shown his mother. In fact, he did not much like his mother's across-the-street neighbor, nor did he entirely trust her judgment, but there was peace of mind in knowing someone was keeping a close eye on his mother, who in the months since his father died, had become lumpy and slow.

"This way, we don't have to economize," Radka said cheerfully. But as Nasko picked his way through the stacks to the chair that awaited him by the fire, he hardly heard her. Clearly this plan had backfired. The wood stacked around the room formed a sort of maze; if the fire ever got out of hand, there was no way to escape. Nasko felt sick. He could imagine the effort that must have gone into this endeavor: bony old Radka traipsing a winter's worth of wood across the street to his mother's house. It was an impressive feat. But what may have been a show of Radka's strength was a demonstration of his mother's weakness. In more lucid times, she would never have agreed to this.

"I'm not sure this was a good idea," he said, the words a mere whisper, so hard and round was the knot in his throat.

Nasko had long known generosity could be a curse. Take his son, Plamen, who in twenty-eight years had only learned how to take—with no notion of what it meant to give in return. Plamen was his fault, as were the pastries, the pressure—he had brought it on himself. But he could not live with the knowledge that a person or family would be cold all winter long. While he couldn't fix every situation, it seemed each winter there was someone who moved him. Someone who had requested that his or her heat be turned off. Someone who, on the day he flipped the switch, discovered, inexplicably, that they had heat. And though they might look at him strangely when they passed him in the square, they would not say anything, lest they jeopardize this holiest of blessings. And Nasko, for his part, would look the other way.

Favors, given and received. Over the years, the weight of so many favors had started to crush him. For although no one ever spoke of them, there seemed a general knowledge of Nasko's oversized heart. As he sat by the fire, he felt a cramp in his chest, difficult to breathe. He summoned the gypsy woman—a moment of her clarity—but the heat, the disappointment were overwhelming.

He was sorry he'd come. He owed it to his mother to bring her cheer. But if he had stayed away, he would not have known of this dangerous arrangement. They'd have been perfectly happy, and nothing would have happened.

Now that he knew, the knowing could not be undone. He stared glumly into the fire's blistering blue embers. Next to the oven's open door, his mother had decorated a makeshift table with a clutter of candles, icons, and a cross. His mother had kept this altar for as long as he could remember, but always in the back of the house, tucked away in the small closet she'd shared with his father. A glance at her now, and it was hard to know what she was looking at—the fire or the altar—her brown eyes cloudy and distant. Though she only sat a few feet away from him, she felt impossibly far away.

They spent the rest of the visit listening to the click of Radka's needles, the hiss and pop of the fire. It was late when Nasko returned to the apartment building. As he climbed the stairs, the corridors of Block 103, Vhod A were as cold as the outdoors. And the choking stink of burning—his clothes? But no. The burning smell was coming from inside the building. He followed it to the top floor. Did not even consider the late hour when he knocked on the door.

That night, Marina baked for the boy, Dobrin, whose perplexed look—*Tea? What tea?*—had made her heart ache. She baked for his parents, with whom she was acquainted only well enough to know they were good people going through a bad time, and today their luck had taken a turn for the worse. She baked for her children, who called and visited just often enough (they were adults now—young and in love—she could not begrudge them that). She baked for her neighbor, Nasko, flipper of the switch, unofficial patron saint of heat, to pay her respects during this time of waiting.

It was not like Marina to throw herself into baking this way. She was not one who sought outlets, releases, escapes. She was not a baker. As a dentist and health-conscious mother of two, she had spent her entire adult life not just avoiding sweets, but urging others to do the same. For more than two decades, Marina had made self-control a way of life, to the point that every deprivation—the pair of shoes *not* purchased, the money *not* spent—was itself a reward.

But on that night, the pendulum had swung in the other direction, and the cookies she produced—basic, crescent-shaped *sladki* sprinkled with sugar—were so sweet, after the first bite, she couldn't stand to eat them. Whether this was because she had trained her palate to reject sugar or because she had been messy with her measurements, she did not know. Nor did she care. For the warm oven, the glass of wine, the mundane task of shaping crescents—these were just the things to occupy her right now.

She was still shaping crescents when the doorbell rang. A burning smell. How could she not smell it? Marina flew to open the oven door, but the two trays of crescents in the oven were already ruined. Standing with the tray in her hand, she recalled the angry yell from downstairs. "Fuck!" the voice had hollered. "Fuck! Fuck! Fuck!" She wondered if *fuck,* the ugly sound of it, might be just the word for the pitiful blackened moons.

DAY TWO: BRUISES THAT HURT

Vladi was gone by 8:30 in the morning. This was something Galia could count on, his 8:30 departure, much as she could the grease on his tie, or the TV, which he turned on the moment he walked into the apartment and which she turned off the moment he left.

The predictability—Galia had discovered that, however unpleasant things might be, she could count on them to pass according to a schedule. She could watch the clock and know when she could breathe easily once again.

And so it was that 8:30 was her happiest time of day. When Vladi walked out the door, it was like the air lifted, and Galia felt so light, she might float away. Even with the baby heavy in her belly, she felt blithe and untethered at the prospect of ten hours without him to recover, rejuvenate, restore.

Only today her happiness flew at half-mast, what with the incident the night before, Vladi's cursing a mere bruise compared to the other, far greater injury. Seeking refuge in the baby's room to avoid Vladi was only a temporary solution. For peace had been compromised. Sure as she was this Mira was the tranquil soul she'd always been, there was someone equally certain this same soul was a bouncing baby Vladi. For Galia, there could be no peace until this was resolved.

Indeed, the levity Galia felt as she flitted down the staircase to retrieve a newspaper from a stand across the road was not so great. On her way back, when she brushed shoulders with her neighbor, Nasko, on the stair, she saw in the down-turned corners of his eyes a greater sadness than she'd noticed before. She wondered if this sadness belonged to him or if it might be a reflection of her own.

Back in the apartment, she put on the tea water to boil and sat down to the paper. "*Trud,*" the paper was called. *Labor*—a name that seemed to speak more to the task of reading the paper than it did to the content it contained. For it was widely accepted that the news stories put forth in Bulgarian papers were more often half truths or untruths, which brought a certain labor—even a gaming aspect—to reading the paper that Galia quite enjoyed. Each day, she read the paper front to back, as though knowing what was going on in the world, however true or untrue, would somehow establish her as part of it. Today, the headline was the cold, of course, and the paper promised no signs of a thaw, which was good news if you lived in Old Mountain. Though Galia was plenty warm, she hoped it was true for the sake of colder friends and neighbors. The wait for central heat would soon be over.

The newspaper went on to offer a series of articles about all things cold or frozen. There were interviews with ice fishermen, evaluations of the warmest fabrics, caps, and coats. Galia had just begun an alarming article on the most effective ways to stay warm when the phone rang.

This would be her mother.

"*Alo?*" Galia said. "*Da . . . da . . . da.*" Lately, when she spoke with her mother, she'd been bristly and unpleasant, and today was no exception. "Nothing, Maika, I'm fine."

But then her mother said she'd run into Petya Docheva in the square and told her she should pay Galia a visit. "I told her you're there. She should just stop by. Won't that be nice?"

Of course this would be nice. Galia would be glad to see Petya, who was the closest friend Galia had ever had. Petya had studied Japanese philology at University and was now living in Japan. Galia could count on a visit from Petya to be honest and interesting, and she looked forward to seeing her old friend.

But something about what her mother had said infuriated Galia, and she hurried to hang up the phone. The panic that gripped her chest had nothing to do with Petya and everything to do with her mother's presumption that *Galia's there*. She was exactly there, and on these cold days, there was nowhere else she could possibly be. And yet, the idea that this was how it was—Galia there making Vladi's dinner, there folding Vladi's clothes, there carrying Vladi's baby, and she would *sooner die* than name this baby Vladi—so incensed Galia she did not know what to do.

Finally, she recalled the tea boiling on the stove, screaming as she would scream if only she could. She recalled her brush with Nasko and wondered if he had been born that way, with eyes that turned down at the corners, or if his eyes had been shaped by the course his life had taken. When Galia thought about how life was shaping her at this very moment, she knew she should feel blessed.

Galia closed her eyes and let a curl of jasmine steam dampen her face. She *would* summon her resolve. But first the paper, which, on this day, Galia tackled with fierce determination, only to find herself mortified by an article that suggested they should all sleep naked together to generate heat. And then on to an article reporting that American women were freezing their fertilized eggs until they were ready to have children. *Cryobiology,* it was called, and this was considered some miracle of science. Galia thought she had never heard of something so awful. As she succumbed to her tears—*cry, cry, cry*—which rolled down her cheeks and spattered the paper in front of her, the silent wails of so many frozen souls pierced her ears. She wanted to claim them, all of them, and name them Mira, each and every one.

The burning smell was there when Nasko woke up, ate his breakfast, walked to the center. It was the first thing to greet him when he opened the door to his office. Even before the cold, it made its presence known. It was as though the smell was trapped in his nostrils. No matter how hard he blew, it would not come out.

"Don't you smell it?" he'd asked his wife, Didi, that morning. For breakfast, she'd heated up a loaf of *kozunak* that had appeared on the doorstep. Though Nasko loved the spongy Easter treat (God bless the woman who made it year round), he could not even taste it for the smoky fumes that plugged his nose.

"Smell what?" Didi had said, the image of innocence. It was not like her to goad him, but it was impossible to understand how she could not smell it, and he had to think this was her intent. He had left the apartment feeling irked and off-balance, and how would he make it through this tetchy, difficult day?

And so Nasko found himself working under a thick haze of irritation. No, he could not guarantee when the heat would go on. No, he did not set the price. No, he could not turn the heat on any sooner, despite the one hundred, two hundred, three hundred *leva* you might be willing to offer. This was not like him. His legendary kindness was the reason people came. That he was willing to listen to how cold you were—this somehow made it better.

But today was not the day. He had been up half the night wrestling with the scene he'd found in his mother's house. It seemed they had just finished with his father, whose mind had failed completely, and now his mother had demonstrated a lapse of her own. Worried as he was—what should he do about all that wood?—he was also angry at her and her magenta hair. He suspected she was not losing her sanity so much as letting go.

Just as Nasko was about to close his door and spare the rest of Old Mountain his terrible mood, his neighbor, Boris appeared at his door. "Oho! Nasko!" Boris said, making himself at home in one of Nasko's chairs. "I knew I'd find you here."

Nasko smiled wanly. Though Boris was his neighbor, he did not consider him a friend. That he was Pavletta's husband— well, he wished he could like him better. But Nasko had little in common with this stocky, track-suited man and could think of nothing to say. Boris could have been anyone. He could have been a perfect stranger, and Nasko would have had more to say than he did to Boris.

But Boris had plenty to say. "You heard about Pavletta," he started, and proceeded to say they'd only be able to heat one room that winter. "But don't worry about us," he said cheer- fully. "We'll be fine."

Nasko struggled to remember what Didi had told him that morning. Something about a crack heard clear across the schoolyard. Something about Pavletta being on crutches all winter long. Nasko had hardly heard her, what with the burning smell and the plates of sweets crowding the apartment, and what was one family to do with so many sweets?

Boris kept on talking. "Pavletta—you know. She'll be able to start the private lessons in our apartment again soon, but without the extra classes at the Technikum—" He shrugged. *"Ami, prosto niama kak."*

Nasko stared dumbly at his neighbor. It was his turn to talk. For as long as Nasko had been in this job, people had been coming to him to confess their shortcomings, and always he had sought to put them at ease. "It is expensive," he would say. "There are lots of families struggling this season." And, "A good space heater will serve you well."

But there had not been a trace of confession in Boris's speech. *"Niama kak,"* he had said with an indifference that bordered on cheer. "There's no way," he had shrugged, as though the matter of heat was completely out of his control. That one could be so free of cares—Nasko could not imagine how this might feel. "I'm sorry to hear that," he finally managed. "How's Pavletta doing?"

"You know, with Pavletta, it's always one thing or another. She'll be fine."

Which was easy for him to say, now, wasn't it? How Nasko loathed this Boris! "Well, please give her my regards," he said crisply.

"I will," Boris said, but he did not budge from his chair. Rather, he looked around the office, taking in the chipped cinderblock walls, a small shag of carpet Didi had brought in, and heavy curtains pulled all the way to one side to proffer a sweeping view of the square. He looked at all these things, then back at Nasko, then back out the window at the relentless gray day.

What was Boris waiting for? Nasko did not understand. They had finished their business. Nasko would log the change in the book. To demonstrate, he picked up his pencil and started to write. He had too much to do. As Boris began to pick idly at the ripped fabric on the arm of his chair, Nasko's irritation festered. There could be only one explanation: Boris was waiting for some reassurance that on the day the switch got flipped, they would, indeed, be fine.

Nasko blew into his cold hands. He was not going to change his mind. Pavletta was a good soul, and the boy—well, Nasko hardly knew the boy, but he was nonetheless hopeful for the forlorn-looking kid, that things would go his way. But Boris he owed nothing. Of course, he didn't owe the gypsy woman anything either, but then, she was not in here asking for favors. Why, that very moment, she was probably knitting an extra sweater. Or counting her *leva* for a space heater. Or calculating how many hours she could afford to light her stove. He could practically see her bent over her bills at her kitchen table, the very image of industry. The slender curve of her neck, the whites of her knuckles—he couldn't have been more proud of her had she been his own daughter.

It softened the heart just to think of her, and for a moment he had managed to forget about Boris. When he looked up to see what had come of him, he found him cheek on hand, lost in a bout of his own contemplation. If Boris was waiting for a favor, that campaign appeared to be abandoned. Instead, this was a man who had nowhere to go.

Stassi said if you're really cold, the best thing to do is to take off your clothes and get in bed with someone else who is naked. The nakedness, he said, it generates heat.

"Shut up," Dobrin said. He did not want to hear about it. On break between classes, he stayed rooted to his chair, bundled in jacket, gloves, and scarf. He did not feel like talking. So far, he'd been assaulted by questions from teachers and students alike, all wondering how his mother was doing, all cringing with disgust and empathy and gratitude that it wasn't them.

"It's true," Stassi said. "It's scientific fact. It was in the paper today."

But this did not prove anything to Dobrin, who could not see Stassi reading the paper—not even an article having to do with nakedness and, thus, sex. "Would you just shut up?" he said, grateful when Ms. Kuneva entered the room, ready to start. He reached into his bag for his English notebook, which was once again incomplete, not even started, only this time, he was not so worried. He had a good excuse.

Then, there was Kuneva standing at his desk. "Dobrin," she said, as the students filed in and took their seats. "I'm sorry to hear about your mother. How's she doing?"

"*Ami*—," he paused, and for a moment, he was not sure he could answer. There was something about the way Kuneva had addressed him, a softness in her voice of one who's known misfortune in every form, that made him feel tender and shaky. "She's okay," he finally managed, eyes on his desk, willing Kuneva not to ask him any more questions.

Mercifully, she moved on. "Ladies and gentlemen, take out your English workbooks," she said. And even though he had not done his homework, Dobrin took this to be an act of kindness, the nicest thing anyone had done for him in a very long time.

The night before, after the salty dinner, the laughter, the *rakiya*, Dobrin had convinced himself things would be okay.

His mother would wake up the next morning feeling better than ever, and not even crutches would slow her down. Or his father would find a job waiting tables at a conference or a private party, and the pay would be enough to get them through the winter. Or his mother would find some money she'd hidden in a box beneath her bed. Or the price of heat would go down, and they would be able to heat the whole apartment after all, with money left over to buy fresh meat for the dogs. As implausible as each of these prospects may have been, the fact of so many possible resolutions made it seem more and more likely one would work out. Dobrin had retired to his bedroom with an empty belly, but a full heart, and some assurance they would find a way to get by.

But as he lay in bed, cold creeping through layers of blanket and numbing his fingers and toes, he overheard a conversation between his parents that eroded his confidence. Even with the covers pulled over his head, he could hear it.

"You're going to have to find work," his mother said in a low, tired voice. Dobrin knew her eyes were still closed.

"Like it's that easy."

"It may not be easy, but we need you to make some money."

"Find me a job, and I'll make you some money."

"I told you. Stefan needs help repairing radiators. I'm sure he'd—"

"Find me a *real* job—"

"It doesn't have to be a real—"

"No, of course not. It just has to be work. That's all that matters to you."

"I work for you and Dobrin. That's what matters to me."

Tatko's laugh was not at all funny. "Work, work, work. It's all you do—and look where it's gotten you." Which was followed by sniffles, then silence, then the sound of Dobrin struggling to breath beneath the covers.

By now, Kuneva had woven her way around the room and arrived at Dobrin's desk to check his homework. He had the book open to a blank assignment. "Dobrin," she said quietly, "I need you to be caught up in your workbook by tomorrow."

Eyes trained on his desk, Dobrin nodded his assent. *Yes, Gospozha, he would have the homework. No, Gospozha, he would not.* In fact, there was no way of knowing whether the work would be done. It had been nearly a week since he'd last done his work; the further he fell behind, the more unlikely it seemed he'd manage to do it.

As Kuneva carried on, Dobrin slumped in his chair, his mind drifting from the unfinished homework to his unhappy parents, crowded around the space heater, and how would they get through the day together? He shifted with discomfort. He did not want to think about it.

He thought instead about what Stassi had said and wondered if it could possibly be true. It would be just like Stassi to sniff out such an article. Dobrin wondered how many people would read it and how many people would try lying naked together in their beds that night. Just the thought of it—an entire country having sex on a single night—was enough to make Dobrin feel hot and delirious. So that, when Kuneva called on him—*Dobrin, can you use the word* negligent *in a sentence?*—all he could do was stare at her blankly and wipe the sweat from his brow.

Marina spotted a possible cavity in number thirty the moment Krassimir Popchev opened his mouth. A sizable spot, and sure enough, the probe sank right into it. It should be treated, of course, rather than left to rot. Still, a half hour into the cleaning, she had failed to mention it, and the longer the appointment went on, the less certain she grew that suggesting a follow-up visit was an appropriate course of treatment.

Popchev's chest was round as a cask of wine and warm, so warm, Marina was disturbingly aware of the searing seam between her forearm and his chest as she leaned in to perform the cleaning. Central heat or no, it was hard to imagine he could need the space heater, and yet he basked before it as anyone might. Marina had come to see her clients during these early weeks of winter as dogs bathing in the sun, soaking in the heat with pure animal need. Popchev's need appeared to be no different from anyone else's, despite the seemingly ample temperatures that radiated from within.

"*Kak e momcheto?*" he'd queried when he'd arrived—the simplest of questions. He was, after all, the closest thing to a father her son had ever known.

But the question had sent Marina into a tailspin, a whirling not unlike what she'd experienced when she finally put head to pillow the night before, purple ring of wine staining a relentless circle in her mind. In her mind, the crack of Pavletta's ankle was loud enough to make her start from her sleep. After a restless night, morning, bleak and cold as it was, came as a relief.

Marina blotted the perspiration from her forehead, the mild queasiness of a hangover having been with her since dawn. Popchev—the fact of his presence—should have calmed her. For to see him now was to see an old friend. Popchev's son, Ivo, had been Drago's best friend growing up; while she had not seen the parents half so much as she'd seen the son, there was a sense that their families were intertwined, the sons close as brothers, the boys having been raised between the two households. Together, they'd done okay.

For sure, she had always liked Popchev. Popchev's wife, Velichka, sold medicinal herbs from their village house up the road, and Marina liked her, too, though she felt closer to Popchev, who was more the parent than his wife and who understood the boys in a way Marina knew she never would. But this afternoon, Popchev's presence in her small office caught her off guard. Flannel shirt tucked into worn jeans. Bushy brows and a shag of beard that climbed high up his cheeks. If one were to judge from hair alone, they might think Popchev somehow less evolved than the rest of them, and perhaps they would be right. Yes, Popchev was a hairy beast of a man, which made other things—the Popchev that asked *How is the boy?* before anything else—seem unexpected, even startling. This on a day when Marina was easily startled, and how had it never before occurred to her that Popchev was the father she should have chosen for her son?

Marina struggled for control. For even if she would no longer allow herself to cry over a pot of beans, that didn't mean the emotions weren't still there, always there, simmering just below the surface, tempting her to dip her spoon in for a taste. Popchev had invited her to do just that.

"He's good," she managed, and surely he was. Military service—however much an agony it may be—was manageable, even good, with a girlfriend who sent packages and welcomed him to Sofia every chance he could get away. "You've heard about Natalia?"

Popchev smiled. "It's good for him," he said. "I wish Ivo had a Natalia."

But Ivo had already survived his military service, having

gone right after high school. Now, he was finishing a degree in forestry, which Marina thought was a perfect choice for a boy who'd grown up hiking the Old Mountain with his father and who'd never cared much for school. She heard herself say, "Ivo has a life," then heard the twins chiding her. *Where did you pick that up, Mom?* Who was their mother to judge who did and didn't have a life?

But Popchev didn't notice. *"Ah taka,"* he sighed, satisfaction seeping from every sweaty pore. "They are good kids, aren't they? We did a good job."

She could smell him now, a blend of body odor and frying meat. Whether his pleasure was triggered by the heat penetrating his frozen core or the triumph of a job well done . . . what did she know? What did it matter?

As Marina probed the soft pink flesh of Popchev's gums, blood appeared. "You could do a better job brushing," she said.

"You tell me that every year."

"You never improve."

"Ami—," he shrugged, smiled. "We all have things we can do better."

He was an imp, this Popchev, a big, impish bear. Headache, heartache notwithstanding, Marina was in just the mood to savor such contradictions. The hairy animal of a man with a heart and gums so fleshy and pink. The gray hairs that peppered his otherwise brown beard—he would be about her age—and still he was as childish as her youngest clients. Better this way than the other way around: the beardless boy facing grown-up problems. The staggering price of heat. A badly broken bone. A union that looked more like an impossible divide.

The day before, when they'd finally made it to the hospital and were waiting for Pavletta to be seen, Marina had suggested she find a phone to call Boris and let him know where they were. But Pavletta had refused. "Please don't," she'd said, breathless with pain. There was no excuse, no effort to explain, and Marina had accepted this, stayed by her side for the length of her stay, then brought her home and helped her settle into the couch. Until yesterday, she and Pavletta had been acquaintances at best. But as she crouched by Pavletta's side, requesting extra pillows, a cup of tea, and *here, Boris, be sure she takes another pill at ten o'clock* . . . by that time, *she* was the insider. Boris was the outsider. And the boy, Dobrin, was caught somewhere in between.

Surprising how quickly these relations could change. As Marina sat up and handed Popchev a cup of water, she saw that his eyes had opened, and he was watching her intently. And there, on the barrel of his chest, was a damp line where her arm had been.

"Well," she said, then lost the words. *You really need to be taking better care of these teeth* was what she meant to say. But then their eyes were locked, their hands caught in an awkward half clasp, and *what* could this be about? Marina did not know—or did she? Rather than look away, she found herself not only meeting his gaze, but boldly staring back.

Come evening, Galia was ready. The meal she had cooked was safe, greaseless, and she knew the apartment smelled good. The peppers were stuffed, the *rakiya* chilled. The conversation on the tip of her tongue.

But then there was Vladi at the door with someone else. And then the *televisor* was on. "Oho!" Boris said of Vladi's TV. "Yours is even bigger than mine!" And then she was serving *lukanka* and salad for the men to eat with their brandy, and she could be certain the dinner would not be touched, the topic of the name would not be discussed—at least not that evening. And then she was eating stuffed peppers alone in the kitchen and listening to the faltering conversation in the room next door. "It's warm in here," said Boris. "Do you realize how warm it is? *Bozhe Gospodi.* It's like the tropics."

"It's too hot," Vladi said. He sounded bothered. "Galia's parents gave us—"

"No, no," Boris said. "It's perfect," and Galia could hear in his voice the relief of one who hadn't been warm in some time.

Galia helped herself to a second pepper, half of a third. She would be lying to herself if she didn't admit she, too, was relieved. A bit disappointed, perhaps, but mostly relieved. It was the same damning feeling she had known all her life. She should be more upset than she was. But she knew the name conversation would happen when it could. In the meantime, she was feeling a strange closeness to Vladi. They had never discussed the temperature in the apartment, and it was comforting to hear he felt the same way she did. Whether Vladi had invited Boris to watch TV or Boris had invited himself, Galia was glad they were sharing their extravagance with one in need.

Not as glad as Boris, though, who seemed to be overwhelmed with gladness. "*Zdrasti,* Galche," he had greeted her, a kiss on the cheek, when she first went in to say hello. Galia was taken aback. "*Gospodin,*" she had responded to his embrace. For although they'd known each other for a long while—as neighbors, and Galia had been Pavletta's student for a handful of years—Galia could not recall ever having exchanged words with him, certainly not names, and she was flattered he should know hers. So flattered that she had not found the words to ask after Pavletta, and how was she feeling? She felt a special softness for her former literature teacher and would have liked to have heard how she was recovering from her fall.

But the moment had passed as so many did, and now she was a room away, and Boris was talking about the TV. "Have you seen Vulkov's?" Boris asked.

Vladi did not respond.

"It's even bigger than this."

More silence.

"It's the biggest TV I've ever seen."

Still nothing. No, Vladi did not have much to say to Boris, who eventually gave up. Galia felt sorry for their guest. If he had come seeking chatter and companionship, well then, he would be disappointed. But each time she went to refill plates and glasses, she noticed he had sunk deeper into the couch. He seemed to be enjoying the big television, the food and drink. She was happy this was enough for him.

Happy and happier still, despite the failed conversation and the knowledge she would spend the next day and the next worried about the name. For as she tidied up the kitchen and prepared for bed, if she had the troubling sense of a chance having slipped away, she also had a surprising sense of gain. To hear Boris flounder about in search of a topic to impress Vladi and to understand he would never succeed was to realize how well she knew her bothered, silent husband. Which made Galia feel like she knew an awful lot.

When she went in to check on Vladi and his guest one last time, she could feel Boris's eyes on her as they had been each time she'd paid them a visit. His gaze was not predatory so much as curious, and she wondered if perhaps he hadn't known she was pregnant—or at least not this far along. She felt a pang of embarrassment on his behalf. She of all people knew the discomfort of words stuck in your throat. As she filled his *rakiya* glass one last time, she suggested a glass of water and was pleased when he said yes.

As Nasko lay in bed, hat pulled down over his ears, he could hear a soccer match on the TV upstairs. He had never been much interested in sport, but over years of listening to soccer through his ceiling and usually through his floor as well, he'd come to take a certain comfort in the sounds of it. The murmur of the crowd, the ecstasy of the announcer: this was the extent of his involvement in the game, and still he could be grateful for these small things regardless of teams, the players, the outcomes. They were sounds of optimism. As he shifted to get comfortable beneath the thick Rhodope blankets layered on the bed, he was grateful for the cheers that insulated him from the thoughts that otherwise might crowd his head.

So absorbed was he by these lively nighttime sounds that Didi had to say his name several times before he heard her. *"Kakvo?"* he finally said, lifting the flap from one ear. They did not keep a space heater in their bedroom, and the air shocked the skin. Nasko had often wondered what it was like for those who lived with the cold all winter—if it continued to be so shocking, or if at some point you got used to it.

"Pavletta's going to need your help," Didi said.

Nasko prickled. "Boris found you."

"No, I haven't seen Boris in days," Didi said. "But I went down to see Pavletta today, and she looks terrible."

"Boris claims they'll be fine."

"Well, Boris is a *glupak,*" Didi said sharply. "She looks terrible, and the boy—," she clucked her tongue. "How would you feel if it was your boy who looked like that?"

Nasko knew what Didi was talking about, the boy's brow so deeply furrowed. In fact, the boy reminded Nasko of his own son. Only with Plamen, it hadn't been a furrowing of the brow, but a slumping of the shoulders—a kind of posturing that had gone from put on to permanent. Now, as Plamen sought to establish himself as a mathematician in Sofia, he couldn't straighten his shoulders even if he tried. Nasko wondered if Plamen didn't regret the choice he'd made as a beleaguered teen. They had warned him—at least they'd tried—but he had been committed to slumping, a choice that now appeared to be a lasting one.

Yes, of course the boy had caught Nasko's attention. When he passed him on the stair, Nasko thought about Plamen—was he getting enough to eat?—and about the boy himself, who he couldn't look at without feeling his own heart ache. No doubt, the boy didn't even know how he knit his brow or the pain that was on his face.

Meanwhile, the boy's father was all *niama kak* this, *niama kak* that. Why should he worry when there were so many to worry on his behalf?

Upstairs, an eruption from the crowd, the announcer. If there was one thing Nasko knew about these matches, it was that they were generally played on foreign soil: Italy, Spain, England. He couldn't imagine Bulgarian sounds, even surrounding soccer, could ever be so cheerful and light.

Of course Didi would know what was going on: she was,

after all, a part of this, these pastries and cakes, this untoward attention. But while she had always taken an interest, she had never attempted to influence his decisions—until now. Nasko felt his irritation soften: his wife's concern was not only genuine but warranted. He pulled the flap of his hat back over his ear and reached for her hand, which was cold even beneath the covers.

Another roar from the crowd. An amazing thing, a brow like that. One of these days, it was bound to knit itself together forever.

DAY THREE: UNINVITED COMPANY

As Dobrin left the schoolyard, he stomped on an empty espresso cup, kicked a candy wrapper, banged his shoe against the gate. When it didn't hurt as much as he wanted it to, he banged it again.

All this stomping and kicking and banging, and not for a moment did he lose his balance. *How* had his mother managed to slip and fall? The more he thought about it, the angrier he got. Where was the ice? Or, as Stassi would say, where was the *goddamn* ice? Goddamn it, he thought—which satisfied him in a way that banging the gate did not. "Goddamn it," he said aloud, and even though he did not know what exactly this meant, he knew it had to do with God, and he needed to be cursing God right now.

Moments earlier, Kuneva had dismissed him for not doing his homework. "Dobrin," she said, "how can we go on like this?"

Dobrin stared at his desk. When Kuneva had walked around to check homework, he had opened his notebook to an assignment from several weeks back he had managed to complete. He had not expected this to fool her, but he had thought this would give her a choice. Either she could put him on the spot, which was the thing she was most likely to do. Or she could walk past his desk and pretend she hadn't noticed. Which would be justifiable, he thought, given the cold, his mother's accident. He was, after all, a colleague's son.

But Kuneva had not chosen in his favor. "I need to ask you to leave until you're ready to start working again," she said in a quiet voice. "I hope we'll see you tomorrow."

Dobrin was stunned. He had never before been kicked out of class. This was a serious punishment—beyond extra homework or having to stay after school. Beyond the Kuneva who screamed and clotted with rage. This was a Kuneva who had given up, he understood, and the fact of this scared him more than purple eyes or a broken ankle. More than a winter boxed in a single room with his parents, which promised to be dreadful.

For, winter would end. The purple eyes were already starting to turn yellow. These were temporary conditions, things that would right themselves without any interference on his part. But the homework situation was one only he could remedy, and the prospect of this . . . if this was a thing he should be able to manage, then why did it feel so *goddamn* unmanageable?

Dobrin sighed. He was making slow progress through the square. There was no reason to hurry. It was cold at school, cold outside, cold at home. There was nowhere to go. The square was desolate, its broad, marble expanse gray and lifeless, save a figure squatting beside a wriggling dog several hundred meters before him. Dobrin did not need to see her face to know who this was.

Years had passed since he'd last seen Petya Docheva. She had to be at least ten years older than him, and yet he had known her for as long as he could remember. He remembered her coming to the end-of-year parties his mother hosted for her students, him in his jammies sitting on the arm of the couch, her squeezed between a couple of classmates, delightfully small and ugly. He had been enthralled with her. For it was obvious even to him that the other students did not like her. And still she carried on, jabbering happily and pushing her glasses further up her nose.

On these nights, after the students moved on to the disco, Petya would stay behind and help his mother clean up, maintaining a continuous chirp: it had been a very good party, *Gospozha!* When everything was cleaned up, she would join them on the *balcon,* with nibbles of *torta,* bites of salami, and biscuits the students had left behind. The dogs loved the cakes. Seeing this, Petya got as quiet as he did, and they listened to the dogs' hungry snuffles in silence.

That had been a long time ago, and as much as Dobrin had been enamored with this small, ugly girl, he did not think of her often. Only when his mother mentioned her—how she had studied Japanese philology and was now living and working in Japan. And when he saw the hairless dog standing in the square.

By now, the dog was extremely old. No one knew exactly how old Krastavitza was, but people said it was a miracle he was still alive. People said Petya had given a small endowment to a local grocery and asked the lady behind the counter to give the dog two hotdogs a day. These same people noted the shop lady had a new coat, a new pocketbook, a new pair of shoes, and what kind of fool was Petya Docheva to think her intentions would be carried out in her absence?

Yet the fact remained, here was the dog, with skittish legs and cloudy eyes and the same tubular body that had earned him the name *Cucumber*. By now, people no longer willed it to die; rather, they were fascinated by how long such a creature could endure.

And endure it did. As Dobrin passed, Petya was down on her hands and knees with the wobbly, whimpering being, which she stroked lovingly on its back, sides, and between the ears as though it had fur. "Have you been a good boy, *milichko*? Do you know how much I missed you? Thank you, *skupi*, for waiting for me."

In that moment, Dobrin was more taken with Petya than he had ever been as a child. Though she was still ugly and small, he was jealous of the sick dog receiving her affection. And he was jealous of the girl herself. All this time, she'd managed to sustain the dog with the mere promise she would return. How else to explain the way the dog lived on and on and on? Food and water could not do that. And if, indeed, the miracle of Krastavitza could be explained so simply and with so much certainty, could it still be a miracle at all?

Dobrin was tempted to turn back and explain to Petya that he, too, needed a miracle. When he had left Kuneva's class that afternoon, there had been complete stillness in the room. No titters. No sneers from Stassi. Not so much as a wheeze from Kuneva, who had retreated to her desk at the front of the room. Dobrin did not need to look at her to see the way she rested her forehead on the palm of her hand and to know she did not believe she would see him tomorrow.

Dobrin did not know if she would see him tomorrow either.

The way he was feeling, it would take a miracle for him to get the work done.

Of course Galia was home when Petya called. Galia made no pretense of coming or going. Rather, she had a teacake in the oven, and she was waiting for her friend, who she hadn't seen since her wedding.

When Petya entered the warm apartment from the cold of the stair, her glasses fogged. As matter of habit, she took them off and wiped them with a mitten. Back on, they fogged again. Japan or no, nothing had changed.

"It's good to see you," Galia said. And it was, truly good to see her friend, who despite the length of their separation, felt more familiar—more like family—than she had in the past.

"I'm glad I ran into your mother," Petya said. Her gladness sounded measured but genuine, which was one thing Galia could count on from Petya: she would always tell the truth.

"Me too," Galia said, tickled by giddiness to be reunited with her friend.

But this would be the extent of their effusiveness. Theirs was not a relationship built on warmth and passion, so much as on circumstance and time—more than a decade of time, hours upon hours with Petya as her private instructor. Back then, Galia had not wanted a tutor any more than Petya had wanted a student. At times (perhaps most of the time), both girls' resentment of the tutorial arrangement had been profound. But now, Galia thought of this relationship as the kindest gift her parents had given her.

"*Eii!*" Petya said, when she could finally see. "Your mom mentioned you were expecting but—wow! When are you due?"

"Another month," Galia smiled, hand on her belly, which was outrageously large, even to her. "Hard to believe, isn't it?"

"A little," Petya said. "I can't imagine that ever happening to me."

Galia had to agree. Difficult as it was to fathom what was happening to her own body, it was even harder to imagine Petya with child. Her friend was every bit as small as she'd always been, which somehow surprised Galia. For here she was, earning a foreigner's income—and undoubtedly a good one—and still she wore the same bright red handknit sweater she'd worn back in high school, which by now had sprouted knots and loose ends. While Galia was mostly relieved to see Petya hadn't changed, she wished the red sweater had gotten lost along the way.

"Come," she said, hanging Petya's coat on a hook. "I'll make some tea." As she led the way to the kitchen, she was aware of her wide, loose hips, her *state,* which was exactly how Petya would regard this pregnancy and so be it. Petya looked celibate as ever in her homely sweater, but something she had said years back . . . the interest was there, surely it was, and wasn't it possible, or *probable,* Petya had indulged her curiosities by now? Even if there really was nothing to report, Galia suspected celibacy in mind and body were not one and the same. And if Petya wanted to entertain prurient curiosities about the activities leading to Galia's condition, well then, such thoughts would only elevate Galia's marriage to a normal level of intimacy, and shouldn't she be proud? No matter how she had reached this point, here she was, married, pregnant, about to become a mother. Pride, true pride, was almost unknowable to Galia, so rarely had she experienced it. But if she had any sense of pride at all, well then, as she welcomed Petya into her kitchen, this was precisely it.

"It's strange to be back here," Petya said. "I feel almost like I've come home."

Galia understood. Though she was still angry at her mother (only two days had passed, but in those two days, Galia had sensed this was an anger without end), it felt right they should meet in the kitchen where they'd spent so many hours doing their homework as girls. When Petya took her seat at the table, it was just like it had always been. Only this time, they had chosen to be there. Galia felt it the moment Petya walked in the door: finally, separated and worlds apart, they were the companions they could never have been as girls. The last time she had seen Petya, at her own wedding, they had both been miserable. The reasons for Galia's misery were obvious from the moment the *orkestara* had shown up outside her parents' window to start the day's festivities, and who, if not her father and mother, was the wedding for? For Petya, the reasons mounted as the night went on, what with her mother, caught in the hungry embrace of Stefan Nachev, losing all inhibition and finally sending the sound system crashing to the floor.

Since then, Galia had heard Petya's mother had taken ill. "How's your mother?" she asked now.

"The same," she said. "Not well." In an instant, her tone hardened. If Galia hadn't known better, she might have thought Petya did not want her mother to get better.

Or perhaps this was what Galia wanted, for she had never much cared for Petya's mother, who had always had a new *gadje* on her arm and a chip on her shoulder where Petya was concerned. She worked hard enough, and it was about time Petya started pulling her weight. Galia had never heard her friend complain, though on the day of the wedding, it was clear the situation had gotten to Petya. Of all the wounds inflicted that night, Galia had often wondered if Petya's complete humiliation was the one that hurt the most.

"I'm not sure when I'll be back," Petya said now. This comment marked a radical change. After so many years of dogged commitment, she might finally walk away. "I don't think she cares to have me around."

Galia pulled the kettle off the stove and set the tea to steep. Petya's mother's lack of interest in her daughter couldn't be more different from her own relationship with her mother— the maddening link of puppet to puppeteer, and how would Galia ever manage to cut the strings? "I told her *you're there*," her mother had said. Not, "I told her *you'd be there.*" Or *"you were there."* But present tense, *"you're there,"* stretching out into infinity, which was a thing Galia feared more than anything else. She needed to know how much time she was looking at and when infinity would come to an end—or if it never would, and she would just carry on in the role that had been divined for her from the day she entered the world, the only child of parents who'd waited and waited and waited for her. The three miscarriages that had preceded Galia stood on the mantel as three Russian dolls. And hallowed, hallowed be the one who survived.

That Petya had the latitude to just walk away and go to Japan—Galia was envious. "I wouldn't blame you for staying away," she said. Then added, "I wish I could do that."

Petya looked surprised. "Really?"

The blink of an eye. The catch in one's breath. How easily

this fury Galia harbored—for Vladi, her mother—could rise. Even Petya thought she should be satisfied with these arrangements, always an arrangement, because nothing Galia could manage on her own would ever be good enough . . . Galia bit her lip. Fuck! Fuck! Fuck! She could fairly hear Vladi screaming in her ears.

"Sorry," Petya said quickly. "Of course you would. I—I just wasn't thinking."

But the mistake had been made. By Petya of all people. Petya, who could go to Japan and never come back. It was a stupid mistake, but Galia's injury was keen. For the Petya she knew did not make mistakes. In an instant, Galia's feeling she was about to be abandoned morphed into an understanding she'd already been left behind.

"Why is it so hard to get it right?" Petya said. "I mean, this business of mothering . . . *we* weren't the problem."

Galia blinked. "I guess I'm about to find out," she said. By then, the sense of confidence, even superiority with which she'd started this conversation—look at this belly! just look at me!—had vanished as quickly and thoroughly as any good feeling she had ever had.

Petya eyed her thoughtfully. "Yeah but—well, who am I to say? I think you're going to be fine."

Petya's reassurance—who *was* she to say—sounded half-hearted at best. After the last few days Galia had had, and likely Petya too, perhaps half a heart was the very most either of them had intact.

Tucking one leg beneath her, Petya dug into a piece of cake. "You heard about Pavletta Georgieva?" she said.

Galia nodded. "They say you could hear the crack clear

across the schoolyard," she managed, a thing everyone was saying, which sparked in Galia some doubt anyone really had heard it.

"So I'm told," Petya said. "Have you seen her?"

Petya's question shamed her—she should have been down to visit. And yet the thought of it was hard for Galia to imagine: how could she just go down and knock on Georgieva's door? This was not her way.

"Not Pavletta. But her husband came up here to watch TV."

"That's weird."

Galia shrugged. It *was* weird, this new "friend" they had. Any magnanimity Galia had felt the night before was now eclipsed by her own small-mindedness. "I need to take them dinner," she said sheepishly. It was the least she could do.

Petya had no response to this, neither dissent nor approval, and afterward, she did not stay long. A plane tomorrow and a thousand things to do. From the baby's window, Galia watched as Petya made her way back toward the center, head bent against the cold, until the only thing Galia could see was an anonymous gray dot bustling through streets of Japan, small and homely and free.

He had not set out for the old church. Rather, he had planned his whole day around going back to visit his mother. It had been a good day, as far as these days went, and he had actually looked forward to the visit. Yes, it was a fine idea they'd had to combine their wood, but would they mind if he restacked it just outside the door? He could come back on the weekend— no trouble at all—and wouldn't the room be nicer without all those cumbersome logs in it? In his mind, he sounded convincing, another problem easily solved.

But as he'd hiked up the mountain, the vision he'd had of this conversation had started to unravel. If it were just his mother, there would be no problem. Easy by nature, his mother was not likely to object to such a simple change. But Radka was a different story altogether. By now their skin would have dried to parchment, and still Radka would object to the idea, if only because it wasn't hers, and Nasko was not in the mood to argue.

And then there was the church poking over the rooftops, its white steeple an appealing contrast to the terra-cotta tiles. Once his gaze fixed on the steeple, crisp and somber against the gray broth of dusk, he knew where he was going. He didn't even notice as he passed his mother's house. If he had seen the bright blaze in the window, he surely would have stopped. The stacks of wood did not obscure a firelight twice as bright as any other light on the street.

Though the church was just a few minutes farther up the mountain, he had not been there since his father died eight months prior—and not for a long time before that. But now he felt a magnetic draw, and he reached it quickly, panting. Inside, the church—a chapel, really—was lit by a dim overhead bulb and the dying light of day. Pausing to catch his breath, Nasko could make out water stains and pocked walls where plaster had crumbled or else been chipped by those who'd helped themselves to the old gold leaf. Though he was not a religious person, he found it unsettling. Nothing was sacred anymore.

As night descended, the church grew dimmer still; the

handful of prayer candles that flickered in red glass cups did little to brighten the church's dreary inner sanctum. Nasko felt his spirits dip. For in fact it had not been such a good day. Even if he could talk his mother and Radka into allowing him to take the wood back outside, there was still the indelible fact that they had moved the wood in the first place, which was, after all, the far bigger problem.

He found a chair along one wall and folded his hands in his lap. Unlike his mother, for whom prayer was central—even during the decades when prayer had not been allowed—Nasko did not pray. He did not know how to pray. For years, he had tried to ignore the small altar she kept, the daily trips to sweep the step and to tend to the prayer candles in the small church. They had known there would be consequences: his mother's illicit activities would undoubtedly be noticed, and somehow, their family would pay a price. Sure enough, Nasko had graduated from University first in his class, but had been the last in his class to find work, a paltry job repairing radiators and setting rat traps in a local motel. Still, he and his father would not deny his mother her faith. And hadn't they, in the deepest hollows of their hearts, been counting on her to pray enough for all of them?

Then, just when they had needed prayer the most—when his father had started on a long, slow, humiliating decline—his mother had given up her daily pilgrimage to the church to tend to his care.

Nasko glowered beneath his cap. Indeed, the day had been a disappointment. That afternoon, from his office window, he had spotted the gypsy woman walking in the square. She held a child in one arm, a bag of groceries in the other, and a boy of five or six walked at her side carrying a loaf of bread. The boy had her same thin build, her same straight posture. Nasko was certain he was a good boy, and he was proud of her for raising such a child. It was reassuring to see such a fine family, and he was more certain than ever they should have heat that winter. But then, as he watched, things had taken a turn. The boy said something to his mother, and she began scolding him. He bore her rebuke for only a few paces before he hurled the loaf of bread into a dirty bank of snow. She scurried to recover it, retrieving the bread, brushing it off, cuffing the boy on the ear. Behind her anger, Nasko could see her damaged pride, her embarrassment: they could press their clothes and walk straight-backed and proper, but they would still be gypsies, wouldn't they? It was the one thing they'd always be.

Behind Nasko, a door opened and closed. Nasko turned to see the girl, Petya Docheva. He wouldn't have known who she was—she had to be younger than his son—but when a woman who looks barely more than a girl comes to pay her mother's heating bill, you take notice. And when monthly dispatches start arriving from Japan, well, you know this is someone extraordinary.

The girl walked to the front of the church and kneeled on a step. Rocking back on her heels, she assumed a pose so still Nasko was almost afraid to breathe. He didn't think she had seen him, and he didn't want to scare her—though he didn't expect a girl who'd made it all the way to Japan would scare so easily.

When he got used to having her there, he started to enjoy her company. There was something about sharing this quiet space that made it feel more sacred, and he felt emboldened to do whatever it was he was there to do. Repent? Search for an answer? Was he really willing to change his mind? Nasko did not think badly of the gypsy woman—certainly not as badly as she thought of herself. His own child had been a good boy, and still he knew these things happened. A loaf of bread thrown into the snow, after all, was not so bad. A wasted loaf of bread was not the worst thing a boy could do. And yet, he could not deny a spell had been broken. If he thought a winter's worth of heat could really ease the load that was theirs by birth, well, he was being a fool.

The girl shifted. Nasko froze, afraid of being discovered. He was not a religious man. He had no business being in this church. He should be with his mother, who at that very moment was huddled before her altar. This time of year, she was waiting for the birth of Christ—a thing his mother anticipated the way most of Old Mountain anticipated heat. He wondered about this girl—what was she praying for? And was her huddled figure so different from the Boris who slumped in his chair? Or the mother who knelt in the snow, brushing furiously at a loaf of bread?

A pang of desperation. Girl or no girl, Nasko was finished with this place. He stood up abruptly, and in so doing, nudged the chair so that its legs scraped the floor.

The girl spun around, her eyes scanning the darkness until she found him in the shadow of the wall. "Oh," she said. "I thought—"

"I'm sorry," Nasko said hastily, and he was. The church was all but black now. He should not be there. And yet, he could not deny the nudge, the scrape, had been intentional. He *wanted* this girl to know that he was there.

Slowly, the girl got to her feet, and whether it was the tall ceiling of the church, the pallor in her face, she looked frightfully small—though not at all vulnerable. She took a step toward him. "I was planning to find you in the morning," she said. "But, perhaps, if you have a minute now . . ."

Marina let herself in. "Pavletta?" she called. It was quiet in the apartment, almost eerily so, and for a moment she feared Pavletta was asleep.

"Marina?"

"I brought some dinner," she said through the closed door of the *hol,* balancing on one foot, then the other as she slipped off her shoes. She found Pavletta exactly where she had left her two days earlier. "I wasn't sure if you would have eaten," she said, stacking the placemats on the dining room table to cushion a hot pan of mishmash.

But the thing Pavletta wanted more than food was *rakiya.* "Will you have one with me?" she asked, and Marina could tell she'd been thinking about the *rakiya* and wondering how long it would be before someone came to pour her one.

How eagerly Marina could ignore her misgivings! The day before, the headache had been fierce and relentless, and she had sworn it would be a good long while before she'd have another drink. But that was yesterday and this was today, when a glass of *rakiya* with a damaged friend was infinitely easier to pardon.

Pavletta directed her to the glasses, the bottle poised on the table, ready to address most any need. Her first sip was a long one; her purple eyes closed with relief. Though Marina was not a drinker, she recognized Pavletta's need, and she was glad she had come when she did.

Marina thought Pavletta looked better—less pained, less puffy—but it was hard to say for sure. That day, everything had looked good to Marina. For the first time in months, she was noticeably not annoyed by the leak in the corner of her living room a hasty patch job did little to disguise, and what would it take for her neighbors to agree the leaky roof had, indeed, become a problem? She was less dissatisfied than usual with the dozen sets of teeth diligently scraped and polished when cleaning barely scratched the surface, and who would ever be able to afford the fillings, the root canals so urgently required? She did what she could: she knew people were not there for the cleaning so much as the heat. By now, the sight of the thermometer stuck at minus five degrees Celsius was starting to look good. For with each freezing cold day, it was more and more likely central heat was just a day away.

Marina sipped slowly at her *rakiya,* oddly enjoying the burn down the back of her throat. "The difference a day makes," she said. The day before, after Popchev had left, she'd suffered haze and confusion and the headache that *would not* go away. But by morning, the skies had cleared, and she was left with the feeling that whatever happened or didn't happen she would be okay. And even though she knew she was hardly one to judge what exactly it meant to have a life, she felt as though she'd had more of a life in the last thirty hours than she'd had in a very long time.

"I'm feeling better," Pavletta said, no matter the unwashed hair, the raccoon eyes. Rest had worked its wonders.

"You look better," Marina said. "Where are Boris and Dobrin?"

"Dobrin is in his room. Doing homework, he says. And Boris is upstairs at Galia and Vladi's." She took another swallow of her drink. "You know Boris. Now that I'm in his spot, he had to find another TV."

It was sad to think this should be the order of things—the TV before all else. And yet the only thing Marina could do was laugh. Already the *rakiya* was getting to her. She could feel it in her legs, on her tongue. She could see how this might become a habit. She wondered if perhaps it should.

"Go ahead and laugh," Pavletta said. "No job. No husband. I feel like I'm on vacation from my life. And it's wonderful."

For some reason, this was funny too, and Marina laughed again. Listening to herself, she knew it was a strange, unpracticed laugh. She was not so used to laughing.

Pavletta eyed her curiously. "You've changed," she said. An accusation. "Something about you has changed."

Which was enough to make Marina sober up. Yes, something had changed. Everything had changed. The looseness in her limbs. If Pavletta was on vacation from her life, well then, Marina, too, had already taken leave of her reality. And this new reality that had her stroking the underside of her hot, sweaty arm a hundred times a day . . . Of course, she had let the cavity go. "I'll see you—soon," she had stumbled. It would have to be soon.

Marina nodded her assent. She owed Pavletta something more. Pavletta, who, in her lowest moment, had told her not to call Boris. To say "Please don't" and nothing more was to share one's darkest secret.

Besides, part of her wanted to talk, the tongue aloose with the spirit. She had thought about calling Sylvia, who was engaged in a scandal of her own. The previous summer, Sylvia had finally admitted her relationship with a man who'd stayed in her building for a spell. The affair was objectionable on every level: the man was Marina's age, married to an invalid, and with a home on the other side of the country. But Sylvia was convinced there was something there, and Marina had to believe she was right, what with the change in Sylvia from storm clouds to sunshine. When Sylvia first told her, Marina had worried. Someday this bubble would burst. It almost had already when the man and his wife returned to their home on the Black Sea coast. But so far, Sylvia and the man—Lazar was his name—were managing to bridge the long distance between them. By Marina's measure, her daughter was the happiest she'd been in years.

Indeed, Marina had gone so far as to pick up the phone to call Sylvia to tell her of this new love in her own life. But there was something about it she couldn't trust. Could she count on Sylvia to be happy for her? Or might she be disgusted instead? And if Drago were to find out—and then Ivo—*Bozhe Gospodi!* The horror of the boys' discovery was unthinkable.

No, she could not tell Sylvia, and so she found herself riding this unimaginable high with no one to talk to. She looked at Pavletta. What was there to say? "You know Popchev?" she said, her voice a whisper, glory in the mere expression of his name.

Pavletta's coon eyes opened wide. "Really?" she said with all the wonder of one who was as new to such affairs as Marina herself.

"Nothing's happened—yet," Marina said, which was true, utterly true, even though it felt like everything had happened and even if nothing more happened, something would still be forever changed.

"Still—"

"I know." To be at this point, to be talking about it . . . it was a scandal so far outside Marina's experience—and clearly

Pavletta's as well—they hardly had the language for what might, what *must* transpire. Marina giggled nervously.

"What will you wear?"

Marina had not yet thought about this. She could not possibly wear the things she owned, which were white and cotton and ridiculous. And to go to a store would be a public admission she could never make.

The *rakiya*—she needed more. She poured them each another glass, then ventured the only thing she could think of. "Nothing?"

Pavletta smiled. "I'm sure he'd be happy with that," she said.

And then silence, as each woman summoned her own lusty imaginings for what such an event might entail—and with a hairy beast like Popchev, no less.

Pavletta recalled the one romance novel she had ever read, a soft, pulpy volume she had hidden away so that Dobrin wouldn't find it. Now she wondered if it would have been so bad if her son had read the novel. Clearly, he had figured out plenty on his own.

Marina, for her part, recalled how solid Popchev's trunk was beneath her arm, and hadn't she leaned in more than she usually did, the flat of her arm pressing hard against his chest as if to test whether this—whatever this might be—could be real? Now that her secret was out, hot, heady, and alive, she was pleased to find she could still feel good about it, great, even. So great, that the thought of wearing nothing at all was less scary than appealing. She leaned forward and put a hand on Pavletta's shoulder. How was it they had hardly known each other till now?

"People have been asking about you," Marina said, and reported some of the day's sightings. Then there were rumblings in Dobrin's bedroom, and it was time for her to go. "Call if there's anything you need," she said.

On her way out, a long-faced Dobrin opened his door. "Oh, hi," he said. He did not look pleased to see her.

"I'm just leaving," she said. "There's mishmash on the table." The savory scramble of cheese, tomato, and egg had been a favorite of the twins, and she had hoped this would make him happy.

But as she pulled the door shut, two shots of rakiya notwithstanding, she was entirely aware that not even mishmash could solve the boy's problems, which clearly continued to fester. Like a cavity that bore through a polished tooth, clean and rotten at its core.

The more Dobrin thought about it, *all* of it, the more furious he got. As he sat in front of his homework, pages and pages of untouched assignments, he wondered how the work would ever get done.

He was holed up in his bedroom with a space heater percolating at his side. The night before, Tatko had gone to watch TV with one of their neighbors and had come back with a heater their neighbor didn't need. "Oho!" Tatko said when he installed it in Dobrin's room. "Your mother goes to work and gets a broken ankle. I watch TV and get a space heater." He laughed. "You want to know how the world works?" He pressed his thumbs to his chest. "Don't ask your mother."

Even though Dobrin had just gotten back from Kuneva's class, his mood as foul as the stink in the boys' bathroom at school, he smiled. He couldn't remember the last time he'd seen his father this happy. Grateful as he was for the extra heater, he was even more grateful to see his father this way.

But then Tatko was gone, Dobrin did not know where, and as he sat before the homework, his momentary good humor also disappeared. It was utterly unreasonable for Kuneva to expect him to do so much work. And what for? Until now, he had managed to scrape by with sloppy attempts at schoolwork. But as cold had gripped them, an entire community wrenched in its vise, he had become more and more skeptical about where English, or any school subjects for that matter, would get him. Look at Kuneva. Even if he mastered the English language (a thing that was never going to happen), he was still going to end up in some mildewing apartment with pigeons whirring in the bathroom vents and the cold everywhere around him. There was nothing to be gained by doing the homework, save that it would make his mother happy.

Truth be told, at the moment, making his mother happy was not his goal. He was angry at her for finding the one tiny patch of ice on the stair. And for wearing ratty underwear and showing it to Stassi. He was angry she was stuck lying on the couch and allowing his father to cook such terrible meals. If she could do something so stupid, then he could, too.

In the next room, he could hear the low murmur of Marina talking to his mother. She had stopped by to see Maika and to bring some dinner. Dobrin had not gone to let her in. Though his stomach grumbled for the food, which smelled delicious and was probably getting cold, he did not much want to see Marina, who would eye him with that same doubtful look. She had come to check up on Maika. Clearly, she had figured out Dobrin could not be trusted.

Now, he could hear them talking about Petya Docheva, who apparently was home for a short visit. Marina said she looked exactly the same, a bit thin in the face, perhaps. They agreed she was an extraordinary girl, and it was kind of her to make such an effort to come back and see her sick mother.

But they did not know the half of it. And if Dobrin was feeling persecuted by Marina and Kuneva and even by his mother, he knew his own persecution was nothing compared to the way Petya Docheva was maligned every day of her life. Even if people acknowledged the miracle of Krastavitza standing in the square, they were never going to give credit to the one who had made it happen.

Dobrin kicked the radiator that purred at his side. "Goddamn it," he said under his breath, then kicked it again.

"Dobrin?" his mother called. He did not answer. For the darkest of his furies had finally surfaced—the one thought he'd been trying to deny: if his mother had broken her head and not her ankle, well then, there would be no homework, no gloating Tatko, no doubting neighbors, *none of it*. And with this most horrid of thoughts, his fury with himself trumped all others.

That night, the upstairs TV seemed to be turned up a notch louder than usual, and Nasko could make out some of the match's finer points. Hamburg versus Madrid. A dominant Bulgarian player called Letchkov. First one goal, then another. Obviously, people were happy.

They were settling, these sounds. Beside him, Didi rustled beneath the covers. It was a wonder, really, how life carried on, how things sorted themselves out one way or another. How a mere girl could happen into a dark church and clear things up just like that. "She was my literature teacher for five years," she said. "Just let me know how much you need." A knot in his throat. If he didn't know better, he would have thought she was doing this for him.

By the time he'd finally left, it had been too late to stop by his mother's, which was probably for the best. He was too boggled by the mystery of it all to talk to her anyway, and what would he say? Was this her secret? Was this how it worked? Ask and you received? Why was it, then, his mother—the kindest, gentlest, most prayerful soul he knew—should have such rotten fortune? As soon as his father had found peace, she'd started giving up, as though willing a life so whole and honestly earned to go up in smoke. Such an ending struck Nasko as tragically unjust. What was the problem? Were her requests not bold enough? Loud enough? Direct enough to be heard and answered?

Or had he, Nasko, just experienced a stroke of beginner's luck, and he should savor it for what it was? Upstairs, another goal, the roar of the crowd almost inaudible beneath the ecstasy of the announcer. The levity of it all bore through the covers, into his very being. Beside him, as Didi continued to stir, puffs of rose and lavender competed with the stink of mothball from the blankets. It was delicious, this smell of his wife under the covers; when it reached his nostrils, he understood just how hungry he was. To touch her—would he be pushing his luck? Worth the risk, he decided. And sure enough, when he reached over and caressed her hip, it was as though she had been waiting.

DAY FOUR: THE SILENCE OF SUNLIGHT

By the fourth day of the cold snap, *Trud*, having reported on the cold for three days straight—and on and off for several weeks prior—was grasping at topics. True, the cold was the only thing people were talking about, but it was no longer news, and there was little left to say about it except there was no end in sight. The paper had already run recipes for twenty-five varieties of soup. Opinion polls—"Hot" or "Cold"—on how people were feeling about the current government. A groundbreaking exposé on Greenland, which *Trud* claimed was colder than the name implied. Galia was bored. Maybe what they needed, rather than this fixation on the cold, was a distraction from it. Articles on hot peppers. Life on the equator. Global warming. She was ready for something new.

That morning, she had considered skipping the paper. The baby had been stirring all night, and she had tossed about uncomfortably, shifting her heavy belly from one side to the other. Come morning, the baby was quiet, and she was exhausted. Vladi was gone by the time she got up. The *hol* she found littered with plates of peanut shells, heaping ashtrays, and empty glasses. In the kitchen, more of the same. Boris had paid them another visit and stayed late into the night. She had not looked at the clock when he left.

Indeed, she had not been so attentive this time around. She had welcomed him, of course. Clearly, this was a person who needed a place to go. But Petya was right. It *was* odd. Suddenly here he was, only two days and already she had the sense his presence was a fixed one. She wasn't comfortable with the way he looked at her—what was it he wanted to say? And she didn't like the way Vladi treated him, as a pesky fly that buzzed at the ear. Swat! Swat! Which was exactly what Vladi did when he had no use for you.

And she was distracted, anyhow, by the thought of Petya getting on a plane the next day—to hell with her mother and

Old Mountain. This might be fine for Petya, *good* for Petya, but where did it leave Galia? As one packed her bags for the last time, here was the other faced with the same mess, the same stink of stale cigarettes. In the fridge, two nights' dinners were barely touched. Soon, her mother would call and "Yes, Mamo, no, Mamo, her visit was fine." The predictability that, just days ago, had been the one thing that could get her through the day now felt airless and tight. Ultimately, she'd gone for the newspaper to get a breath of fresh air, only to be rewarded with a series of articles all stuck on a single note, and wasn't it time to move on?

A flip of the page, and here was something different. The headline read "Cold Wars"—of course—but the article that followed spoke of rising divorce rates in Bulgaria, and what was happening to the country's youth? The article compared the failing "love marriages" in Bulgaria to arranged marriages in India: how a man and a woman start out hardly knowing each other, and then grow together; whereas in Bulgaria and other places where men and women choose one another, they grow apart.

It was a different type of article for sure. And a different day, a different Galia who read this article. Three days ago, she would have felt indifferent to such news. Until the subject of the name had come up, she would never have even considered her own agency in the beginning, middle, or end of her marriage. Now, control over this one matter—their child's identity—had become of utmost importance. While the struggle over the name felt monumental enough, Galia had to wonder if something even larger might be at stake. The article sparked optimism: either she or Vladi would grow together in their marriage (for Galia, the less desirable outcome by far), or they would get divorced, and she could take her Mira, and they would wander freely about the streets of Japan.

Oh, it was silly to even hope, and yet on this stagnant, scratchy day, even this remote hope was one she had to entertain. Could they dislodge themselves from their perpetuity and resolve this marriage—if you could call it that—once and for all?

She would start by telling Vladi the baby's name was Mira. Then, she would tell him she had not cooked dinner, because there were two dinners in the fridge, and she was sorry if he didn't like leftovers, but this was a shameful waste. And she would tell him she did not like the way he treated Boris; if he could not be nice to him, he should ask him to please go home.

No, she would start by going down to see Pavletta Georgieva and telling her how sorry she was and here were a couple dishes she had made. Surely, they could use some food. (Vladi could eat peanuts. At least they wouldn't stain his tie.)

No, even before paying a visit to her literature teacher, she would pack up more of the baby clothes, Vladi's ties, her clothes, the extra heaters—so many things they didn't need— and she would take them someplace, she did not know where. Just the thought of it, and already she felt lighter. So light, in fact, that without thinking—had she ever eaten breakfast?— she was wrapped in her coat and out the door before the telephone could ring. When her mother called, she would not be there. And that would be the truth.

Stassi said Kuneva didn't really mean Dobrin couldn't come back to class. He said she was a girl, and that was the way girls were. They said one thing and meant another, and you could never take them at face value.

Dobrin was not so sure. Until then, his only significant experience with a girl had been with his mother, and as far as he could tell, she meant what she said. When she said, "I can't buy you a chocolate bar today," there were no *leva* left in her wallet. When she said, "My head hurts," there was a grimace on her face and wetness on her cheeks. And when she said from her settle on the sofa, "I hope you don't grow up to be like your father," there was an empty *rakiya* glass on the table, a bandage on her foot, a garbage can stuffed to overflowing, and no sign of Tatko anywhere.

But when Stassi cared enough, he could be convincing. They were in math class, the first class of the day, and their teacher, Shterionova, told them there would be a quiz the next day. "How much do you want to bet she doesn't mean that?" Stassi said. It was true, Shterionova often threatened tests with all the menace she could muster and then seemed to forget about them the very next day.

Kuneva, Shterionova . . . Dobrin could only hope Stassi was right on both accounts.

The night before, he had managed to get through four of his English homework assignments. This had taken him three hours, and there were still five assignments left to go. Today, Kuneva would give them another, and then there would be six assignments left to do. And Tatko would still be off doing whatever Tatko did, and his mother would still be stuck on the couch. The only thing worse than the stillness in the apartment, no Tatko, no TV, was the hushed classroom the day before—the quiet in Kuneva's voice, the pall over the students as Dobrin had made his shameful exit. No, there could be no doubt Kuneva had meant exactly what she said, and why test it with five unfinished assignments only to be humiliated again?

"Besides," Stassi whispered in a loud voice. "With the cold and all, she's probably getting laid." Getting laid—and in particular, Kuneva getting laid—was Stassi's favorite topic. For if crabby old Kuneva could get laid (and they had a theory she not only *could* but *did*), then this was certain hope it could happen to anyone.

A chorus of snickers around the room, and a glare from Shterionova. She might be scattered but she was not deaf.

But the snickers, the glare were exactly the reaction Stassi was looking for. "People are nicer when they're getting laid," he whispered even more forcefully. More snickers. Another glare.

Dobrin elbowed Stassi sharply in the side. By now it was clear this dialogue had nothing to do with Dobrin's five missing homework assignments and everything to do with getting attention and what a fool Dobrin was for even trying to believe Stassi cared.

"Ow," Stassi giggled, and Dobrin elbowed him again.

"*Stiga tolkova,*" Shterionova said, trying to sound cross. But as Dobrin, red-faced, stared at his teacher—*he* was not the one to blame—wasn't that a blush in her cheek? A trace of a smile in the corner of her mouth? And if Dobrin could be certain of any one thing—another jab at Stassi, another "ow"—he was certain Shterionova *had* gotten laid the night before, and judging from the benevolent look on her face, it had been very pleasant, indeed.

Marina's fingers ached. They were the hands of an old person—but not for long. Already, the cancellations were coming for the following days. With the thermometer seemingly frozen at minus five degrees, heat had become a foregone conclusion, and who needed clean teeth when there was so much warmth? Around them. Inside them. Already, they could feel it.

In prior years, the cancellations had bothered her. It was one thing to time your visit to the dentist coincident with the heater; it was another to cancel so abruptly, so unabashedly, when heat was no longer needed. Furthermore, the short-sightedness of forsaking the long-term health of one's teeth for a hunk of yellow cheese, a crate of beer—however you celebrat-ed the end of the cold—was discouraging to say the least. What kind of heathens were they, caring less for their teeth than they did for a bite of cheese?

But this year was different. Rubbing her knuckles, she was relieved, happy even for the cancellations. The drive that had propelled her through five years of busy seasons had disap-peared. And as she worked her way through another set of teeth—"You really need to be brushing twice a day"—she found herself watching the door, her whole person abuzz with expectation that the next person would be the one she was waiting for.

Divorce. A failed marriage. A failure of any sort, but par-ticularly one of this magnitude—it was the most liberating thought Galia had had in a long time. Once this possibility had occurred to her, it seemed infinitely easier than trying to confront Vladi about the name, and she was animated down to the tips of her toes, which she could not see beneath her belly, so much as feel, a tingling that was less like frostbite and more like simply being alive. The sooner she could end this joyless marriage, the better, as far as she, and more important, Mira, were concerned.

She hardly even noticed the baby's weight as she skipped

through the square. So invigorating was the cold, she was not sorry to have forgotten her hat and gloves. If she caught a cold, well then, this failure of another variety would also make her happy.

Though she hadn't started out with a destination in mind, she was not surprised to find herself wending her way to the bus station. Petya had mentioned she would be leaving on the 9:45 bus to Poduene. If she hurried, Galia could be there just in time to say good-bye. At once it seemed very important to see her friend one last time. For even if she did manage with the divorce, she did not know how she and Mira would get to Japan. She could find the money. But the actual execution was hard to visualize. She could not count on it happening, which made it all the more urgent she reach Petya now.

The square, so wide and bright, was busier than it should have been on such a cold December day. Though the temperatures were bitter, the sun was threatening to shine on the small town of Old Mountain for the first time in a long while. Whether it was the trickle of sun, or the promise of heat, or whether Galia's own mood was coloring her perspective, the general populace of Old Mountain seemed several degrees happier than usual. Even Krastavitza, who curled in a cement planter amid the greasy discards of pastry papers and empty bags of crisps, fairly glowed with contentment. Galia could guess Petya had preceded her on this pristine morning. And sure enough, when she reached the bus station, her friend was already there.

By now, the morning bustle to Sofia had already come and gone, and Petya alone waited for a bus. Perched on a worn blue duffel, plastic cup of tea cradled in her hands, it was clear she'd been crying. She looked neither surprised nor happy to see

Galia. "You didn't have to come," she said, lips barely lifted from the edge of her cup, then turned her gaze to a pothole that pocked the vacant lot.

How had Galia pictured this parting? A hug? A peck on the cheek? A surge of pent-up gratitude gushing out, a great outpouring of thanks finally, earnestly expressed? For once, she had not deliberated, and this is what she got for her haste: a glimpse of her friend so hollowed out it was painful to look at. This was a side of Petya she did not want to see.

Petya wiped a tear from her cheek. "It's that dog," she said. "How do you say good-bye to a goddamn dog?" The tears continued to come, spilling from her chin and soaking into her coat. As if to stop them, she sipped fiercely at her tea.

"He's lived too long as it is," Galia offered. "He needs to die."

"Of course he does!" Petya shot back. "So why the hell is he still alive?"

For once, Galia did not mind being snapped at. Even liked it. This was more like the Petya she knew. The Petya who lived life according to principle and intention, regardless of the choices others made. The Petya she admired more than anyone and whom she would almost certainly never see again. For when Petya made a decision, that was the way it was. The thought struck Galia as a sharp pain. Her Mira would never know her.

Petya glanced at her, then looked away. "You can't cry," she said, the tears still coming. "He's my dog, anyway. Always has been."

Galia heard the bus before she could see it, its thunderous rumble an anomaly on this blindingly bright day.

"Besides, you're going to have a baby," she said. "You won't need a dog." Wiping her tears on her sleeve, she stood up and hoisted her bag onto her shoulder. "Think I'll get a seat?" she said, searching for her ticket.

"I hope so," Galia whispered, ashamed. She could not blame this on a dog.

Petya stopped rifling her pockets, and as the bus pulled into the station, she gave Galia a small, hard hug. "You're going to be a good mom," she whispered. "I know it."

Dobrin banged his shoe against the gate on his way out of school. This time it hurt; no need to do it again. Of course Kuneva had meant what she said. Stassi knew that better than anyone. And even though Dobrin had not been fool enough to go to Kuneva's class, he nevertheless felt a great hatred for Stassi, who thought nothing of hurling Dobrin into harm's way. Just the thought of more humiliation, more shame—Dobrin did not have to experience it again to know how harmful it would be.

Another hour before Maika would expect him home. Not a *lev* in his pocket (even if he did have money, he could not have spent it). From Dobrin's blackened perspective, the scene on the square was bright enough to sting the eyes. Ridiculous it should be so bright and so cold at the same goddamn time. The slabs of marble beneath his feet pitched at every angle, offering ample opportunity for a fall, and here Maika, why not here? or here? or here?

And there was the dog lying in a planter, peaceful in the sun. No fur coat to speak of, and still it could be happy. When Dobrin sat down on the edge of the planter, the dog lifted its head and rested it on Dobrin's leg. "It's okay, *milichko*," he whispered. But it was not okay. Even a dog could see that.

Dobrin caressed a bald patch on the dog's head. The skin,

which was usually a bluish black, had turned a deep purple, infused with scarlet from the cold. It looked like a bruise— one covering the dog's entire body—and Dobrin adjusted his caress to be gentler and gentler. It was impossible to believe it didn't hurt, such a bruise. And yet, his mother claimed the rings around her eyes didn't hurt. And later, when Dobrin took off his shoes and socks, he would be pleasantly surprised to find a painless bruise on his gate-kicking foot. It was the most satisfying thing he had done in some time.

No, the visible bruises, bad as they may look, seemed not to hurt as much as the invisible ones, the ache that ringed his mother's hips from lying on the couch for so long, the bruise on his heart, which hurt mightily at the moment. Hard to pinpoint what exactly had put it there—and to know whether it would ever go away.

From his office window, Nasko watched the neighbor boy pet the hairless dog. Mindless of the bustle around him, the boy was fully absorbed in his activity, and of course, the dog enjoyed the attention. Though Nasko nursed a nagging fear for the diseases the dog might carry, he was grateful these two had found each other. They seemed a rightful pair.

It was lunchtime, and the soup Didi had packed in a thermos for Nasko's lunch had gone cold. Not even a thermos—not even a good one—worked on such a day. Just a few bites, and all Nasko could taste was waxy chicken fat. He screwed the cap back on the thermos. A shame, he thought. It was the first day he'd had an appetite in some time.

Still he allowed himself these minutes to gaze out the window and to plumb a moment of satisfaction. This sunshine bathing the square—he was somehow responsible. Come tomorrow, they would be on the other side of this hump, this old mountain, and things would be okay.

There was Kuneva, now, talking to the boy. Even from this distance he could fairly hear her talking in the way Kuneva talked to children. Always an edge in her voice—a rim between warmth and irritability, care and crankiness. As a parent, he'd found it difficult to know which side of the border Plamen had stood on. He guessed Kuneva had not decided how she felt about this tall, sullen, well-intentioned child, and whose fault was that? As much as he loved his son, he knew Plamen did not make it easy.

These were the places his mind could go now that things were more or less decided. The soft, pink, tender places—there were too many. And shame on him for failing to get to the dentist once again.

Then, mother, boy, and baby were making their way up the square once again. Today, the boy was eating a piece of *banitsa* as he walked, and his mother carried both bread and baby. This was a better day. Nasko could feel it. The mother said something to the boy, pulled up his collar to cover the back of his neck. There were no smiles. No, she was not the smiling type. But there was a warmth there, nonetheless. A premonition that things would be okay.

Vladi wasn't home five minutes when Boris arrived. "Oho!" Boris said when Galia opened the door, as though his arrival should be a great surprise.

"*Vlezete*," she said. "We were waiting for you." Inviting him into the *hol*, she motioned to the couch, poured him a drink. "*Zapovyadaite*," she said.

"Oho!" Boris said, somehow surprised again on this, the third night of such treatment. It piqued Galia's irritation in a way she could not help, so trite and inauthentic, and how could life possibly be so full of surprises?

In fact, there were surprises to be had that evening, but not so much from Boris. By the time she'd gotten home from the bus station, she was spent. Physically, emotionally, there was nothing left. And so, the phone, which rang every fifteen minutes, did not get answered. The dinner did not get made. The apartment did not get cleaned. It wasn't until the sun had started to drop, an orange halo limning the mountain's girth, that Galia was able to lift herself from the couch. She'd had just enough time to deliver the casseroles to Pavletta Georgieva and take a shower before Vladi got home. When Vladi walked in, he found the mess he'd left behind the night before. Galia did not apologize.

But Vladi had not reacted to the state of the flat or to Galia, herself, who was just stepping out of the shower. Rather, he had taken off his tie, opened a beer, and cleared off a spot on the table for his feet. Flipping on the TV, he had dropped into his chair with all the detachment of one who could care less, so long as he had a chair to sink into.

Yes, Galia's irritation was piqued, more than piqued. Ducking so as to not block the *televisor,* she scooped angrily at the dirty dishes, carting one load off to the kitchen, then coming back for another. She couldn't stand the mess any longer. All day long, she had put up with it, and what for? Not even so much as a grunt, a raised eyebrow, a sideward glance. It was reminiscent of the baby—a thing Vladi had not acknowledged for four months. And if it took four months for one to acknowledge the fact of one's own baby, well then, perhaps divorce was the right answer after all.

A sink of hot, soapy water was just the thing. Slipping her hands into it, already Galia felt more in control. A clean kitchen would help her clear her head. A clean kitchen was good for that.

In the next room, the TV broadcast a match Galia thought she'd heard before—but she'd never known Vladi to be deterred from watching a match a second, third, or fourth time. Meanwhile, Boris was making his obligatory attempts at conversation. *"Ami—,"* he said. "When is the baby due?"

"Another month," Vladi said, bored, always bored. Galia was starting to wonder if it was his own damn fault he should be so bored all the time. If she didn't notice anything, she would be bored, too.

"It's going to change your life," Boris said.

"That's what they say." Swat! How easily Vladi could dismiss a person—perhaps this was the thing Galia hated most. If Vladi had just one drop of decency, maybe divorce would not be necessary. Just because Boris could be so frightfully irritating was no excuse.

But Vladi's dismissal was not enough for Boris, who kept pressing. "But in ways you can't expect," he said. "When I look at my son—," he started, then paused.

From the TV, an eruption. Someone had scored. Galia, still at the sink, waited for Boris to finish his sentence. *When I look at my son,* what? He must complete his thought. Here, the guy was nothing but cheer despite his wife's badly broken ankle. And his son . . . That afternoon, when she'd dropped the dishes off, the boy had answered the door. Galia had been better at keeping a blank face, but she knew how he felt, the wrenched face betraying the contorted heart inside. When he looked at his son, what exactly did Boris see?

But now it was Galia's turn to be surprised. For when the match quieted again, the only sound was a sniffle. First one, then another and another. Could Boris be crying? Galia had never let Vladi see her cry. For her stony husband to see her so compromised was a thought more painful than pain itself. If she got upset, she could always catch herself, and the fact that he noticed so little worked to her advantage. Now to imagine the scene in the other room—at once, her exasperation with Boris turned into embarrassment on his behalf, and she willed him another *rakiya,* another space heater, another goal, whatever it might take to make the moment go away.

But it was Vladi himself who came to Boris's rescue. "Yeah, well, we're going to name it Vladi. Vladislav if it's a boy, Vladislava if it's a girl," he said, his own voice weighted not with embarrassment but pride, as though he could already imagine how it might feel to gaze into the face of his child.

This was just enough to help Boris recover. "Well, then, here's to Vladi," he said, and she could hear the sounds of *rakiya* being poured.

"Here's to Vladi," Vladi said, with more warmth in his voice than Galia thought she had ever heard.

Here's to Vladi. As she dried her hands on a towel, she recalled the countless wedding toasts, which had struck her as an utter sham. Could she have been wrong all this time? *Vladi.* For once, the name struck her as passable. Perhaps *Vladimir. Vladimira.* She could call her *Mira* for short. "What do you think?" she whispered. For the rest of the evening, her belly felt taut and ripe. She had eaten nothing all day, and still she was content and round and full.

From her perch before the blazing fire, Radka chirped happily. That evening's episode of *Dallas* had been a good one, and do you ever watch it, Nasko? You really should.

Nasko smiled. Already they were off to a better start. With coat, hat, and scarf discarded at the door, he had only to wait for his blood to thin, so the heat might feel more tolerable. In the meantime, *Dallas* seemed like a fine topic, and yes, of course he had seen it, not that evening, but from time to time. Here at his mother's house, and back at the apartment, where Didi watched it religiously. She was not a religious person, his Didi, but she never missed *Dallas*.

"Well, it's too bad you missed it tonight, Nasko," Radka said, fingering the piece of knitting in her hands. "It was a good one."

Nasko nodded, then looked to his mother, who had not said a word since he'd arrived. "*Kak si,* Maika?" he asked, a hand on her knee. Her black polyester dress was hot to the touch. Her face was flushed with heat.

"I'm fine," she said softly, looking away from the fire only briefly to meet his gaze.

"She always says that," Radka snapped, and in an instant, the mood turned. "Does she look fine to you?"

Magenta hair notwithstanding—Radka, no doubt, was responsible—Nasko had to admit his mother looked as fine as she'd looked in a long time. But Radka didn't allow him to answer.

"I keep telling her, you can't be fine all the time. There have to be times when you're more than fine. Or less than fine. But you can't be fine all the time and expect people to believe it."

Nasko was not sure what to make of Radka's theory, but he was not there to pick an argument. Rather, he was there to bide his time until he could flip the switch, and he was happy to spend this time with his mother. He was feeling more than fine, his job all but finished. He had already decided he was not going to mar this fine day by bringing up the wood and what to do about it. He certainly was not going to debate the issue of his mother's fineness with Radka, and what did she of all people know about being fine?

"Five hundred years under the Turkish yoke, and she still thinks we're all just fine," Radka continued. "How many more years should we have endured for your mother to understand we're not so fine at all?"

Nasko stared into the fire. He had hoped for more from this visit. He was not sure what. After his trip to the church the night before, he felt a newfound kinship with his mother. Even to be sitting this close to her, close enough to lay a hand on her knee—even that was something.

And then, as they sat, mother and son with eyes trained on the fire, Radka knitting fervently, an ember the size of a five-*stotinki* coin flew from the fire and landed on the altar.

Nasko jumped to his feet, looking for something to put it out.

"What?" Radka shouted. "What on earth is the matter with you?"

But when Nasko looked back to the altar, the ember was already out, and there was nothing to say, except this was exactly why the wood needed to be moved. A more persistent ember, and the whole house would burn down.

"You scared me half to death," Radka continued, though

already she had resumed her stitching. "What are you doing jumping around like that?"

There was no answer, of course, and Nasko settled back into his chair feeling foolish and tense. He had seen an ember. He was certain of it. And how was it the faded silk flowers, the photo of his father, the icon on the thinnest, driest piece of yellowed paper, had not gone up in flames?

Meanwhile, his mother hadn't budged, not even when he jumped, nor had she lifted her eyes from the fire. Rather, she had held her gaze steady on the altar, the fire. With the altar positioned directly before the blaze, they were one and the same.

Then Nasko noticed a charred ring burnt into the floor around the wood-burning stove that had not been there before, the product of a thousand such embers having shot from the fire. And all over the altar, blackened spots pocked the table, photo, flowers. To see was to know: those embers had died as this one had by her request. Each time, the fire complied.

Popchev's beard smelled of onion and pickled carrots. His chest and legs, a mat of fur, tickled the skin. His groin was moist at Marina's hip. And he was hot, so hot, the heat was more than she could stand.

"Aren't you hot?" she said, peeling back the blanket to leave only a thin sheet between them and the frigid air. A few moments more, and she had to get out. "I'll be right back," she said, rising from the bed and blazing a naked trail through their strewn clothing toward the bathroom door. She could feel his eyes on her back, her lithe buttocks, as she picked her way across the floor. She felt more brazen and damp and delicious than she'd ever felt before.

The contrast between the bed and the open air was shocking, and by the time she reached the bathroom, her nipples were hard, her skin pimpled. A pause in front of the mirror, and she couldn't help but touch her breast, trying to recall the roughness of his hand, the kneading eagerness of his touch. She shuddered with delight, dropped her hand to the edge of the sink, then reached up and touched again.

Cold as she was, she could not stop looking at herself. Her eyes were bloodshot with overwork, crinkled at the corners from so many years of peering into open mouths. Her usually porcelain skin was pink from heat, cold, the exhilarating transition from one to the other. Any moment now, the central heat would go on, and these days would be over, and then what?

After work, she'd bought a bottle of wine, hurried home, taken a shower. When he'd failed to make an appearance at her office that day, she'd known he would find her here. She'd known this in the way one knew things. Like the day her mother died. She'd woken up that morning knowing her mother had died during the night. And though she was not the least bit prepared for it—alone, the twins still babies—it somehow helped to know and to formulate her own understanding before anyone, namely her father, could apply the callous touch of words.

She'd known of Sylvia's affair months before Sylvia confessed it to her. The smoke on her clothes. The lift in her voice. She had known, too, there must be something objectionable about this relationship. By the time Sylvia finally broke the news, details like his age and marital status seemed paltry, given the possibilities. Marina found she could actually be happy, delighted even, for a love that was clearly satisfying, if precarious, and you know, Sylvia, I'd love you, no matter who.

She knew, absolutely, there was something going on with

Pavletta's boy, and what was he doing leaving school so early? Two days in a row, Marina had seen him leaving the school, kicking the gate. She worried for him as if he were her own son, and swollen eyes not withstanding, was it possible Pavletta could not see? Or else she saw, but what to do?

Yes, she'd known Popchev would come. As it turned out, wine, words were not necessary. In the same way Marina conducted all her work, they'd wasted little time. And if she had worried that after so many years, she would be embarrassed or ashamed or even repulsed, this had not been the case. Not for a moment. Rather, she was left feeling holy. Hallowed. Whole.

At last, the cold had penetrated deep, too deep, and she hurried back to the bed. "*Bozhe Gospodi,* it's cold," she said, pressing into Popchev's side.

"Then what took you so long?" he said, wrapping his arms around her.

"I'm not sure," she said, already too warm again. Hot. Cold. These cursed, blessed days there was no middle ground.

DAY FIVE: A GODDAMN MIRACLE

Technically, Nasko should wait until 2:34 A.M., which would mark the exact passage of ninety-six hours of freezing temperatures. In earlier years, he would have waited until precisely this time. But when he arrived back at the office at 12:15, this seemed late enough. Who at that hour would even notice?

Dobrin was awake when the heat went on. He had gone to bed too early, and the apartment was too quiet, and his father was out again, and where the hell was he?

The long afternoon had turned into an even longer evening. Without a TV to watch, a father to distract him, Dobrin had struggled with what to do. Maika had instructed Dobrin to heat some of the food their neighbor brought, and Dobrin had taken a large portion to the dogs on the *balcon*. The dogs simpered obligingly, their icy noses reminding Dobrin he should stop feeling so goddamn sorry for himself. At least he had a space heater and a room of his own.

Speaking of heaters, at the moment, there was an odd burning smell. If Dobrin didn't know better, he'd think the space heater was burning the carpet. But this was a nice space heater, far nicer than the one his family had bought the year before, and in the two days they'd had it, there'd been no problems. Likely, the smell came from someone else's apartment, and how bad could a little fire be on a night as cold as this one?

Dobrin sighed. He wasn't going to be able to fall asleep, haunted as he was by the burning smell, the unfinished homework, the conversation he'd had with Kuneva that afternoon. She'd caught him lingering in the square. "I was disappointed you weren't in class," she said, to which Dobrin could only bow his head. He was disappointed, too.

She told him she had let the class out early because of the cold and given them a night off from homework. "This should give you a chance to catch up," she said. "But tomorrow there will be heat, and there will be homework."

Dobrin didn't doubt this. "Yes, *Gospozha*," he'd said, which was enough to satisfy Kuneva, and at last she went away.

A week earlier, any direct address from Kuneva, let alone this attention, this concern, would have unnerved Dobrin: he did not talk to teachers, especially not Kuneva, any more than school required. But as she'd left him alone with that pathetic old dog, part of him had been sorry to see her go.

Ujas, Dobrin thought. *Golyam ujas.* To have developed any degree of fondness for Kuneva—he could not think of anything more disgusting, not even the thought of so many people lying in bed naked together, an image that continued to disturb him, no matter how hard he tried to push it out of his mind. He flopped over in bed—*why* wasn't he asleep?—and banged his knuckles on the radiator above his head, which was warm. Hot. The heat was on in his bedroom. How could that be?

In the following minutes and hours, a thousand thoughts reeled through his head, not the least of which was Tatko, and had he been the one to make this happen? But try as he might, Dobrin could not imagine this. The truth was, he did not have enough faith in his father to believe he could manage such a favor. As he turned this conundrum over and over in his mind, his thoughts kept going back to that bruised and hairless dog that lived on and on and on, and how could this be? Dobrin did not know what to think, except he was warm, hot even, and there were only two English homework assignments left to go. And he was not going to sleep anyway, so he might as well . . .

As Nasko climbed the stairs of Block 103, Vhod A, he was greeted by the familiar burning smell of the old radiators coming to life, their erratic click and thrum just barely audible through the closed apartment doors. The smell, the sounds— these were good signs, evidence things were as they should be.

He was just rounding the first-floor landing when Boris came bounding down the stairs. "Oho!" he said. "You've been working your magic, have you? Does this mean what I think it means?" Boris clapped him on the shoulder as though Nasko's shoulder were his to clap. "Bravo, Nasko! You did it again!"

For much of the day and evening, Nasko had been looking forward to climbing these stairs, to pulling closed the door to his apartment, and to finding Didi, his Didi, with her irresistible smell of rose and lavender, and what had happened that he, they, should feel this way? Now, here was one more hurdle, Boris, a man completely unknowable to him. The only thing Nasko could think as he absorbed Boris's blunt blows to his shoulder was how grateful he was to the small, black-haired girl. For on this endless night, he was certain that, left to his own devices, he would not have given Boris heat. And Pavletta would wake up cold the next morning. And the boy's brow would knit and furrow until it knotted right in the middle. And Didi would give him the cold shoulder for the entire winter to come, and had his heart gone and shriveled up, abandoning a friend and neighbor in this way?

Indeed, the only reason he could look forward to seeing Didi now was because of the girl, Petya. Blessed be that girl, ephemeral ember that she was on the coldest, darkest night. Truth be told, if Nasko could make another request—how easily this could become a habit—he'd like to ask for Boris to go away. But he could not be so selfish, not after what the girl had done for him. Instead, he asked that the girl with her short black hair, knobby red sweater, fogged glasses—please, may she never change.

The overnight flight was a smooth one. The plane was not full—there were not so many people who traveled from Bulgaria to Japan—and the seat between Petya and the Japanese man on the aisle was empty. She requested apple juice. He chose wine—one, then another in quick succession. She closed her eyes to fend off conversation.

At the airport, every item in her bag had been removed and examined by security. She was used to this: apparently, she fit some sort of profile, and she could not remember a time in any airport when they had not brought in the drug-sniffing dog to peruse the contents of her bag. Even these dogs, so trained and intense, took a liking to her, and the dog that afternoon was no exception. After examining her things, the dog began whimpering and chewing on Petya's red sweater. By the time the sweater could be extracted from its mouth, it had been reduced to a rag, which, Petya conceded, was not so bad. The sweater was an old one, she said. The dog could have it—and please, he should not be punished.

The air seeping in around the plane's window casing was cold and persistent. Already, Petya missed the old red sweater. She stuffed a pillow in the window well, laid her head against it, and still the cold air rifled her hair, chilled her side. She should have asked for tea. After four days in below-freezing temperatures, the cold knew just where to go, burrowing straight to the bone and then staying there, lest her great escape be too easy.

As it turned out, the chill would not go away. It was there year-round, even in the mug and swelter of a Tokyo July, when the only thing worse than the hot, humid air that steamed off every last surface was the cold that blasted through vents invariably pointed at her. Petya would come to see it as a penance of sorts: was it so wrong to leave? When her Japanese friends would ask her about her hometown, even though the weather was not so different from Tokyo temperatures, the great cold was what she would speak of most of all.

Galia waited until she was certain Vladi was asleep before she got up to turn off the heaters. It felt wonderful to go into each room and to flip the switches, each one a privilege they did not deserve. Flip. Flip. Flip. She wished every action could be so easy.

They would not need the space heaters for another year. By then, this Vladi, this Mira—whoever this was—would be almost a year old, its very own person. And who knew where they would be by then? Japan, perhaps. She knew they could love Japan. Or else here, with the baby's daddy. That evening had sparked a hope in her that maybe, just maybe, this baby could love her daddy. As she'd listened in on the conversation between Vladi and Boris, the thought had occurred to her that love was possible. Perhaps she had underestimated Vladi's capacity for compassion—and if she tried hard enough, she might be able to love in return.

But as she returned to the bedroom and Vladi, she had her doubts. He lay on his stomach, legs sprawled wide, his regular position. After two years of marriage, Galia was still disgusted by this sight. She had never gotten used to his body, his thighs like tree trunks, their broad circumference wearing thin patches in the crotch of every pair of pants. That he was down to his underwear now only made it worse. For the thousandth time, she wished he would sleep beneath the covers.

As it was, she could not bring herself to rejoin him in the bed. Instead, she sought refuge in the baby's room, taking a seat in the rocking chair, which these days was more comfortable than the bed anyway. Even with the lights off, the tidy stacks of blankets and clothes looked bright and white. A flutter in her belly—the baby? her? For just a few more weeks, she could savor their being a single whole.

Across the courtyard, a lighted window illuminated the darkness. Through the living room shears, she could make out the top of her mother's head, could all but see her mother sitting there with a cup of tea, miffed by the day, and *why, Galche, did you not answer the phone?* When Vladi got home, Galia had had to pick up, but could only manage to be caustic and elusive. *We have guests now, Mamo. I really must go.*

Seeing the light, she felt sorry, for certainly she was the reason her mother was awake. *What's wrong, Galche? Why won't you tell me what's wrong?* She could still hear the pain in her mother's voice—a pain that would only have intensified if Galia had told her the truth: she wished she were the one on a flight to Japan. If she were on a plane right now, she would like a Coke with a wedge of lemon, no ice, please. That would be her celebration.

But she doubted very much Petya was celebrating. She, in her bright red sweater, was not one for indulgences. Earlier that day, she had looked so ravaged—this was *not* just about the dog. No, not even Petya could make that sound convincing.

Galia stared at the bright yellow square across the courtyard. On her mother's mantel she could make out the row of Russian dolls. Soon, very soon, her body would cleave itself in two, and there would be a Vladi to contend with, a Mira to cherish as Galia had never cherished anything before. Was it possible even after the baby left her womb, the space would still be filled? It was the same hope her mother harbored as she waited by the phone.

Another truth—one she loathed to admit: they were not so different, she and her mother. And another one, as she eyed the Russian dolls, the tired hair, the damning patch of light: she, Galia, could never take flight.

At first, she thought something was burning. She was a light sleeper, the kind who woke to the scuttle of a cockroach, the flush of a toilet two stories up. Now that the baby could share a room with her big brother, she was starting to sleep better. Still, she left the doors open so she could hear the sighs and swallows. What was it she found it so difficult to trust?

This smell. Her first thought was the stove. But it was cold, as were the oven, coffee pot, curlers. She stood in the bathroom for several minutes staring at the bathroom vent—at once, an unlikely source of such a smell, and yet the only possible source she could think of. Perhaps there was a problem on another floor? But the bathroom smelled even less than the rest of the apartment. As she caught sight of herself in the mirror, she felt too tired for this, and when had she gotten so thin? The bones of her nose, the plate of her breastbone—they were bone and nothing more.

She passed through the apartment a second and third time before she realized it was warm. Not exactly warm, but warmer, and why should that be? On a whim, she checked the radiator and found it hot to the touch. She pulled her hand back and gasped. Something had gone wrong.

Burrowing her scalded fingers into the folds of her nightgown, she sank into a hard chair. How had this happened? They were honest people. She had gone to the man with the down-turned eyes and told him in the plainest language she could find they would not be able to afford heat. She had bundled the baby in her crib, tight as a mummy, using the heaviest blankets she had. And the boy—well, he was just like her, thin and restless as a leaf. There was no use covering him with blankets only to have them kicked off. His nose would run all winter long.

A lick of fury—could this be a test? Was she, with her gypsy-brown skin, being put to a test? Was he waiting to see if she would turn herself in?

Rarely did she allow herself to cry, but the frustration of it all—they were good people, anyone could see that. How many bottles of bleach and cans of starch would it take for them to rise above the color of their skin?

Were it not for the children, she would march right over there and tell the man he had made a mistake. She would knock on his door in the middle of the night and make him switch it off right away. She did not want this catching up with them.

But what mother in her right mind could make that choice? What mother should have such a choice to make? Pulling her knees to her chest, she cried until the tears of rage and gratitude had soaked her nightgown and the baby woke to the first rays of dawn.

"I've got to go," Popchev said, and of course he did.

It was daylight by then. Marina did not know how he would make it home without being spotted. Which was a shame—any blemish, the things people would think, when there could be nothing wrong with such a night.

But Popchev seemed worry-free as he slipped on his jeans and plaid flannel shirt, humming a tuneless tune. He kissed her at the door. "Same time next year?" he grinned, and once again, she felt coy, lovely, irresistible—as she hadn't in years.

Standing at the bedroom window, she hugged her arms to her chest and watched him make his way up the path. Between the heat inside and the sunlight outside, you could almost believe it was warm, balmy. Popchev in his black jeans and olive green parka was a dark spot against the crisp brightness. So many colors. Blue sky. White, yellow, and orange apartment blocks. Green dumpsters with red and blue political slogans. Courtyards, a khaki tundra, and a brilliant Pepsi sign. To Marina, the apartments of Old Mountain had never looked more beautiful.

Popchev's gait was wide, hands stuffed into pockets. She could still hear his tuneless tune. *Same time next year?* This, of course, had happened before with some other blind and willing woman. On some level, she'd suspected it, given the ease with which they'd taken up, the flirt and flurry, the clasped hand. She hadn't had time to think, but of course he had. He had planned this all along.

Still, her only regret was that it was over.

That was the thing about these days: they eventually ended. Life returned to normal. With Sylvia and Drago, it was the TV they turned to. They would be rapt as zombies for a week, maybe two. And then they'd be back to normal, the occasional bickering, and what's for dinner, Mamo? I'm hungry.

With her clients, the workload would slow to a trickle. There would be some follow-up with the people she'd just seen, the most conscientious of whom would take care of their cavities before they became problems. The others would wait months, even years, until their issues became acute. As a result, a disproportionate amount of her time was given to patients in agony. "You really should be brushing twice a day," she'd say, as she drilled and filled. It was hard to feel sorry.

Popchev would be one of those. "I need to tell you there's a tooth that needs attention," she'd said as soon as he'd arrived that evening. There. She'd told him. She'd felt lighter immediately.

"Right now, my tooth is the last thing that needs attention," he'd said, as he'd groped at her clothes. The next time she saw him, lust would be replaced by pain, and the desperation would be of an entirely different form.

They were, after all, a people of hardship. Five hundred years under the Turkish yoke. Marina found it amusing, not the history itself, but the pride with which people recalled it. If they could endure that, they could endure a toothache or four days of freezing cold temperatures. They could endure anything.

People said there was a lady up the hill who knitted sweaters that were too beautiful to wear. An old history teacher with no one to knit for—they said she was good enough to be a knitter for *Dallas*.

They said each of the sweaters was marked by a signature black patch—the "eye" of the sweater, she called it, a reminder of the darkness from which all color sprang forth.

When Marina had first heard about her, she'd had little interest in such a jaded old lady. Who wanted a reminder of their suffering? But over time, Marina's curiosity had grown. People say the sweaters are extraordinary. You would never wear them, they say, but they truly are something to behold.

Now, as she watched Popchev disappear between the brilliantly colored apartment blocks, there was no doubt in her mind the black patch did matter. Without the darkness, the colors would not be half so bright, and the brilliance of this beautiful morning would be tragically lost. Same time next year? She hoped so. She hoped Popchev would be her ritual, along with the giant space heater and a few more bottles of wine.

Between now and then, she had some time to kill, a period of waiting. Feeling rich and luxurious and frightfully sated, Marina had half a mind to strap on her boots and go find that old lady up the hill. Perhaps it was time to see those sweaters.

The sponge of his nose was dry as the dirt. One of the more sizable patches of fur on his tubular torso was frozen to the ground. His legs were brittle as dead twigs. It would take nothing to make them snap. In fact, the body itself was easy to ignore. Hot, cold, hungry, and full were things he could not feel. The boy who'd caressed his skin so tenderly the day before—he couldn't feel his touch so much as his kindness.

Happiness and sadness, these were the senses still intact. As the sun rose over the mountain, he did not feel its warming rays, but rather the brightness of a new day. The girl had told him she would not be back. She had told him it was time for him to let go. These were things he understood only as much as he did the warm mutterings of his name, *"Bozhe,* Krastavitza," as people scurried through the square. But if letting go was what the girl wanted, it was easy to comply. For the body was long gone. And the spirit had only to rest on the warm breath of wind that straggled through Old Mountain that day and drifted up to the sky.

Cynthia Morrison Phoel served as a Peace Corps volunteer in a Bulgarian town not unlike the one in her stories. She holds degrees from Cornell University and the Warren Wilson MFA Program for Writers. Her work has appeared in *The Missouri Review*, *The Gettysburg Review*, and *Harvard Review*. She lives near Boston with her husband and three children.